Song for Susie Epp

Elma Schemenauer

Published by Farland Press, 2024.

This is a work of fiction. Similarities to real people, places, or events are entirely coincidental.

SONG FOR SUSIE EPP

First edition. June 17, 2024.

Copyright © 2024 Elma Schemenauer.

ISBN: 978-0921718079

Written by Elma Schemenauer.

"I did then what I knew how to do. Now that I know better, I do better."

–Maya Angelou

"To love is to be vulnerable."

–C.S. Lewis

"The open spread of plain and sky felt strangely sheltering now. It was a contradiction. The place with nowhere to hide had become a refuge."

–Dora Dueck

Cover photograph by Robert S. Schemenauer

CHAPTER 1

N*ear Wells Gray Park, British Columbia, February 21, 1970*
I sat on a log beside a frozen lake three hundred miles from home, psyching myself up with Aunt Frieda's words. *Keep your chin up, Susie. A little courage goes a long way.*

On nearby logs and benches, other young people laughed and chatted as they laced their skates. Their breaths clouded in the morning air. Some were already out on the lake, gliding and swirling across the ice in groups and hand-holding pairs.

My thrift-store skates lay on the log beside me. As I put them on, I prayed I'd make some friends before I headed home to Vancouver. My prayer was a bold one. I only had three days left and I wasn't good at friendship.

Actually I did okay with the seniors in the care home where I sometimes worked. Golden-agers loved me but people around my age—twenty—tended not to. They found me too serious or too naïve. Or something.

But things could change. Young people from across British Columbia had come to this sports festival to skate, ski, snowshoe, and admire frozen waterfalls. Surely one or two of them would enjoy meeting me.

I donned the red hat and mittens I'd knitted for the festival and stepped onto the ice. My stomach fluttering with anticipation, I glided toward the oval that had been cleared and smoothed for skating. Merging with the other skaters, I cruised along beside a narrow-faced girl who wore a ban-the-bomb button like mine. She skated with her hands behind her back and had a dreamy look in her eyes, as if she liked poetry and maybe wrote it. I offered a friendly smile.

She skated away as if she hadn't seen me. Maybe she hadn't.

Swallowing my disappointment, I maneuvered toward two bearded guys in leather jackets. I smiled and said hi as if I didn't care whether they answered or not.

"What's up, Buttercup?" said the one with the ponytail.

Before I could respond, his companion pulled him away. They swooped toward a pair of lacquer-haired girls a few yards ahead of me. The guys offered the girls their arms. The girls shook their heads. The guys shrugged and sped off.

Why hadn't one of those guys asked me to skate—or both of them? I wasn't bad-looking. My skin had cleared up and I wasn't as scrawny as I'd been as a teenager. My eyes were big, brown, and only slightly crossed. My hair was a decent shade of brown. Maybe guys would pay more attention to me if I was with a girlfriend.

In the crowd ahead, a short girl zipped around and between the other skaters, disappearing and reappearing like a rabbit in a magic trick. She wore a Simon Fraser University crest on her jacket. Summoning all my courage, I detoured past a lanky couple skating with their arms around each other, dodged a few other skaters, and caught up with the girl. "Excuse me. I saw your crest. How do you like SFU?"

She smiled, the braces on her teeth flashing. "It's great."

"So you'd recommend it? I'm at the University of British Columbia but I'm thinking of transferring."

"You won't be sorry. SFU's a groovy place, fresh and forward-thinking." She glanced at her watch. "Excuse me. I've got to go and meet my friends at the lodge."

"Sure." My heart sagging with disappointment, I watched her hurry away. I felt like escaping to my bed in the lodge, eating a bag of caramel creams, and sleeping until lunchtime or whenever.

No, that would be cowardly and uncool, the sort of thing my mother would do.

What would Aunt Frieda say? *Never despair, Susie. Nil desperandum.*

Okay, Aunt Frieda, I'll try again. But I need a break first.

I left the oval, skated around a bunch of kids playing ice baseball, and headed for the island farther up the lake. The ice wasn't Zamboni-smooth up that way but I was relieved to get away from the crowd.

As I approached the south end of the island, a Canada jay whistled from a birch tree. I gave an answering whistle, then skated around the eastern edge of the island. I was passing the snow-covered beach when a red fox emerged from a clump of willows. The animal stared at me, its eyes bright, one black foot raised. A second later, it streaked away, a flash of red on white. Beautiful.

Feeling more cheerful, I turned and headed back toward the oval. As I passed the benches on shore, a foghorn voice called, "Hey, Red Hat."

Surprised, I pivoted on my blades and slid to a stop a few feet from Ervino Sousa, a beak-nosed guy I took chemistry with at university. He was leaning against a bench made out of a car seat.

Ervino jerked his thumb toward a sturdy-looking fellow who sat on the bench lacing his skates. "Somebody here wants to meet you."

Distrust nibbled at my insides. Were they making fun of me?

"Can you come closer?" Ervino called. "I lost track of your name. Sorry."

"It's Susie." I coasted toward him.

The guy on the bench tied his skate laces, his hands big and square. As he raised his head to adjust his scarf, I noticed he had a firmer jawline than Ervino's and a more settled-looking face. Maybe he was a few years older than Ervino. His cheeks were round as apples, his eyes almost as blue as his jacket.

"This is my friend Simon," Ervino said. "From Sage City." Ervino jerked his head toward me. "Simon, meet Susie from Vancouver."

I gulped. "I'm pleased to meet you, Simon."

"Susie. That's a nice name," Simon said in a voice as smooth as honey. As he wobbled onto the ice, he gave me a slow smile that seemed to come from some sunny place the outside world could never touch. He offered me a grey-mittened hand. "Would you like to skate?"

I shrugged. "Why not?" I didn't want to seem too eager but in my mind I was shouting *Thank you, God. Thank you, Ervino.*

Simon clutched my hand, his grip like warm steel through his mitten. His touch had a homecoming feel mixed with an electrical sensation that scrambled my nerves. Nice but scary.

Ervino gave us a jaunty wave. "Have fun, guys."

As Simon and I headed toward the oval, he kept his gaze fixed on his feet. Left foot, stagger, right foot, left foot, skid, right foot. I propped him up, trying to anticipate his moves and keep him from falling. I felt sorry for him though I was kind of glad he was awkward. It meant he needed me.

"Shall we head up to the island?" I asked, thinking we'd do better with more space around us.

"We could try but I'm not skating too well, as you may have noticed."

I didn't know what to say. Simon was a horrible skater. It was brave of him to even venture onto the ice, let alone ask anyone to skate with him.

"These aren't my skates," he added as I steered us toward the island. "They're Ervino's. I borrowed them."

"Don't you have skates of your own?"

"They're at home."

"Why didn't you bring them?"

"I didn't come here to skate," Simon said. "I came to pick up some veterinary supplies. Ervino brought them from Vancouver for me. His parents own an animal supply company."

"Are you a veterinarian?"

"No, my brother is. I work in his clinic."

"That must be interesting."

"It is."

I guided Simon around a clump of cattails frozen into the ice. "I think those skates are too big for you. That's probably why you're having trouble."

"Probably." Simon watched his feet for a few moments, then risked a glance at me. "What else do you study at university, besides chemistry with Ervino?"

"Botany, toxicology, therapeutics, and Russian. I want to be a pharmacist."

No, maybe that sounded too boastful. "Or a pharmacy technician."

"You could help a lot of people that way."

"Yes, and I think I'd enjoy it." My mother's pill addiction had sparked my interest but I didn't bother mentioning that to Simon.

"What does the Russian language have to do with pharmacy?"

"Nothing in particular," I said, guiding him over a rough patch in the ice. "But we're supposed to take one foreign language. I chose Russian."

His eyebrows quirked up. "Are you Russian?"

"No." I paused. "It's complicated. My grandparents are Mennonites. They came from Russia but they have Dutch, German, and Polish roots."

"Something like my ancestors," Simon said.

"What?" I almost dropped his hand. "Don't tell me you're a Mennonite too." There were tons of them in the Fraser Valley but I wasn't sure about the rest of the province.

"My last name is Epp," Simon said. "Some of my relatives' names are Wiebe, Sawatzky, and Unrau. What does that tell you?"

"Enough," I replied with a laugh. "Is there a Mennonite church in Sage City?"

"Yes, we have a small church," Simon said. "I lead the choir."

"So you must be a good singer."

He shrugged. "People seem to think so."

As we neared the island, a raven croaked from a spruce tree. Another raven answered, farther inland. "I saw a fox up here earlier," I said.

"Where?"

"Around the bend, on the beach. Red fox."

We stumble-skated around the eastern edge of the island. As we slowed to a stop alongside the beach, Simon peered down into the snow. "Those are probably your fox's pawprints." He pointed. "See the four toes with the triangular lobe behind?"

I nodded. "Looks like the fox couldn't decide which way to go." Its prints veered to the right, then left and back again.

Simon shook his head. "It was probably listening for mice. See over there?" He raised his free arm, swaying on his skates. "You can see where it reared onto its hind legs, jumped, and dived headfirst into a snowbank."

"Mice are under the snow?"

"That's where they live in winter, in snow burrows."

I was impressed. "How do you know?"

Simon shrugged. "I'm interested in animals, wild and tame." He glanced at his watch. "I should leave soon. My brother's expecting me."

A cold hand squeezed my heart. This dreamy guy in a blue jacket with matching eyes had asked me to skate, just like that. Now he was going to disappear, just like that. "It's almost lunchtime," I said in a small voice. "They're having a wiener roast."

"I'd love to stay and eat but I need to get back to the clinic."

Was that true or just an excuse to get away from me? "Could you phone your brother and tell him you'll be late?"

"No, sorry. Saturdays are our busiest days."

I almost drowned in a wave of disappointment.

In gloomy silence we retraced our route around the eastern edge of the island. The wind tossed bits of ice into our faces. My nose started running.

As I dug a tissue out of my pocket, Simon said, "It's a pity Mennonites don't dance. I'd make a better dancer than a skater." He glanced at his feet. "Wearing these things anyway."

I wiped my nose. "Why are you even trying to skate?"

"I saw a cute girl in a red hat, and I wanted to meet her."

My heart did a backflip. Maybe there was hope after all. "You could have waited until I came to shore."

"I waited half an hour but you didn't show any sign of quitting. When Ervino said he knew you, I borrowed his skates and got him to introduce us." Simon squeezed my hand. "I'd like to keep in touch with you, Susie. How about writing me a letter when you get home?"

My heart stood on its hind legs like the fox, its ears twitching with hope. "I might do that," I said, trying not to sound too keen. "What's your address?"

"I'll give it to you as soon as I get these blessed skates off."

CHAPTER 2

When I arrived home in Vancouver, fog was swirling through the streets. It made a stranger of the rowhouse I'd lived in all my life.

As I carried my suitcase up the wet walkway, memories of meeting Simon gave my feet wings. Anxiety about my mother dragged them down. What condition would I find her in? I never knew what to expect. I unlocked the door. "Mom, I'm home."

The entryway was silent except for the fluorescent fixture droning in the ceiling. I removed my jacket and boots, left them, padded to the door of my mother's bedroom, and knocked.

No answer.

Peeking inside, I caught a whiff of the menthol cream she put on her feet to soften her calluses. She wasn't there.

I hurried into the living room. The green quilt Aunt Frieda and I had made lay rumpled on the carpet along with several used tissues, a blue sock, a few sunflower seeds, and a magazine with Premier Bennett on the cover. Dirty dishes littered the coffee table. One plate was upside down, leaking something grey. Probably sardines, judging by the smell.

I checked the kitchen and found Mom sitting at the table in her ratty pink housecoat. She had a dopey grin on her face and her eyes looked glassy. One of her hands swatted at something that wasn't there.

Too many tranquillizers, or maybe a mixture of tranquillizers and painkillers.

"My little girrrl," she slurred.

"That's me, Mom," I said though I didn't feel like her little girl. I felt like her mother, forced into a role I wasn't ready for. My sister Coralie didn't live at home anymore, smart girl. But I stayed and kept trying. God knows I tried.

I kissed Mom's cheek and gave her a little backrub. Then I cleaned up the mess in the living room and retreated to my bedroom to unpack my suitcase.

In the past, I had sometimes locked my mother's pills into my typewriter case to keep them away from her. But I had quit doing that. She always managed to get more of whatever she wanted—Phenobarbital, Valium,

Dexedrine, Hydrocone. Years of working as a nurse's aide had provided her with 'useful' connections.

Whenever Mom obtained her pills from whatever source, she'd swallow five, six, or more at a time—whatever it took to float her into a happy bubble. Sadly, her bubbles always burst.

When Mom's dope-sickness got too bad, Dad took her to a rehabilitation centre where the staff managed to wean her off the drugs. After one of those sessions, she might stay clean for weeks. Then something would upset her, like a TV tube blowing or an argument with Coralie, and she'd go back to eating pills.

I did my best not to aggravate my mother. I certainly wouldn't tell her about Simon. She'd worry about me writing to a guy I hardly knew. She had been a worrywart for as long as I could remember. I could just imagine what she'd say. *Susie, what do you really know about the guy? He could be dangerous. He might blackmail you, or double-cross you, or corrupt your morals.*

I couldn't picture sweet, awkward Simon doing anything of the kind. He was a good person; I just knew it. He had even been considerate enough to suggest I write to him rather than phone. Long distance calls were expensive. A postage stamp cost six cents.

How was Mom doing? I checked on her, found her sleeping on the couch, and laid a quilt over her. Then I returned to my bedroom, took a sheet of mauve stationery out of my desk, and wrote:

February 24, 1970

Dear Simon,

It was nice meeting you at the sports festival. A choir sang in the lodge on Sunday morning. They made me think of you leading your choir in Sage City. On Sunday afternoon I tried snowshoeing and liked it. On Monday I went on a tour to Helmcken Falls. As you may know, it's the fourth-highest waterfall in Canada.

I got home on the bus okay except for a bunch of mountain sheep blocking the highway near Lillooet. The driver honked at them but they didn't move so we just waited until they wandered away.

I hope to hear from you.

Sincerely, Susie Rempel

Did Simon really want to keep in touch with me? I wondered as I dropped my letter into the mailbox. Maybe he had suggested it on the spur of the moment and changed his mind later.

After eight days of hoping and second-guessing, I found a letter from him in the mailbox at the end of our walkway. There it sat, a miracle in a caramel-coloured envelope. I scooped it out and opened it on the walkway while cars growled past on the street. A radio in a Ford Thunderbird blared "We all live in a yellow submarine."

Simon's handwriting was large and blocky.

March 1, 1970

Dear Susie,

I'm glad you enjoyed the rest of your time at the festival. Too bad about the mountain sheep on the highway. But you have to admit they're beautiful animals with their heart-shaped faces and curved horns.

How are your university classes going? Ervino told me you're a more serious student than most.

Our receptionist at the veterinary clinic, Betty, has sciatica. She can hardly walk. She still answers the phone, makes appointments, and does paperwork, but she can't help us with the animals like she used to. She's considering retirement. We'll be sad to see her go.

My brother Wally's wife, Myrtlemay, teaches grade six. She persuaded me to give a talk on birds that stay in Sage City all winter, like magpie, chickadee, starling, eagle, and grouse. I think the students enjoyed it. They sent me thank you notes afterwards. I've got them stuck to my refrigerator with magnets. Your letter is in a place of honour on the freezer, ha ha.

I hope you and your family are well. Please write again and tell me what you're up to.

Yours truly, Simon Epp

The letter gave me a warm happy glow inside. I answered it immediately. Every few days after that, our letters crossed the mountains and valleys between us.

Simon's letters never called me his girlfriend or sweetheart or anything like that. But just knowing he cared enough to write so often made me feel worthwhile and special.

Not wanting my parents to see his letters, I locked them in my typewriter case. I also made a point of picking up our mail myself, usually on my way home from university.

Mom never picked up the mail; she was afraid there might be spiders in the mailbox. However, Dad sometimes collected it when I was late getting home.

"You got a letter from S. Epp," he announced one afternoon when I dragged myself into the house dripping wet from getting caught in the rain.

I peeled off my soggy jacket and hung it over the chair by the door. "It's not a big deal. Just a pen pal."

A sulphury, tomatoey aroma drifted out of the kitchen. Probably cabbage rolls from the restaurant where Dad washed dishes and peeled vegetables. He often brought home food that didn't sell and couldn't be kept until the next day.

He peered at the return address. "Apparently S. Epp lives in Sage City." The bottom third of Dad's face sagged from not putting his teeth in. He seldom wore them; they hurt his mouth.

"Yeah, Sage City." I pushed wet hair off my face. "One of the sunniest cities in British Columbia. It's probably not raining there."

Dad checked the envelope again. "Looks like a man's handwriting."

"Might be. Might not." Attempting a playful smile, I reached for the envelope.

Dad waved it up, down, and sideways, just out of my reach. When I finally managed to grab it, he gave me a toothless grin, his eyes sparkling with—what? Pride maybe. His uncool daughter had actually captured a man's attention. Maybe I wasn't destined to be a perennial wallflower after all.

For Easter, Simon sent me a box of chocolate eggs. I was allergic to chocolate but I didn't tell him. I just thanked him for his thoughtful gift. Then I donated it to the seniors' care home where I sometimes worked at the front desk.

I enjoyed the care home, especially the residents' stories about their first train rides, jobs, fishing trips, and romances. The manager wanted me there full-time in the summer but Simon had another idea. A week after Easter, he wrote:

April 6, 1970

Dear Susie,

Betty retired and Wally hired a new receptionist. Unfortunately she isn't doing well. She's afraid of the animals, gets the files mixed up, and makes mistakes in the billings. I'm sure you'd do better. I suggested to Wally that he offer you the job. His letter is enclosed. It would be fun to spend the summer working together, wouldn't it?

It would indeed. The prospect sent my heart careening around in my chest, bumping against my ribs. My fingers trembled, making the paper rattle as I unfolded Wally's letter.

April 6, 1970

Dear Miss Rempel,

Simon told me about your education and work experience. Based on his recommendation, I'm willing to offer you employment from May 1 until your autumn semester begins. The job would involve office and front-desk duties plus some animal care. Remuneration would be a hundred dollars a week plus a small living allowance, paid on Fridays. I look forward to hearing from you.

Sincerely,

Waldemar (Wally) Epp, DVM

That sounded great. I loved animals and the pay was higher than in the seniors' home. But Sage City was two hundred miles from Vancouver. What would Mom and Dad say? I'd never lived away from home before.

CHAPTER 3

On Sunday morning I hurried home from church, gearing myself up to tell my parents about Dr. Epp's offer.

As I crunched up the gravel walkway, Dad glanced over from weeding the garden, his shoulders hunched in a denim shirt I'd mended. "The irises are budding. Did you notice?"

"Yeah, I saw them when I left for church."

Dad straightened to his full five feet, five inches. "They should do well this spring, after all that rain."

"They should," I said, "but I might be gone before they bloom."

Dad's forehead wrinkled. "Where do you plan on going? Hawaii? Timbuktu? The far side of the moon?"

I laughed. "Nowhere that exotic." I turned toward the door. "Let's go inside. I need to talk to you and Mom."

The house reeked of carbolic soap. I disliked its tarry medicinal smell but Mom said carbolic was a super germ-killer. Germs were everywhere, just waiting to make her sick or kill her.

She was pacing the living-room floor in her green uniform from when she was a nurse's aide. Her shoulders twitched under the shiny fabric. Her hands fluttered, probably from too many diet pills. They energized her though not always in a good way.

"Sit down, woman," Dad said. "Our daughter needs to talk to us."

Mom stopped pacing and turned her mocha-brown eyes on me. "You're in trouble, Susie." It was a statement, not a question.

"No, it's good news." I suspected she wouldn't consider it good.

Dad kicked his shoes off and settled into his recliner chair.

Mom perched on the edge of the couch, her knees bouncing with pill-induced energy.

I sat beside her, filled my lungs with carbolic-scented air, and told my parents about my pen pal and the job his veterinarian brother had offered me.

"Too dangerous," Mom said when I'd finished.

"Not as dangerous as flying to the moon," Dad observed.

Mom scowled at him. "Shut up, Reuben. If you can't say anything reasonable, don't say anything at all."

She angled her body toward me. "You need to be careful about men you don't know. You can't judge a person's character just from letters. Simon might take advantage of you. You could get pregnant like your cousin Velda."

"I can resist temptation," I said. Not that I'd had any experience resisting the sort of temptation that could get a girl pregnant. "Anyway Simon's not that kind of guy. He leads the choir in the Mennonite church in Sage City."

"Score a point for Simon," Dad said. "We don't do too well in the church department ourselves."

Mom threw him a look that could have stripped the varnish off the coffee table. "You could go to church, Reuben. It wouldn't hurt you to get up early once in a while."

"What about you? I don't see you rushing to the bus stop with your Bible every Sunday morning."

Until a few years ago, our whole family had attended church. Aunt Frieda and Uncle Milford had picked us up and taken us. But our lives changed after they moved away.

Tears gathered in my mother's eyes. A big one rolled down her cheek.

I patted her arm. "Listening to church on the radio is almost as good as going in person." We often tuned in the *Back to the Bible* broadcast from Lincoln, Nebraska.

Mom gave me a watery smile. "You understand me better than him over there." She jerked a nod at my father. "I think you'd better stay home this summer. You could work in the old folks' place again. You enjoy that, don't you?"

"Sure but I can't stay home forever." I loved my parents but I needed a break from them. A long break.

Mom frowned at a stain on her sleeve, spat on a couple of fingers, and scrubbed at it. "You're only twenty. You need somebody to keep an eye on you."

I almost laughed. Mom was often too zoned out on pills to keep an eye on anybody.

I squared my shoulders. "Coralie was only eighteen when she left home."

"That was different," Mom said. "Your sister only moved five blocks away, and she has roommates."

"Right, but—"

"Who are Simon and his brother's parents?" Mom asked. "Do you even know?"

"They must be smart people," Dad said, "if they've got a son that's a veterinarian."

I shot him a grateful look. "Simon and Wally's mother's name is Adeline," I said. "She farms in Saskatchewan. Adeline's husband was Isaac but he passed away." I paused for dramatic effect. "He was related to Theodore H. Epp."

Mom raised her eyebrows. "The *Back to the Bible* pastor?"

I nodded and pressed my advantage. "Simon said his family always listened to *Back to the Bible* when he was growing up. He still listens."

"Interesting." Mom frowned at a spike of cuticle beside her thumbnail, leaned over, and bit it off. "Where would you live in Sage City?"

"There are places that take boarders. Simon sent me a list."

"I don't want you living with strangers."

Dad heaved himself out of his chair. "I think my second-cousin Lena Neufeld still lives in Sage City." He padded toward the kitchen. "Maybe Susie could stay with her."

"I hear she's not a good housekeeper," Mom called after him.

I followed Dad into the kitchen, picking up one of Mom's stray socks along the way. "Do you have Lena's phone number?"

"No, but you can probably get it from Information."

As my father dumped a container of beef stew into a saucepan, I called Information, the dial of our rotary phone clicking as it spun.

CHAPTER 4

When I returned to the living room, my mother was doing arm flings and knee bends—both at the same time. "Guess what, Mom."

"What?" she puffed.

"Lena said seventy dollars a month for both room and board. That's reasonable, right?"

Mom nodded.

However, she still wasn't keen on having me move. On the other hand, she didn't entirely oppose the idea.

That was typical Mom. When I was a kid, her dithering kept me on edge. If I asked permission to do something like go to the playground, or try on her jewellery, or sleep with my nightlight on, I seldom got a straight answer. Even when Mom said yes, she often made me feel guilty about doing whatever she'd said I could do.

Regarding the job in Sage City, I forged ahead despite Mom's shilly-shallying. Dad had given me the green light, so I phoned Dr. Epp and accepted his offer.

Ten days later I packed my suitcases and said goodbye to my family. With a mixture of nostalgia and relief, I boarded the bus for Sage City.

Simon met me at the depot, wearing a leather vest with fringes—quite trendy. He looked slimmer than before and his hair was longer. He'd mentioned in one of his letters that he was growing it out because I'd said crewcuts were going out of style.

The sky was clear, the city golden in the late-afternoon light. Pine trees and greening sagebrush dotted the mountainsides. "Welcome to Sage City," Simon said with a slow smile.

I saw bashfulness and uncertainty in his eyes. Or maybe I imagined them because I felt bashful and uncertain myself. Was Simon my boyfriend or potential boyfriend? If so, how should I act with him? I'd never had a boyfriend or even gone out on a date.

"How was your trip?" he asked, his big square hands clasping the handles of my suitcases.

"Fine, thanks." I swung my backpack over my shoulders.

As we headed into the parking lot, Simon adjusting his steps to mine, I wished I could think of something interesting to say to him. I would have if I'd been writing to him instead of seeing him in person.

A pair of mourning doves ambled across the lot near Simon's Volkswagen Beetle, their heads bobbing. As we approached the birds, they flapped up into a cottonwood tree and sat there cuddling, sure of their relationship.

"I've met Mrs. Neufeld a few times," Simon said, opening the passenger door of his Beetle for me. "I think she'll be a good landlady."

"I've never met her but she sounded nice on the phone."

Simon nodded, put my suitcases in the trunk, went around to the driver's side, and slid in. Feeling his big warm body so close to mine made my pulse beat faster. He smelled of shampoo and apples, or maybe there were apples in the car. I glanced into the backseat but didn't see any, just a neatly folded jacket and a newspaper open to the sports page.

The tiny blond hairs on the backs of Simon's hands gleamed as he turned the key in the ignition. Over the thrumming of the engine, he said, "Mrs. Neufeld brought her turtles to our clinic a few months ago."

"I didn't know she kept turtles." Dad hadn't told me much about his second-cousin except that she was a retired telephone operator whose husband had died of cancer.

"She doesn't have turtles anymore," Simon said, shifting into first gear. He signalled, then pulled out into a street of two- and three-storey buildings with glass storefronts.

"What happened to them?"

"They died, unfortunately," Simon said, shifting into second.

I dared to give him a teasing grin. "What kind of a clinic are you and your brother running if you can't even keep turtles alive? I read somewhere that they can live to be a hundred."

"Mrs. Neufeld's turtles weren't so lucky." Simon turned onto a street lined with frame houses, some with flowering shrubs outside. "They were beautiful animals—yellow-bellied sliders—but they had a respiratory infection that Wally couldn't find the right medication for." Simon wheeled the Volkswagen onto a street that sloped down toward the river. "Our clinic does better with dogs, horses, and cattle."

"I look forward to seeing the clinic."

Simon gave me a sideways grin. "That's a nice positive attitude in an employee."

Was I only an employee to him? Maybe he was joking.

"Wally wants to meet you tomorrow morning at eight," he said. "Do you know how to get to the clinic?"

"I can probably find my way on the bus," I said. "I photocopied the bus schedule in the library, also a map of Sage City."

"You're organized."

"I try to be. Maybe my organizational skills will gain me a few points as an employee."

Simon's smile curved toward his dimples. "They can't hurt." He eased the Volkswagen past several houses, then stopped in front of an almond-coloured bungalow with a grey roof. "This should be the place."

"It looks homey," I said. I liked the colours though the roof sagged a bit.

"Let's go and say hello to Mrs. Neufeld first. We can come back for your luggage."

As we walked up the driveway, I noticed lace valances at the tops of my landlady's windows. Maybe she enjoyed needlework. If so, she and I could crochet or knit together in the evenings, unless I had a date with Simon. Would he ask me out on dates or would we only see each other at work?

The door was grey with a chrome mail slot. I knocked and waited.

No answer.

Simon shrugged. "Maybe she's not home."

"That's odd. I told her I planned to arrive around this time." Glancing around, I noticed a sheet of blue-lined paper taped to the bottom of the door. I pulled it off and read.

> I'm sorry, Susie. My daughter got sick. I have to go to Kelowna and babysit her kids. I don't know how long I'll be gone. Please make yourself at home. Evelyn Baines in the yellow house next door will give you the key. Your bedroom is the one with the blue wallpaper. If you have any problems, go to Evelyn. She'll take care of you. Your second-cousin-aunt, Lena Neufeld. P.S. We can cut your rent in half since you'll need to make your own meals. Help yourself to whatever you can find in the refrigerator and cupboards.

I slumped against the almond-coloured siding; it felt cold on my back. "I've never lived alone before." My voice came out small. "I've never even lived away from home."

My mother's voice scratched at the back of my mind. *It'll be scary, Susie. All those rooms and nobody there but you. You'll jump every time you hear a noise. What about mice? Burglars? Rapists?*

"Don't worry," Simon said. "It'll be fun, an adventure."

A small butterfly of freedom fluttered in my heart. "I guess so."

"You won't spend much time alone here anyway. You'll be at the clinic five days a week."

"Right."

He shifted from one wide foot to the other. "We can eat in a restaurant some evenings. On Sunday mornings, we can go to church. Sunday afternoons, we can go for drives or hikes." His voice rose with enthusiasm. "Sometimes there are concerts or baseball games in the parks."

So Simon did plan to ask me out on dates. I was glad though I couldn't help feeling crowded. I wasn't accustomed to spending much time with anyone besides members of my own family. "You sound like you've got my life all planned for me."

Simon's cheeks reddened. "I didn't mean it like that. I was just trying to be friendly. I don't want you getting bored and lonely in Sage City."

I smiled. "I appreciate that. I look forward to not getting bored and lonely."

Simon returned my smile, then glanced toward the house next door. "Shall we go and get that key?"

CHAPTER 5

On the three-month anniversary of my move to Sage City, I rose before six in the morning. In my slippers and flannel pyjamas, I padded down Lena's pink-carpeted stairway, my heart swelling with gratitude for the way my life was turning out.

I loved my job. I enjoyed living alone in Lena's house while she stayed in Kelowna helping her family. My dad admired my independence though my mom wanted me to come home. Simon and I were becoming more comfortable with each other.

Today he and I were going to drive out into the country with our boss, his brother Wally. We planned to vaccinate cattle at a couple of ranches. Between ranches we'd have a picnic lunch in a canyon with interesting rock formations. I had volunteered to bring a pineapple upside-down cake for lunch.

My mouth curving into a smile, I pirouetted through the kitchen door and across the linoleum floor to the counter. Before moving to Sage City, I wouldn't have known how to make a pineapple upside-down cake, but I had learned a few things from Lena's cookbooks. I was taking a mixing bowl out of a cupboard when a knock at the back door made me jump. "Who's there?"

"Good morning, Susie," a tenor voice called.

"Simon!" Oh, no! My hair was wild, my face unwashed. I set the bowl on the counter, smoothed my hair, wiped the sleep from my eyes, and hurried to the door. "What are you doing here?" I cracked the door open a few inches. "I thought we weren't leaving until eight o'clock. It's not even six-fifteen."

"I came to say good morning to my girlfriend." Simon had recently started calling me that, though he never held my hand or kissed me or anything along that line. Our Mennonite church had rules about courting behaviour.

"I'm a mess," I said, smoothing my pyjama top. Simon had never seen me in pyjamas, even modest ones like those I was wearing. Obviously meeting one's boyfriend in pyjamas would be against the rules. But I couldn't do anything about it now.

Simon eased the door open a bit wider. "You're too pretty to ever be a mess."

"Flatterer." A blush warmed the roots of my hair. "What brings you here so early?"

"I suppose I should have phoned but I wanted to tell you in person."

"Tell me what?" Had something happened to Wally or his wife?

Simon fiddled with the zipper of his windbreaker. "Can I come in for a few minutes?"

"I guess so." Many Mennonites would frown on me for inviting a man inside when I was alone in the house. But they weren't here and the wind was cool.

"I hope you're feeling adaptable this morning," Simon said, following me into the kitchen.

"What do you mean?" I offered him a chair, then sat across the table from him.

"Wally changed Okanaga's medication. He needs you to stay here and give it to her."

I pictured the racehorse in her stall at the clinic, her eyes watery, her breathing raspy. She needed help, sure. I just wished I wasn't the one being asked to provide it. I'd been looking forward to driving out into the country with Simon and Wally.

"Okanaga needs the new antibiotic every six hours," Simon said. "Wally gave it to her at five this morning so she'll need it again at eleven. It's in the refrigerator with her name on it."

"Right." I was pleased that Wally trusted me to take care of Okanaga by myself. On the other hand, I didn't like the idea of getting left behind.

"Give Okanaga the new antibiotic the same way we did the other one," Simon said. "Slide the big syringe into the corner of her mouth, away from her teeth. If you have any trouble or notice anything unusual, call Dr. Redshaw right away."

"Okay, but how will you and Wally manage without me?"

Simon gave me a cautious smile. "We'll miss your pineapple cake for sure, but we've got someone else to help with the vaccinations. "She—"

I jerked my head up. "She?"

Simon crossed his arms, then uncrossed them. "A friend of our mother's."

"Where did she come from all of a sudden?"

"She and Mother drove out from Dayspring, Saskatchewan."

"That's a long way. Did you know they were coming?"

"Nope," Simon said. "They didn't bother telling us."

"Why not?"

He shrugged. "Some Saskatchewan people are like that. They just show up."

"Are you looking forward to spending time with your mother?" Wally's wife called her a fire-breathing dragon.

"Of course I look forward to it. She's my mother, eh?"

My eyes narrowed. "So you're taking her and her friend into the country instead of me."

"Not Mother. She doesn't want to go

"Why not?"

"She's tired of travelling, she says." Simon jingled his truck keys. "I'd better shove off. I want to do a few things before we leave."

"Hold on a minute," I said, following him to the door. "If your mother's not going, there'll be room for me in the van. Maybe someone else could give Okanaga her antibiotic."

"Nobody else is available today," Simon said. "Max has the flu and Gayle is on holidays."

"What about someone from Dr. Redshaw's clinic?"

Simon laid a warm hand on my shoulder, making my heart shift into a higher gear. "We'd be delighted to have you come along. If you can find a substitute, great. Let me know before eight and we'll pick you up."

After he left, I showered and dressed, then blew my hair dry. By the time I'd eaten breakfast, I figured Dr. Redshaw would be in his clinic. As I reached for the phone to call him, it rang.

Simon's mother, Mrs. Epp, was on the line. She wanted to meet for a cup of tea before I gave Okanaga her medication.

I twisted the phone cord around my fingers, wondering why she wanted to meet me without Simon. I was tempted to say no. The woman sounded scary, plus I'd had zero experience in meeting a boyfriend's parents. On the other hand, I'd need to meet her sooner or later if Simon and I stayed together. I might as well get it over with.

CHAPTER 6

I arrived at the Back Home Café at nine-thirty sharp, my stomach fluttering like a moth in a Mason jar. The fire-breathing dragon from Saskatchewan—otherwise known as Simon's mother, Mrs. Epp—stood over a red Formica table, scrubbing it with a handful of paper napkins. I recognized her from the snapshot Simon carried in his wallet. She was a tall sixty-plus woman with wide legs and hips sloping up to narrow shoulders and a small round head. Her steel-wool hair was held in place by a hairnet. I didn't like the hairnet but it gave her an air of practicality. Or realism. Or something.

I cleared my throat. "Good morning, Mrs. Epp."

"Morning, Susie." She clumped over to the garbage can near the counter and threw her napkins in, her knuckles grazing the swinging lid. "My Simon," she said, returning to the freshly scrubbed table. "I think God made him out of leftovers."

That was quite an opener. Whatever happened to small talk? "Why do you say that?"

Mrs. Epp plunked herself onto a chair. "I didn't mean nothing bad." Her voice squawked like a crow's.

"Oh?" I seated myself across from her. Photos of local wildlife peered out from the wall behind her. Hawk, eagle, coyote, bear, cougar.

Mrs. Epp fingered the collar of her old-fashioned mauve dress. "I just meant Simon was born after I thought I didn't have no bolts and nuts left to make another baby. When I got pregnant with that little *benjel,* I was going through The Change already. I had hot flashes, sore joints, very close veins, forget*somkeit*—the whole shootin' match."

The waitress, whose name tag said Linda, was moving from table to table setting out ketchup bottles. She clamped her pink lips together as if suppressing a laugh. Maybe she had never heard anyone mix bad English with Mennonite Low German the way Simon's mother did.

Linda plunked a ketchup bottle down on a nearby table and approached us, raising a penciled eyebrow.

Mrs. Epp jerked a nod at her. "We'll have two teas, please."

I would have preferred coffee but I didn't have the guts to say so.

Mrs. Epp lifted the edge of her hairnet and tucked a couple of stray curls underneath it. "Simon says you're good at typewriting. Did they learn you that in high school?"

"Yes, but I've been out of high school for a few years now. I'm working my way through university." Maybe that would impress the woman. I needed to win her over or at least persuade her to tolerate me. She was the mother of the man I loved.

Linda brought our tea. As she set it down, Mrs. Epp asked, "Does it give pie in your café?"

Linda's lips twitched into a half-smile or maybe a smirk. "We've got strawberry pie and lemon meringue today."

"I'll take one piece strawberry and two pieces lamon."

Really? Wally's wife, Myrtlemay, had told me her mother-in-law enjoyed food but three pieces of pie seemed excessive. Gross actually. "I'll have lemon pie," I told Linda. "Just one piece."

After she left, Mrs. Epp leaned back in her chair. "My son Wally, he's a wonderful good veterinarian."

"He is," I said with genuine enthusiasm. "He has a sixth sense when it comes to animals."

She poured cream into her tea. "My Wally, he gets things done. But my Simon—" She flung her hand out as if shooing a fly. "He doesn't make something from himself. When he finished high school, he wanted to be a teacher like Wally's wife. So I said, *'Na yo,* Simon, remember you had romantic fever when you were small. Your heart is maybe too weak for teaching but we can anyways try. I'll send you to teacher college.' But before he finished teacher college, he quit and went to Bible School at Caronport. He didn't finish that neither."

"No, but he learned a lot about the Bible at Caronport." I didn't like hearing Mrs. Epp badmouth her son. Why was she doing that? A mother should be proud of her children.

As Linda arrived with our pie, Mrs. Epp grabbed her fork. "But Simon didn't become a preacher or a missionary or even a Sunday School superintendent." She attacked her closer piece of lemon meringue. "After Caronport, he moved himself away to Seattle, where his sister lives. He wanted to study fish science. Salmons and trouts and stuff."

I traced fork lines in my meringue. "Sometimes it takes a while for a person to settle on a career."

Mrs. Epp raised a forkful of lemon pie and peered at it. "He didn't make nothing from his fish science neither."

"I think it helps him with his veterinary work."

"Not much. Mostly Wally teaches him. Simon is lucky he's hooked on with Wally and Myrtlemay. But they can't keep care of him forever." Her voice had a serrated edge to it. "He needs a with-helper."

"A what?"

"A with-helper. A wife that can make something from him. Like Bethany Banman."

My heart stumbled over a few beats. "Who?"

Mrs. Epp finished her first piece of lemon pie, pushed the plate aside, and pulled the strawberry pie into position. "Simon must have told you about Bethany. He was sweet on her in high school. In teacher college too."

"He mentioned her," I admitted, watching Mrs. Epp's fork break through the pie crust and mush it down into the strawberry filling. The crust was thick and brown, glittering with sugar. "Wasn't Bethany the girl who painted pictures of horses and tractors and stuff on the other kids' lunch-pails?"

"That was her." Mrs. Epp's voice softened. "That girl is artistic like crazy. She learned herself to be an art teacher. Then she married herself with a fish farmer. He had a fish farm south of Dayspring but he got water on his brains and died."

"That's awful."

"Of course awful but now Bethany has that fish farm by herself. She's got twelve people working for her. Twelve! Lots of money, no husband."

"I don't think Simon would be interested in her anymore." I hoped he wouldn't.

Ignoring my comment, Mrs. Epp ran her gaze over my meagre bosom. "Bethany's not skinny like a mouse. She's filled out real nice."

"Are you saying she's fat?" I asked, misunderstanding on purpose.

Mrs. Epp scowled at me like I was a beetle in the sugar bowl. "I mean Bethany's shaped just right."

I'd never been shaped just right—too scrawny—but Simon liked me the way I was. On the other hand, maybe he and the rich, filled-out Bethany Banman really would be interested in each other. Strange things happen.

"My Simon should marry himself with Bethany," Mrs. Epp announced, chasing a runaway strawberry with her fork.

"But he loves me," I protested. He'd never said the actual words but I knew I was good for him. Wally and Myrtlemay thought so too. They said Simon was livelier and happier since he'd met me.

The dragon flashed her eyes. "You should go to Vancouver back and leave my son alone."

"I won't do that, Mrs. Epp." I sharpened my eyes. "I've got a job here and I'm good at it. Wally says I'm the best summer help he ever had."

"You've got spunk, Susie." Mrs. Epp smiled. She actually smiled at me. "I like spunk. But you're young and green. Young people don't know always what's good for them. Simon's wrong for you. You need a younger *kjeadel*, a go-getter with more fire and drive." She pushed her hairnet higher on her forehead. "It must give lots of those kind in Vancouver."

"But I like Simon."

Mrs. Epp sipped her tea, her gaze fixed on something in mid-air. "As soon as he's *befriet* with Bethany, he'll be rich. He can help her with her fishes, help her count her money, and live nice and close to his mom."

I felt like I was floating in a soup of wretchedness. "I've gotta leave." I fumbled with my purse. "I don't feel good."

"What's loose with you?" Mrs. Epp squawked. "Woman troubles?"

"Something like that." I pulled a two-dollar bill out of my purse and threw it on the table. "You can pay for my pie and tea out of that." I lurched out of my chair. The café swirled around me, a blur of tables, chairs, and wildlife photographs.

Mrs. Epp lunged toward me, grabbing my arm. "No, Susie, I'll pay." She tucked the bill into my purse. "Bethany gave me a discount coupon."

I wheeled around, the sudden motion making me dizzier than I already was. "Where would she get a discount coupon for this café?"

Simon's mother tightened her grip on my arm. "The café reached it to her when she bought sandwiches for the picnic with my boys."

I blinked, trying to stop the swirling or slow it down. "So she's with Simon and Wally right now?"

"Yes." Triumphant smile.

What a schemer Mrs. Epp was! What a dirty rotten schemer! And what about her son Simon? Maybe he wasn't a model of integrity either. He'd let me think his mother's friend was some sixty-plus matron when she was really his former girlfriend. I needed to find out where I stood with that man. I yanked my arm out of his mother's grasp and stumbled out of the café.

The sidewalk rose and fell under my feet. Struggling to stay vertical, I staggered around to the alley at the back of the café. Behind one of the garbage bins, I sank into the weeds and let my tears flow.

I longed to retreat to Lena's house, crawl into bed, and stay there. But I couldn't, not yet anyway. Wally and Simon were depending on me to give Okanaga her medication. I fumbled tissues out of my pocket, blew my nose, and lurched to my feet.

CHAPTER 7

The barn behind Wally's veterinary clinic smelled of hay and animal sweat. Okanaga's halter chain rattled. I approached her stall armed with the plastic syringe full of medication. She greeted me with a low whinny.

"How's our girl?" I murmured, patting her dappled forehead. "We'll soon have you feeling better. You'll see." I aimed the syringe at the corner of the horse's mouth. Then I inserted the tip as gently as I could, avoiding her teeth, and pumped the liquid in. As I stroked her neck to help her swallow, I told her about the scheming Mrs. Epp and how I might lose Simon to Bethany. Okanaga listened with sympathy in her watery eyes.

Feeling a bit better, I wandered into the office to start reorganizing the patient files. It was a tedious job that I'd been putting off. I figured I might as well tackle it since I was there anyway.

I was sitting at my desk sorting the first folder when the phone rang. Wondering who would call when the clinic was closed, I grabbed the receiver. "Sun City Veterinary."

"Hello, Susie." A breathless voice. My mother's. Mom often sounded like she was afraid a brick wall would fall on her.

"Hi, Mom." I tried not to sound like her. "What's up?"

"I'm worried about you." She gulped. "Simon's mother phoned."

"Mrs. Epp called you?" The gall of that woman! "Where did she get your number?"

"I don't know."

The dragon must be more devious than I'd thought. "What did she want?"

"She wants you to move back to Vancouver and leave her son alone."

"Yeah, well, I'm not going to do that."

"Maybe you should." Mom's voice went high and thin. "I'm afraid she'll hurt you somehow."

"I can take care of myself." I longed to tell Mom about the filled-out Bethany and how she might steal Simon away from me. But I'd start bawling if I did, and I knew Mom's nerves would go haywire if I cried.

"You don't sound good," she said.

"I'm fine, Mom. Mrs. Epp is just visiting in Sage City, okay. She'll go home soon and things will settle down." Hopefully.

"I really think you should come home."

"It's too late to get a good summer job in Vancouver."

"You could still get on at the old folks' home."

"But I like Sage City. Listen, Mom, I'll call you later, okay? I've got stuff to do."

I returned to Wally's filing, trying to ignore the tightness that was creeping into the back of my neck. By two o'clock, when I went to check on Okanaga, I had a headache. I gave the horse a shoulder rub along with a few encouraging words. Then I wandered into the lunch room and ate half a leftover pizza. I found some aspirins in the cupboard, took two with a glass of milk, and returned to the files.

By three-thirty, the ache in my head was a vice squeezing my temples. Time to go home. I returned the files in the cabinet, separating out the ones I'd reorganized. Then I said goodbye to Okanaga and emerged blinking into the sunlight, locking the door behind me.

I had my choice of two routes to Lena's house. I could follow the streets through a residential area and past the typewriter shop to my turnoff. Or I could hike down to the river and take the path along the water. The river route was prettier and more peaceful.

The Cutbank River was one of my favourite things about Sage City. I loved the gentle way it flowed between its gravel banks. As I crunched along the path by the water, the lapping of the waves along the shoreline eased the tightness in my temples.

I rounded a bend and reached the picnic area near the outdoor stairway that led up to the shopping mall. The maple tree Simon and I had climbed a few days earlier stood like a sentinel near the bottom of the stairs.

My heart warmed at the memory of us sitting high among its leafy branches, eating oatmeal cookies. Simon and I had heard children chasing each other around the picnic tables. We'd caught snatches of conversation from the parking lot at the top of the stairs. But we'd sat smug and secure in our hideaway, knowing that nobody was likely to see us.

I swallowed a sob. Simon was with the beautiful Bethany at the Holmquist ranch. Or maybe they were back from the ranch, sitting in some cozy café gazing into each other's eyes. The thought worsened my headache and sapped my energy. I schlepped myself over to the maple tree, slumped onto the ground underneath it, and leaned against the trunk.

I don't know how long I sat there but I must have nodded off because I dreamt I was trying to read a prescription while a customer went into convulsions, frothing at the mouth. Then a crow squawked.

What was a crow doing in this dream? It didn't belong. There it was again. My eyes snapped open. The squawking sound seemed to come from the parking lot at the top of the stairs. As I listened, it formed itself into words. "Fish farm. Bethany. Good-looking woman."

Mrs. Epp! I bolted upright, my back as straight as the tree trunk. I couldn't face that woman again, not so soon anyway. I wanted to talk to Simon but not her.

Her voice croaked toward me again. "Too bad Bethany didn't come along with—"

Simon interrupted his mother, his voice fainter than hers. "I'm sure Bethany's happier at the mall." He paused. "Shall we go down and look at the river. Can you manage the stairs?"

Mrs. Epp snorted. "For sure. Easy. But let's first get our jackets from the car."

Oh, no. They'd be down here soon. I needed to hide but where?

The maple tree. If I climbed it and sat still, they might not see me.

I scrambled to my feet and grabbed a low-hanging branch, heaved myself onto it, and scrambled up through the branches almost to the top. There, I shrank back among the leaves, watching Simon and his mother descend the stairs. He held her arm though she didn't look like she needed help.

My head still ached. Fatigue dragged at my arms and legs. I hugged the tree trunk, breathing its woody scent and yearning for my room in Lena's house. Unfortunately I couldn't go there until Simon and his mother left.

That could take a while, from the looks of things. Mrs. Epp toddled over to the bench near my tree, her head bobbing like a crow's. As she plunked herself down, Simon started toeing the gravel, probably looking for fossils as he often did when we came here. He swept his shoe around in a half-circle, pushed aside the top layer of pebbles, and peered at the ones underneath.

He picked up a reddish stone about the size of a fist. "Here's a nice one, Mother. It's not a fossil but the texture is interesting." He crunched over to her and gave her the stone.

She weighed it in her hand. "You should give it to Bethany. She paints on stones. Sceneries."

Simon shrugged. "Why don't you give it to Bethany if you think she'd like it?"

The ache in my head eased. If Simon was interested in Bethany, he'd give her the stone himself, wouldn't he?

Mrs. Epp moved toward one end of the bench. "Sit yourself, Simon. We need to talk."

"I can talk standing up."

She patted the spot beside her. "Simon, I said sit yourself."

He sighed and perched on the edge of the bench.

Mrs. Epp lifted her hairnet and fluffed up her curls under it. "I met your little friend Susie this morning."

"Yes?" Simon's voice crept out cautiously, like a barn cat. "And?"

Mrs. Epp let the hairnet snap back into place. "She needs to move herself back to Vancouver."

"What? No." Simon sat up straighter. "Susie can't leave. She's the best summer help Wally and I ever had."

My face warmed with pride.

"Susie is wrong for you," Mrs. Epp said as if telling a child how to tie its shoelaces. "She's too young and green. You're twenty-six years old. You need a grownup wife."

"She's grown up enough for me."

I felt like cheering.

His mother hauled in a breath. "And Susie's parents would drag you down. Her pop is a dishwasher in a crumble-down café. Imagine. A dishwasher only."

Simon wheeled around to face his mother. "How do you know that? I never told you."

"I phoned to the mom from Susie. I asked."

Simon groaned. "Mother, how could you?"

She crossed her arms over her bottom-heavy chest. "I won't let you throw your life away on such a low-class family like that."

"Dishwashing is honest work," Simon said. "There's nothing wrong with it."

There wasn't. My dad enjoyed his job, humming while he worked. If more people were like my father, this world would be a better place.

Mrs. Epp's voice grated up through the branches. "Susie's mom is a sissy. She cried on the phone."

"She has weak nerves," Simon said. "She can't help it. Anyway Susie is much braver than her mother."

I was glad he considered me brave. I wasn't really. I just forged ahead in spite of my fears.

Mrs. Epp grabbed Simon's arm and shook it. "You should marry yourself with Bethany Banman. She comes from such good people. Her grandpa was a preacher in Russia. And her *gross-onkel* was something in the czar's government."

"What?"

Mrs. Epp shrugged. "I don't know. Something important."

Simon left the bench and started pacing. "I'll make up my own mind about marrying, if and when the time comes."

"But Simon," his mother bleated, "I know God wants you to marry yourself with Bethany. Think on your poor passed-away pop. He always wanted you to do God's will."

I'd never met Simon's father but I couldn't help wondering if his impression of God's will would be the same as his wife's.

Simon glanced at his watch. "Speaking of Bethany, aren't you supposed to meet her for supper?"

"Supper!" Mrs. Epp lurched off the bench. "It flew right out from my mind." She loped toward the staircase, then lurched to a halt. "Simon, aren't you coming with?"

"You go ahead, Mother."

"But you need to come. I told the restaurant three people."

"Tell them I can't make it." Did he flick a glance up into my tree or was that my imagination? "I've got something else to do."

"What?"

"Something important."

"What can be so important that my son can't eat *oventkost* with his poor old mother? I came all the way from Dayspring to see you. Now you don't even want to know from me."

"You exaggerate, Mother. Of course I want to 'know from' you. I look forward to spending more time with you but not right now." He shooed her away. "You'd better run along. You don't want to keep Bethany waiting."

CHAPTER 8

Cool air breezed up from the river. I shivered on my branch high in the maple tree. My right leg was stiff from sitting still but I forced myself to remain motionless and silent while Mrs. Epp clumped up the stairs toward the mall. After she'd gone, Simon sauntered over to my tree and leaned against it, whistling through his teeth.

Why didn't he go away and do whatever was so urgent that he couldn't eat supper with his mother? I needed to get out of this tree or at least move.

Simon peered up through the branches. "Susie, suppose you tell me what you're doing up there."

My toes curled with embarrassment. How long had he known I was here? "Bird-watching?" I ventured. It was the first thought that came to mind.

He faked a frown. "Eavesdropping, more likely."

"Not on purpose." Trying to work the stiffness out of my leg, I tightened my muscles, then relaxed them. "I was here before you and your mother showed up."

"You look cold."

"I'm not," I said, shivering.

"You'd better come down. I wouldn't want my favourite co-worker catching pneumonia."

Had Simon already downgraded me from girlfriend to co-worker? "Did you have fun with Bethany Banman?" I asked, not attempting to keep the sarcasm out of my voice.

"Come down and I'll tell you."

I could have challenged Simon to come up and get me but I was too cold and discouraged. I worked my way down the tree, one branch at a time.

As I hopped onto the ground, Simon removed his jacket and helped me put it on. "Would you like to go out for dinner? *L'Assiette* is only a few blocks away."

"I'm not dressed for *L'Assiette*."

"Me neither. They'll let us in anyway."

"I'm not hungry." If Simon planned to break up with me, I didn't want it happening in public.

"Shall we take a drive? What about Seymour Lookout?"

I shrugged. "Sure, if you like." The Lookout was a good place to watch the sun go down.

Nobody else was at the Lookout when we arrived. Not even a breeze stirred the sagebrush. Simon parked near the fence at the top of the hill.

"All right, Simon," I said as he switched off the ignition. "Tell me what's up between you and Bethany. Let's get it over with."

"There's not much to tell. My mother tends to—" He grabbed my arm. "Susie, look."

Following his pointing finger, I saw a couple of meadowlarks flitting from one sagebrush to another. The fading light glinted on the male's yellow chest.

The female, in sensible brown feathers, fluttered to the ground and began pacing around in the grass and weeds. The male swooped up to a fencepost, opened his beak, and poured out a loud, warbling song.

The female ignored him, jabbing her beak into the ground. She poked around a bit, then raised her head and gobbled something, probably a bug or a worm.

The male repeated his song, adding an extra warble at the end.

"What do you think he sang?" Simon asked.

I shrugged. "I don't know. Maybe *Come, come, the noodles are done.* That's what my dad would say."

Simon laughed. "I don't think that was it."

"What about *I left my pretty sister at home?* That would be my Aunt Frieda's version."

Simon shook his head. "Wrong again."

"So what do you think he sang?" I asked, watching the birds flutter toward the creek.

Simon cleared his throat, swallowed, and cleared it again. *Come, come, won't you please marry me?*"

I sucked in a breath. "I assume you're speaking for the bird."

"No." He gulped. His Adam's apple bobbed. "I'm speaking for myself."

My heart did a cartwheel. "You mean you want me to marry you?"

He nodded.

"All of a sudden?" I asked in a voice that didn't sound like mine. "Just like that?"

"You wanna get married, don't you?" His voice broke. "To me?"

"I think so but not until after...."

"After what?"

"After a while," I said. "I'm only twenty years old. I'm not ready to be a wife." I was just getting accustomed to being a girlfriend.

Simon put his arm around me. "Twenty is old enough. Come on, Susie. Say you'll be my lifetime pal."

Pal didn't sound as scary as wife. "What about Bethany Banman?"

"Bethany doesn't need me. You do."

I pulled away from him. "I can take care of myself. I'm not a charity case."

"Of course not. But life is better when people share it. Like it says in the Bible, *Two are better than one. If two lie together, then they have heat: but how can one be warm* alone?"

My pulse quickened at the thought of lying beside Simon. "Are you sure that's in the Bible?"

"Ecclesiastes." Simon kissed me. "I love you, Susie. Marry me before my mother finds a way to stop us."

"What about my university classes?"

"Could you do them by correspondence?"

"Maybe. But your mother hates me." How could our marriage work, given the way she felt about me?

"Mother doesn't hate anybody. She's a Mennonite."

"Yeah, well." I didn't think Mrs. Epp acted like a Mennonite or a Christian of any kind, but it wouldn't be nice to tell her son that.

"Don't worry. Mother will come around once we're married."

"What if she doesn't? I'm not a good cook or housekeeper. Nobody taught me how to do things properly." Homemaking skills would be important to a woman like Mrs. Epp. I pictured her scowling at my scorched stews and streaky windows.

Simon laid his hand on my knee. "I'll help you with the cooking and housework. It'll be fun."

"I don't know." My voice wobbled because of Simon's hand on my knee. "How can we even plan a wedding with your mother—"

"I hadn't figured on Mother attending our wedding."

"What?"

"We can just wait until she goes home, then get Pastor Ewart to marry us in his office."

I lifted Simon's hand off my knee. "I don't like that idea. It's too cold and business-like."

"We can invite your Vancouver relatives and friends if you like."

"But not your mother?" A proper wedding included both sides.

"Mother wouldn't need to know. She'll be hundreds of miles away. We can visit her on our honeymoon and tell her then."

"Some honeymoon. I can just imagine how mad she'd be. Anyway it wouldn't be fair. Your mother loves you. You can't leave her out of your wedding."

He sighed. "Okay, if you insist on involving Mother, let's get it over with. Come to Wally and Myrtlemay's for breakfast on Thursday. We'll break it to her then."

CHAPTER 9

Wally and Myrtlemay's house was a rambling log place set back from the street. Petunias grew in barrels on the porch—red, white, and purple. The flowers' clove-like aroma teased my nostrils as I rang the doorbell, bracing myself for the showdown with Simon's mother.

Myrtlemay came to the door wearing a grey pantsuit that complemented her stately figure. Her hair hung over her shoulders in two shiny black braids.

"Good morning, Susie," she said, her face kind and motherly. "I'm afraid Simon's not here. He said to tell you he's sorry he can't come for breakfast."

"What?"

Myrtlemay nodded toward the veterinary clinic across the street. "He's helping Wally do emergency surgery. A police dog got knifed in the eye."

I sucked in a breath. "That poor dog! Shall I go and help?"

"They don't need you yet. Wally wants you to come after breakfast." She stepped out onto the porch, her dark eyes shining. "I hear you got engaged."

I gave her a crooked grin. "Where'd you get that idea?"

"Simon told Mother Epp before he went to the clinic."

My grin faded. "He told her already?" I had pictured us telling her together.

Myrtlemay took a watering-can from between two of the barrels. "He figured he should prepare her before you arrived."

"Why didn't he tell me he wouldn't be here? He could have phoned."

"He tried," she said, running water from the outdoor tap into the can. "He didn't get an answer. You must have left already."

I backed away from her, not sure whether to leave or stay. "What did Mrs. Epp say?" Was there any chance of the dragon pulling in her claws?

Myrtlemay watered the petunias in the barrel closer to the door. "She's against you two getting married."

"Big surprise."

Myrtlemay pinched off a couple of dried-up blossoms. "Susie, you need to learn to stand up to her."

"I already stood up to her. It didn't work."

"It gets easier with time."

"How much time?"

Myrtlemay gave me a wry grin. "The first twenty years are the hardest."

I groaned.

She set the watering can down and took my arm. "I'm joking. Come on. Let's go in and tackle her together."

I pulled away from her.

"Trust me," she said. "I have a hunch that things will turn out fine."

I hoped she was right. She'd been right before, on less important matters such as: What crème rinse could I use to make my hair shine like hers? Should I shave my legs? What should I give Simon for his birthday?

My heart fluttering, I followed her inside and along the hall to the dining room.

Simon's mother wasn't there.

I peered around the ivy-covered trellis that separated the dining room from the kitchen. The dragon stood at the kitchen counter, glaring out the window. I cleared my throat. "Good morning, Mrs. Epp."

She jumped, then stiffened, her change in posture the only evidence that she'd heard me.

"Courage," Myrtlemay whispered, squeezing my elbow. Then in a loud upbeat voice, she said, "Susie, maybe you'd like to set the table."

"How many of us will there be? Will Mrs. Epp's friend join us?"

Myrtlemay shook her head. "Bethany's visiting relatives in Vernon. She won't be back for a few days."

I breathed a sigh of relief. I could happily do without meeting the rich filled-out widow.

I followed Myrtlemay into the kitchen, trying to summon enough courage to speak to Simon's mother again. Before I could say anything, she thrust a pan into the oven, shut the door, and wheeled around to face me. "How could you trap my Simon?"

I stared at her. "What do you mean?"

Mrs. Epp shook a thick finger at me. "I know what you were doing, naked with Simon in your boarding house."

"Naked?" My voice rose. "I've never been naked with Simon. Even if I had been, it wouldn't be any of your business."

"Careful, Susie," Myrtlemay murmured.

"Sorry, Mrs. Epp." I wasn't very sorry. "I didn't mean to sound disrespectful."

She fixed her gaze on my stomach, then jerked her head up. *"Du best schwanga, nicht?"*

"Pregnant?" Myrtlemay blurted. She didn't know much Low German but she understood that. "How can you even suggest such a thing?"

"It's true, *nicht?*" Mrs. Epp's eyes narrowed to slits.

"Of course not," I said. She evidently didn't know what a cautious suitor her son was.

"So why do you want to marry yourself so quick?"

I considered yelling *erauf, frü* (down, woman), but this was no time for flippancy. Simon's and my future might hang on what happened next. Please, God, show me what to do.

An image of my weedy Uncle Milford came to mind. Maybe it was an answer to my prayer, maybe not. In any case, it gave me an idea. "Okay, Mrs. Epp, you want me to move to Vancouver. I'll do better than Vancouver. I'll move to Toronto and work for my Uncle Milford in his law office. He and Aunt Frieda will be glad to have me."

"You have a lawyer uncle?" Mrs. Epp asked in a reedy voice. "In Toronto?"

"Yes, Toronto, Ontario," I said, opening the cutlery drawer. "And my stomach will stay as flat as it is now because I'm *not pregnant.*" Realizing I was shouting, I lowered my voice. "And I think Simon will follow me to Toronto. In fact, I'm pretty sure he will." My confidence increased as I spoke.

"Such a big city," Mrs. Epp bleated. "So far away. What could my Simon make from himself in Toronto?"

I suppressed a smile. The dragon was eating my story like it was breakfast. Maybe she wasn't as smart as I thought.

Myrtlemay took a pile of plates out of the cupboard. "Susie's uncle might even have a job for Simon."

Thank goodness for Myrtlemay. She was on my side and she had an imagination.

"Yes," I said, trying to sound casual. "Uncle Milford is an environmental lawyer. He might be interested in someone with Simon's background." This was a stretch, especially since Simon didn't have a degree in science or anything else.

Mrs. Epp clutched at her heart. "Toronto! You'd really tempt my boy away to Toronto?"

I took knives, forks, and spoons from the drawer, wondering how far Myrtlemay and I could push the dragon.

"Susie's aunt is such a stylish woman," Myrtlemay murmured. "I'm sure she'll arrange a beautiful wedding for Susie and Simon."

Right on, Myrtlemay. If only Aunt Frieda were here, too! She was as overbearing as Mrs. Epp but artistic and nice.

"Na yo." Mrs. Epp stared at me like I was from outer space.

The oven timer dinged.

Myrtlemay went to the stove and turned the oven off.

A moment later, Simon burst in through the kitchen door. "Susie." He gasped for breath. "Could you run over to the Mollgards' house and get their dog?"

"Sure. Why?"

"Wally had to remove the police dog's eye." Spots of urgency burned in Simon's cheeks. "He packed the socket but it might still hemorrhage. If it does, we'll need the Mollgards' dog for a transfusion. Wally wants her standing by. I phoned the Mollgards. They'll have their dog ready."

"I'm on my way." I pushed past him, heading for the door.

Mrs. Epp loped after me. "Stop one minute, Susie, before you get that *hund*. I can make your wedding just as good as your Toronto aunt. Better even."

The dragon was taking the bait.

Simon twitched his head around. "What's going on?"

I gave Simon a small nod, my hand on the doorknob. "I'll tell you later."

Mrs. Epp seized my arm. "You and Simon can marry yourselves in the Mannonite church by my house. The church ladies will make you such a wonderful-nice supper! Sausages, buns, potato salad, dill pickles, borscht—"

"Mother," Simon said, "what are you saying? I thought you were against Susie and me getting married."

"I was at first doubtful but now...." She bunched her shoulders toward her earlobes, then let them fall. "What can a poor mother do? Young people want to steer their own canoe."

Myrtlemay squeezed my shoulder. "Welcome to the family, Susie."

Mrs. Epp spread her arms. "Come here. Give me a kiss."

I complied, relieved to be accepted or at least tolerated as her future daughter-in-law. At the same time, I couldn't help wondering what kind of a life I was letting myself in for.

CHAPTER 10

After some discussion, Simon and I decided to accept his mother's offer to 'make the wedding' in her Mennonite church thirteen miles east of Dayspring, Saskatchewan. The woman had her faults but she was a born organizer and leader, unlike my parents.

A few days before the wedding, Simon and I drove out to Adeline's place—a green and white farmhouse with a lean-to porch. She assigned an upstairs bedroom to Simon, and the guest-room on the main floor to me.

At ten o'clock on the big day—October 17, 1970—Simon drove over to the church to help set up tables for the reception. I retreated to the guest-room, where I took my wedding dress out of its garment-bag.

Oh, no! There were long creases in the skirt. It needed pressing but I had tons of other things to do, and the wedding was supposed to start at three.

I hung the dress over my arm and hurried along the hall toward Adeline's kitchen to get her iron and ironing board.

The whir of her electric beater greeted me. She stood at the counter in a beige housedress, whipping cream to put on my wedding cake. This was a revolting idea in my opinion. She'd already crammed the cake with maraschino cherries and nuts when she was making it. Then she'd added half an inch of almond icing. The last thing that cake needed was whipped cream, but I didn't have time to argue with her.

As I took the ironing board out of the pantry, Adeline wheeled around, beater in hand. "Susie! What do you have there?" She silenced the beater, wiped her hands on a towel, and snatched the dress from me. "This isn't your bride drass, is it?"

"Actually it is." Adeline had handled the other preparations for the wedding but I'd sewed my own dress and I was proud of it. The fabric was a silver-white silk that made my skin glow. The style of the dress—fit 'n flare—did wonders for my scrawny figure. I had planned to surprise everyone with the dress. Why had I stupidly let Adeline see it?

She held the neckline against my collarbone and squinted at my legs in their faded blue jeans, evidently gauging where the hem would fall. "This can't be a bride drass. It's too short."

I blinked. It had never crossed my mind that the dress was too short. I was a city girl; I took short skirts for granted. Women in Sage City wore shorter ones, even to the Mennonite Church.

Adeline flapped the hem against my legs. "Your bare knees will show."

"It covers the tops of them." My voice wobbled. "Anyway my knees won't be bare. I'll wear pantyhose." I wished I had someone to help me defend the dress. Simon was sophisticated enough to like the style but he wasn't here. My bridesmaid, Valerie, had helped me choose the pattern but she wasn't due to arrive until just before the wedding. My sister, Coralie, was in the hospital with a broken leg.

My mother wouldn't be much use either. She was probably pacing her hotel room right now, trying to decide which pills she needed to get her through the wedding. The less pressure I put on her and my father, the better. They were out of their depth with Simon's relatives, especially his mother.

Adeline shook my dress as if that might lengthen it. "A bride drass should come right down to the feet."

I'd considered making a longer dress but decided against it because Valerie said my legs were my best feature. That would make sense to Simon but not to his mother. I almost told Adeline, "My wedding, my dress. If you don't like it, tough." But I swallowed the words. I didn't want to alienate my future mother-in-law. I lowered my chin and peered up at her, little-girl style. "I sewed this dress myself. I put a lot of work into it."

She turned the skirt inside out and examined the stitches. "Very neat, the seams."

"Thank you. And isn't the fabric beautiful? It's raw silk from China."

"Very nice."

Maybe I was making progress. I barged ahead. "But silk is expensive. That's why I made the skirt short." That might make sense to a penny pincher like Adeline.

She gave me a sour look. "You could have bought polyester and sewed a longer drass for cheaper. And polyester doesn't wrinkle neither."

"My Aunt Frieda said I should get silk. She never uses polyester in the dresses she makes for her clients in Toronto."

"I'd like to meet your fancy *taunte* sometime," Adeline said. "But this drass...." Her eyes fretted over it.

Why couldn't she have kept her opinion to herself? On the other hand, why hadn't I realized that such a short dress would be unsuitable for a wedding in her antediluvian church?

There wasn't anything we could do about the dress now. The kitchen clock ticked like a time bomb. Almost ten-thirty and I still needed to take a bath, wash my hair and curl it, and then—

"*Na yo.*" Adeline seemed to reach a decision. She yanked the oilcloth off the kitchen table, laid my dress on the bare grey Formica, and loped over to her linen cupboard. She opened a drawer, pulled out several tablecloths, and piled them on her arm.

"What are you doing?" I squeaked. "You're not thinking of sewing a tablecloth onto my beautiful dress, are you?"

Ignoring my query, Adeline brought the tablecloths to the table and held one against my dress. She squinted at it, then gave a dismissive grunt. She tried another. "No, this one's too yellow." She set it aside and tried another. "This one, too heavy." Suddenly she snatched a semi-transparent white cloth from the middle of the pile. "How's by this one, Susie?"

She was asking my opinion. Hard to believe.

As she lifted a corner of the tablecloth, sunlight danced through the butterflies woven into the fabric. I couldn't help admiring those silvery butterflies. Where had Adeline obtained such a tablecloth? It didn't seem to belong in her kitchen with its plastic curtains and tractor calendar. Someone must have given it to her. She shook out the cloth. "Well?"

"It's not horrible," I admitted, "but we don't have time for sewing. The wedding starts in four and a half hours."

"Put on the drass once," Adeline barked. "We'll pin the butterfly cloth on and see how it looks like."

My stomach clenched in rebellion. Or was that a cramp? "We don't have time," I said. "You need to finish whipping the cream and slicing the meat. I need to shampoo and curl my hair. We've gotta go to the garden and pick flowers for my bouquet, eat, change our clothes, and—"

Adeline waved off my protests as if they were flies. "Put on the *kjleet,*" she said, fetching her sewing basket from the shelf above the tractor calendar.

I clenched my fists. "No." The word sounded good so I repeated it. "No. I won't let you change one thread of my dress."

Her knuckles whitened on the handle of her sewing basket. "What will people think?"

"Let them think whatever they want to. But you're not changing this dress." I scooped it off the table.

"Susie, listen to me once. You're young yet. You'll be sorry if—"

"If you say one more word against this dress, I'll hem it up even shorter." Her eyes bulged. "You wouldn't."

"I would," I said, my stomach cramping again. I was bluffing; I hoped she wouldn't realize that. "I've got a sewing kit in my suitcase."

She clutched the side of her head. "A person could die from such a daughter-law like you."

My heart was racing out of bounds. I clutched my dress, escaped to the guest-room, and collapsed onto the bed.

I lay there for half an hour, taking deep breaths and begging my heart to slow down. When it finally did, sort of, I got up and returned to the kitchen with my dress, which still needed pressing.

Adeline stood at the counter arranging slices of ham, roast beef, and bologna on a serving platter. She gave me an almost timid look. "You didn't hem it up, did you."

"Actually," I said, getting the ironing board out of the pantry, "I didn't."

"Thank the dear God. Now let's hurry ourselves. We don't want to be late."

CHAPTER 11

Crickets chirped in the grass as Adeline and I scurried up the steps of the Mennonite church. We were ten minutes late for my wedding according to the clock in her Chevy.

"Where were you?" my bridesmaid, Valerie, demanded as we hurried into the foyer.

"Don't ask." I jerked a nod at Adeline, who was brushing something invisible off her polyester suit.

Valerie frowned at me. "Simon and Wally have been standing at the altar for twenty minutes already."

The door of the sanctuary burst open. The pastor's son, Morgan Warkentin, hurried out, wearing an usher ribbon on his lapel. He offered Adeline his arm. "I can seat you now, Mrs. Epp." Morgan glanced at me. "Then we'll start the wedding, okay?"

"Just—give me a—few minutes." I had a cramp in my stomach and a sticky feeling in my underwear. Dear God, don't let my period be starting already. It wasn't due for another two weeks.

Valerie took my arm. "What's the matter, Susie? Are you nervous?"

I waited until the doors shut behind Morgan and Adeline, then whispered, "I need a pad."

Valerie rolled her eyes. "Are you sure?"

I felt a trickle between my legs. "Pretty sure." I glanced at the tiny pink purse hanging from Valerie's wrist and realized she couldn't provide what I needed.

She steered me toward the washroom. "Maybe there's a dispenser in here."

The walls were bare except for paper-towel holders and photos of Mennonite missionaries.

"Think." Valerie's voice rose. "Who might have something?"

My mind stumbled over the possibilities. "My mom?" Mom always carried a giant purse containing everything she might want or need—pills of various kinds, sunflower seeds, extra eyeglasses, flashlight, Scotch tape, sanitary supplies.

Valerie's face brightened. "I'll go and get her."

As my bridesmaid hurried out of the washroom, the strains of a hymn filtered in from the sanctuary: "Holy God, we praise Thy name; Lord of all, we bow before Thee." The congregation were singing in four-part harmony, which came as naturally to Mennonites as pinching pennies. Good for them. Singing would help pass the time during the delay I was causing, or that Adeline had caused. If she hadn't driven me into such a frenzy, my period wouldn't have started early.

Poor Simon and Wally were probably still standing at the altar with everybody staring at them.

As the first stanza of the hymn came in for a landing, Valerie hurried in with my mother. Mom wore a blue dress and hat, quite smart. Her eyes had an I'm-not-home look—too many pills—but she managed to produce what I needed, thank God. Moments later I emerged from a washroom cubicle feeling calm and in control.

I was washing my hands when Adeline charged in. "Susie, what's taking so long? People think you're backing out from marrying yourself with my Simon."

"Coming." I dried my hands and headed toward the door, almost lighthearted.

As I walked up the aisle on my father's arm, I kept my eyes fixed on my bridegroom. He stood at the altar looking stalwart in his navy-blue suit and smiling as if he and I were the only two people in the sanctuary. The guy had waited more than half an hour with the congregation watching him but he could still smile.

Simon Epp was the miracle of my life. Even if I hadn't believed in God before meeting him, that alone would have convinced me.

I returned Simon's smile, took my place beside him, and felt a gush between my legs. How were we going to deal with that on our wedding night? I stood up straighter. My sweetheart and I would figure it out. We had a lifetime to figure things out.

Pastor Warkentin stood broad-shouldered in a charcoal suit, his black hair silvery above his swarthy face. He smiled, looked out over the congregation, and admitted he'd been late for his own wedding thirty years earlier.

Several people chuckled, probably recalling the event or at least having heard the story.

The pastor continued. "My wife, Tina, was a believer when we got married. But I'm sorry to say I was a doubter. I didn't come to the Lord until years later." The pastor's eyes searched my face and then Simon's. "However, I think you two are both believers." He paused, waiting for a response.

Simon and I glanced at each other and nodded.

The pastor scanned the congregation. "Salvation through faith in Christ is a priceless gift." His voice rumbled through the building. "Simon and Susie's love for each other is also priceless."

I said a silent Amen.

The pastor launched into his sermon. One of his main points was that Simon and I should let our love inspire us to treat other people in a loving way. I prayed it would, especially with regard to my mother-in-law. Thankfully I wouldn't need to spend much time with her. Simon and I planned to move into the basement apartment in Wally and Myrtlemay's house. Adeline would be two days' drive away.

CHAPTER 12

*F**our years later*
 Afternoon sunlight slanted in through the windows of Adeline's kitchen. Outside, cattle grazed in the pasture, pushing snow aside with their red-brown heads and munching the frozen grass underneath. It was Christmas Day 1974. Simon and I were eating dinner at his mother's house east of Dayspring, Saskatchewan. We had arrived from Sage City the day before. Our one-month-old baby, Norine, slept in her crib in the living room. Our three-year-old, Emily, sat on a booster chair beside her grandmother.

Adeline ladled gravy onto Emily's mashed potatoes. "See what a nice gravy Oma made? Lots of goose fat. That's the secret."

I pushed a forkful of green beans around my plate, wishing we could talk about something other than food for a change.

Simon helped himself to more roast goose. "That's quite a cyclone they had in Australia."

Adeline struck her hand against her forehead. "Oh, no! I forgot the marshmallow salad! It went right out from my mind. I'll get it."

"What were you saying, Simon?" I asked as his mother hustled over to the refrigerator.

"I said that's an awful storm they had down in Australia. Hundreds of homes destroyed. Many people injured. Thousands evacuated. I wonder if—"

"Here the salad is," Adeline shrieked, airlifting it onto the table. She plopped it down, forked a miniature marshmallow off the top, and stuffed it into Emily's mouth.

Emily chewed and swallowed, her grey eyes bulging. The little girl had a long face like mine. She had my dark hair but her eyes were Adeline's, at least at that moment. Emily loved her Oma. I was pleased about that but I shouldn't have let them sit together. Adeline was feeding her too much.

The woman's preoccupation with food was bizarre. In a normal household, we could have continued the conversation Simon had started. We could have discussed the damage the cyclone had caused and the challenges faced by the injured people and evacuees. We could have prayed for them.

But I knew from experience that there was no point trying to converse normally at any meal Adeline cooked. She'd squelch any attempts, especially from me. Of course she wanted us to appreciate her hard work. That was understandable but still.

For the next few minutes, my mother-in-law's comments dominated the airwaves. "You're not eating your peas. Is something loose with them? Have some more drassing. Have some pickles. Ruby Fehr gave me the racipe. It's a new one from Schteinbach."

Finally Adeline rose and began gathering the plates, evidently having determined that we'd eaten as much of the main course as we could. "Susie." She tossed my name over her shoulder. "Could you put on the kettle once? We'll have tea with our cake."

I suppressed a groan as I pushed my chair back. Serving cake after such a huge meal seemed excessive. I would have served fruit or a milk pudding.

"I like chocolate cake," Adeline said, taking the dinner plates off the table. "Simon and Emily like chocolate cake. But I made a white *kuchen* because our Susie is allergic by chocolate."

I groaned aloud that time. She was forcing everyone to suffer for my sake. That meant I couldn't avoid eating at least some cake. If I refused, I'd seem like an ingrate.

I grabbed the kettle, banged it down into the sink, and cranked on the water full blast. As I set the kettle on the stove, Adeline barged out to her closed-in porch. Moments later she returned with her cake. It was shaped like a football field and slathered with evil-looking green frosting. "Susie," she said, depositing the cake on the table, "could you bring me that tin once?" She jerked her head toward a red tin on the china cabinet. "I made a surprise for you."

I fetched the tin, my heart quaking. Adeline's surprises had a way of embarrassing me.

She removed the lid with a flourish. "Here the cake dacorations are. They're the twalve days from Christmas." She held up a disk of white chocolate the size of a silver dollar. "See." She tilted the disk so it caught the light. "Here's the partridge." She jabbed a finger at the long-tailed bird embossed on the disk.

I threw my husband a pleading look, hoping he'd speak up for me. I didn't often challenge Adeline personally because I loved Simon, and he loved his mother. He wanted us to get along on the few occasions when we spent time together.

He wiped his mouth with his napkin. "Mother, it was nice of you to make the fancy chocolate but you know chocolate makes Susie sick. You said so yourself."

Adeline's nostrils flared. "Doctor Hoag says people can eat white chocolate even if they're allergic by brown."

"How does he know that?" I dared to ask.

Adeline frowned at me. "He reads doctor magazines. He knows."

I'd never eaten white chocolate. I wasn't sure if it would bother me but I didn't want to experiment, especially since I was still recovering from Norine's birth.

I retreated to the living room to check on the baby, almost wishing she'd start fussing so I'd have an excuse to avoid both cake and chocolate.

No such luck. Norine was asleep, a solid little mound under a quilt that Adeline had embroidered with pink roses. I pulled the quilt higher over her shoulders and left the room.

As I stepped back into the kitchen, Adeline looped her arm around Emily. "Help me sing, Sweetie." *On the first day from Christmas,* Adeline sang. Emily chimed in, knowing the song from the radio. *My true love gave to me a partridge in a pear tree.* Adeline beamed at the child, then took another chocolate disk from the tin. "Here's the two turtledoves." She and Emily sang *Two turtledoves.* She set the disk on a saucer and extracted a third. "Three French hens."

Emily reached for the chocolate hens. "Lemme see the chickens, Oma."

"They're sweet, Dear, just like you. Do you want to eat them?" Adeline slid the chocolate disk into the child's mouth. Emily sank her teeth into it.

Adeline shot me a triumphant look. "I made the twalve days special for you. Ruby Fehr learned me how and she borrowed me the moulds."

"I appreciate that, Mother Epp," I said, taking the teapot out of the cupboard. I did appreciate it but I sensed an underlying current of cruelty. If not cruelty, at least insensitivity. Chocolate gave me diarrhea, cramps, and shaky hands and legs. Whenever I told Adeline that, she changed the subject.

Maybe she thought I imagined my symptoms or developed them on purpose to annoy her.

I poured boiling water over the tea bags in the pot. As I carried it to the table, Adeline began serving her cake. Into each piece she inserted a chocolate disk, slanting it at a jaunty angle.

I never liked Adeline's cakes; she made them too sweet. But I couldn't refuse altogether. "Could you cut me a smaller piece, please?"

My mother-in-law clicked her teeth together like she did when she was annoyed. Then she plunged her knife into the corner of the cake and hacked out a piece. It was smaller than the others but had twice as much frosting. She inserted the chocolate disk embossed with six-geese-a-laying and plunked the plate down in front of me.

Everyone else dug in but the longer I stared at my cake, the less I felt like eating it. Finally I faked a smile and pushed it aside. "I'll save this for later."

Adeline clicked her teeth again. Simon scowled at me. I knew what he was thinking: *Why can't you humour Mother? Just eat a bite or two. Feeding us is her way of showing she loves us.* He had said that more than once but I wasn't sure. I suspected feeding us was her way of controlling us. She felt compelled to dominate our lives including what we ate, when, and in what quantities. When our consumption didn't meet her expectations, she tried to make us feel guilty.

I refused to fall into the guilt trap, most of the time.

I poured the tea and sipped mine while the others ate in silence. From time to time, Adeline scowled at me as if I'd broken a rule like *Don't blow your nose on the tablecloth.*

After dinner Simon retreated to the living room to check on Norine. I stayed in the kitchen, scraping the dishes over the garbage can while Adeline put the leftovers away. I poised my plate over the can, tempted to discard my cake and bury it in potato peelings. I might have gotten away with it if Adeline hadn't wheeled around at the critical moment. "You're not going to waste that *kuchen,* are you?" Her eyes drilled into mine. "Wasting food is a sin. You know that."

"Of course I wouldn't waste it," I said, setting the plate on the counter.

Adeline plucked the chocolate disk out of my cake. "Emily," she called to the little girl, who was dozing in the rocking chair near the west window. "Come here, Dear. Oma has a chocolate for you. Your mom didn't want it."

The child roused herself. As she wandered over, I snatched the chocolate disk out of Adeline's hand. "That's the last thing Emily needs."

"She likes it."

"Well, she's not getting it." I dropped the disk into the garbage can.

Adeline sucked a breath through her teeth. "Simon," she bleated.

Her son didn't respond. He was miles away or pretending to be, watching the news on TV while giving Norine her bottle.

Suddenly Emily slumped forward, clutching her stomach.

I put my arm around her. "What's the matter?"

"My tummy feels bad."

"No wonder, after everything Oma fed you."

Ignoring Adeline's thundercloud look, I hurried to the closet and got Emily's jacket and boots. "Let's go to the outhouse. The fresh air will do us good." We could have visited the indoor bathroom, but we needed a change of scene.

A pale sun hovered over the horizon as Emily and I crunched through the snow toward the outhouse. We were almost there when she doubled over, her face greenish. She stared down into the snow for a moment, then threw up her dinner. When she was done, I scooped up a handful of clean snow and washed her face. As I dried it with a tissue, she gave me a trembly smile.

"How do you feel?" I asked.

"Okay."

"Your tummy's not sick anymore?"

"No." She kicked at the snow, then scooped up a handful. "Can we play snowball?"

"Sure, why not?"

I scooped up more snow and helped her make a snowball. I overhanded it into the field beyond the outhouse. Emily's laughter rang clear as we ran to retrieve the snowball. We picked it up and packed more snow around it. Emily threw the reconstituted snowball. We ran through the whiskery stems of harvested wheat and retrieved the snowball.

We reconstructed it a second time, and I threw it again. By that time, we were far out in the field. The horizon was darkening from pink to purple.

"We'd better get back to Oma's house," I said. Adeline would scold me, asking where we'd been for so long. Maybe I'd tell her it was none of her business, or maybe I wouldn't have the courage. One thing I knew for sure. I was never going to let her feed my kid that much again.

CHAPTER 13

On Boxing Day afternoon, Simon's brother Wally and his wife, Myrtlemay, came to Adeline's house for coffee and cake. They'd been visiting her parents in Davidson, twenty-five miles away.

Wally was a big, not overly handsome man in his mid-forties. His shoulders sloped up to a short neck and a seal-like head that seemed too small for his body. Usually he ate two pieces of any cake served, but that afternoon he didn't seem interested in cake. He hunched over the table, staring down at the poinsettias his mother had embroidered on the tablecloth.

Suddenly he bobbed his head up and blurted, "I'm going to put my veterinary practice up for sale."

"What?" Everybody stared at him.

The colour drained out of Simon's face. "Why would you sell? You're doing great in Sage City. Everybody likes you."

Wally raised a shoulder and let it fall. "I'm thinking of buying Sol's practice."

"What did you said?" Adeline asked. "You mean Sol in Davidson?"

"Right. Sol Keshev," Wally said. "He's retiring."

Adeline flung her hand up in a hallelujah gesture. "If you and Myrtlemay move yourselves to Davidson, you'll be close by me. Half an hour driving only. Less in summer."

"We'll be even closer to my parents," Myrtlemay said. "They need help. My dad's Parkinson's disease is getting worse."

Simon scrubbed his fingers across his forehead. "I can understand you wanting to live near your folks but what about Susie and me and the kids? I'll be out of a job."

"Where would we live?" I asked, my heart fluttering. I loved our apartment in Wally and Myrtlemay's house. It was a cozy refuge with its fireplace, sagebrush wallpaper, and cowhide rugs.

Wally laid a brotherly hand on Simon's arm. "You can work for me in Davidson. There'll be lots of—"

I choked on nothing, reaching for my coffee. "Surely you don't expect us to move to Davidson just like that."

Wally shrugged. "Davidson isn't a bad place."

It wasn't. It was bigger than Dayspring and located on a major highway. But my mother-in-law would be only half an hour away.

Myrtlemay turned to me. "You could buy a nice house in Davidson. Real estate is cheaper than in Sage City."

Simon's face was regaining its colour. What was he thinking? A smile flickered between him and his mother. Maybe the idea of living near her was beginning to appeal to him. He loved her though her pushiness sometimes drove him crazy.

I clenched my fist, digging my fingernails into my palm. We couldn't move to Davidson. Adeline would hijack our lives. She'd tell us what to eat, how to arrange our furniture, how to raise our kids, how to breathe. She'd consider it motherly guidance. For me it would be torture. I was only twenty-five years old. I wasn't experienced enough or forceful enough to resist her influence on a long-term basis. I'd be old before I was forty, worn out from trying.

My mother-in-law reached across the table and laid her hand over mine. "Davidson wouldn't be a bad town to land up in," she said almost humbly. "It's got a nice park. Two grocery stores. A hospital, even a drugstore."

I sat with my hand in my mother-in-law's, silently acknowledging the connection between us. I didn't love Adeline and I wasn't sure how much she loved me, if at all. But she and I shared strong ties. Family ties and ties of familiarity and duty. Unfortunately that didn't mean we could live close together without throwing tea cups at each other. Plates, frying pans, butcher knives. "Simon and I—" I managed to say around the lump in my throat. "We couldn't move. We just couldn't."

He kicked me under the table.

"Think on your children," Adeline shrieked. "It would be wonderful-nice for them to have an Oma so close by! Only half an hour."

I drew a breath to protest, then blew it out, realizing I wouldn't get far without my husband's support. My wishes didn't count for as much in this family as Simon's. I wasn't related by blood, and blood is thick.

CHAPTER 14

The veterinary practice sold at the end of March, along with Wally and Myrtlemay's house. The new owners, a veterinarian couple from Edmonton, weren't interested in hiring Simon or me. However, they agreed to let us continue renting the basement apartment until the first of May, when they and their children would move in.

Early one morning near the end of April, I stood in our bedroom ironing Simon's blue shirt while he hovered nearby. The shirt didn't need ironing in my opinion, but he wanted to look extra-good in case the coordinator of substitute teachers phoned with a job for him. Myrtlemay had used her influence to have his name added to the roster.

The coordinator wouldn't call before seven but my husband was already as nervous as a dragonfly. If he had still been working for Wally, he would have slept later and eaten breakfast with me and the kids before bounding out the door, whistling on his way to the clinic.

But his clinic days were over unless we moved to Davidson. I couldn't do that. Also, as I'd told Simon more than once, it was time we tackled life on our own, independent of relatives.

Simon opened the door of the furnace room, which doubled as a walk-in closet. He yanked the string to turn on the light, then peered in at his neckties. "Which tie would go good with that shirt?" He ran his fingers over one tie, straightened another, and moved a third slightly to the left. If he'd still been my easygoing sweetheart, the sight of his bare torso might have tempted me to lure him back to bed for half an hour. But watching him fuss with his ties just made me mad.

I slammed the iron down on his shirt. "Why can't you learn to iron your own shirts if they need ironing so bad? I should be sewing while the girls are still asleep." The money I made sewing and knitting was an important part of our income, more important than Simon liked to admit.

"Well, pardon me for spoiling your plans." Simon disappeared into the furnace room, closing the door behind him.

I nosed the iron over the left sleeve of his shirt, feeling guilty for making him mad.

A few minutes later, Simon slunk out wearing a paint-splattered green T-shirt.

"Why are you wearing that old thing?" I asked, putting the freshly ironed shirt on a hanger.

"It's good enough for a has-been," he said, slouching toward the kitchen.

I followed. "You're not a has-been. Please don't say that."

He turned in the doorway with a raincloud of misery in his eyes. "I've got no job, no prospects. I work one day a week if I'm lucky."

I went and put my arm around him. "You'll get more teaching assignments. You'll see. It just takes time for people to catch on to how good you are." I smiled at my husband. "Remember how impressed the teachers at Gleneagles Secondary were with how you handled those hoodlums who glued their other substitute to a chair?"

He grunted.

I squeezed his shoulder. "A lot of people don't have your knack for dealing with teenagers."

"Yeah, well, I enjoy working with them but that doesn't count for much apparently."

It didn't. Neither did the fact that Simon had worked in a veterinary clinic for years, and had partial degrees in education and marine biology. The Sage City School Board put a higher value on a completed education degree.

He pulled away from me and headed for the refrigerator. "Do we have any cheese?"

"Sorry, we're out. Could you have peanut butter this morning?"

"Never mind. I'll just eat a banana."

"You need more than a banana," I said, trying to sound encouraging. "Who knows what kinds of hoodlums you'll have the privilege of teaching today?"

Simon grabbed a banana from the bowl on the counter. "The coordinator won't call."

I nodded toward his blue shirt, which I'd hung on a doorknob. "You'd better put that shirt on in case she does." Simon usually had only an hour between the call and the time he needed to leave the apartment. Less than an hour if the school happened to be out of town.

"If there's a science job," Simon said, peeling the banana, "the coordinator will give it to some rancher's wife who doesn't know the difference between a fruit fly and shoo-fly pie."

I dropped two slices of bread into the toaster. "That's a nice positive attitude. Just what we need around here."

Simon ate his banana in gloomy silence.

"I'm sorry," I said. He didn't like sarcasm, especially from me.

"Don't apologize." Simon's voice sounded as flat as the kitchen counter. "You have every right to consider me a failure."

"You're not a failure." The toast popped up. I grabbed both slices, slapped them onto plates, and buttered them. "You have the potential to become a good teacher but you can only go so far as a substitute. You need to finish your degree so you can get a proper job."

"I'm too old to go back to college. Anyway I've got a family to feed. I should forget about teaching and take the first full-time job I can find." He grabbed the newspaper off the counter and flipped to the want-ads. "How's this? *Irwin's Service Station needs gas-pump attendant. Must be—*"

The phone rang and Simon lunged toward it, the eagerness in his face painful to see.

After he left for his precious day of teaching, I sat down at the table with the newspaper and scanned the *For Rent* ads. We needed to find another apartment soon. However, the search had been discouraging so far. Most were beyond our budget.

CHAPTER 15

The apartment I found for us was a third-floor walk-up with streaky walls and ink-stained parquet floors. The place smelled like fried food and sour milk. The rent was two hundred dollars a month but we managed to have it reduced to a hundred and fifty in exchange for cleaning and painting the place.

Our new apartment had large windows facing south and a balcony overlooking the college campus. Simon soon found a job as a janitor at the college, and was able to quit substitute teaching. He worked evenings, which left his days free to take classes toward his education degree.

Not long after we moved in, Fayleen Friesen from our church offered me two thousand dollars to make dresses for her wedding—her own dress and those of her four bridesmaids. I was delighted with Fayleen's generous offer. My fingers itched to get started but I didn't want to unpack my sewing stuff until Simon and I got the apartment in better shape. Anyway she wasn't getting married until November so there was no rush.

One Saturday morning in May, I was filling holes in the living-room walls and Simon was cleaning the oven when the phone rang. He wiped his hands and grabbed it. "Hello? Mother, how're things? No, the kids aren't here. Susie's friend Valerie and her mom are babysitting them today."

Simon pointed toward our bedroom, where the extension phone was. He liked me to participate in conversations with his mother.

I meandered into the bedroom, taking my time. As I picked up the receiver, I heard Adeline shriek, "Ross Forbes. The principal by the Dayspring School." She gulped. "Simon, he has a job for you. Teaching science in high school."

Simon gave a sneeze-like laugh. "You're dreaming, Mother. The school board wouldn't hire me without a degree in education."

"Ross says they won't care," Adeline scream-shouted. "I told him you've got an almost-degree in fish science. And you know what he said?"

"No, what?"

"He said 'We need somebody like your son in Dayspring. He can teach at the school and in his spare time he can help the fish farmers with their trouts and stuff.'"

The idea of moving to Dayspring gave me goosebumps. It was only a village, not even a town like Davidson. Worse, Dayspring was only twelve miles from Adeline's house.

"Susie," she screeched, "are you there?"

"Hello, Mother Epp."

"What's loose with you? You don't sound good."

"Susie's fine," Simon said. "She's just tired from getting the walls ready to paint."

"*Na yo.* You won't need to paint in Dayspring. Ross has a bungalow for you, right near Knutson Lake. He'll rent it to you cheap. It's already painted and wallpapered real nice."

Simon remained silent, probably because he was painfully aware of my reluctance to move.

"Simon, why don't you say nothing?" Adeline bellowed. "Are we off-connected already?"

"No." Simon sighed. "We're fully connected."

"The school board wants to talk to you. You'll come for an interview, *nicht?*"

"I'll think about it," Simon said. "Susie and I will discuss it."

"Don't discuss too long. Ross might find somebody else."

"I'll get back to you, Mother."

After we hung up, I slumped down on the bed. Simon and I were doing fine in Sage City. He was on course to finishing his degree and finding a full-time job. Why did his mother have to interfere?

I heard my husband's footsteps creak on the floorboards in the hall. A moment later he stood in the bedroom doorway, his face arranged in the casual expression he assumed when hoping to persuade me of something he knew I wouldn't like. "So Susie, whaddaya think?" Simon sat down beside me, making the bed sag. "I should at least meet the school board and principal, shouldn't I? It would be interesting to hear what they have to say."

"It would," I admitted. "But that job would be a dead end for you. If you could even get it." I leaned against his shoulder, breathing his scent—apples and honey; it was a natural scent that almost never left him. "You can't go far as a teacher without a degree in education. You should stay in Sage City and finish it."

Simon kneaded my tired neck muscles. "If I was teaching in Dayspring, I could work toward my degree at summer school in Saskatoon."

"Maybe but—"

"Susie, don't you see? This job could be my big chance."

"Or maybe it's no chance at all. You know how your mother exaggerates. I think it's too good to be true."

"But—" Simon said.

"You should phone the school board and see how interested they are. Maybe they wouldn't even consider you."

"I can phone them, sure, but I have a hunch this is for real."

I stared down at the bedspread—orange flowers on a beige background. "What would I do in a backwater like Dayspring besides fight with your mother?"

Simon's fingers danced up and down my spine as if it was a piano keyboard. "You could take in sewing and knitting jobs."

"People in small towns do their own sewing and knitting."

"But they don't have magic fingers like yours. Customers would come from miles around."

"Right." I snorted. "The crows and gophers would beg me to make their wedding dresses."

Simon sighed. "Could we at least pray about this?"

"Go ahead." I couldn't very well argue against praying.

He bowed his head. "Dear heavenly Father, you know about this opportunity. You know the people involved. Please give me wisdom for the interview." He took a breath. "And please help me get the job if it's your will."

My silent prayer contradicted his.

Simon raised his head. "So when shall we go to Dayspring?"

"I don't know," I said. "I'm awfully busy here. Couldn't you go alone?"

"Mother would be disappointed."

I didn't know how disappointed Adeline would be, except about not seeing her grandchildren. I often felt like a third leg on a goose around that woman.

CHAPTER 16

Ten days later, I sat on an orange chair in the lobby of our apartment building, waiting for Simon to return from Dayspring. The sulphury aroma of cabbage rolls drifted down the stairs; our neighbours were cooking lunch. Norine bounced up and down on my lap, her blonde curls bobbing. "Dadda. Dadda."

Four-year-old Emily stood at the window in her thrift-store jacket and jeans, her nose pressed against the glass. Every time a vehicle nosed its way into the parking lot, she hopped from one foot to the other, doing a little dance of anticipation.

I was as excited about seeing Simon as the girls were but I was also exhausted. My eyes burned and my arms tingled with fatigue. I'd stayed up all night making a Bar Mitzvah suit for a boy on our street. The Bar Mitzvah was still a couple of weeks away but he wanted the suit for a piano recital tonight. His parents had offered me an extra twenty dollars to finish it early. Considering the state of Simon's and my finances, I couldn't refuse.

Norine grinned up at me, her new tooth white as milk. "Dadda?"

"Soon, Sweetheart." I retied her shoe. Soon Simon would be here and I'd know what our future held or didn't hold.

"There he is," Emily shrieked. "That's Daddy's car."

I gathered Norine into my arms, lurched to my feet, and herded Emily outside. The wind whistled around our building, whipping the weed-choked geraniums in the pots near the door. We hurried around the geraniums and out to the parking lot, where Simon was lifting his suitcase out of the Volkswagen. "Welcome home," I called.

Simon turned and I knew in an instant that my husband had changed in some fundamental way. There was a new light in his eyes, a new tilt to his head. "How was your trip?" I asked, hurrying toward him.

"Fine." Simon set his suitcase down and kissed me, then Norine.

"Daddy!" Emily tugged at his jacket. "Where'd you get the pretty flowers?"

I hadn't noticed but Simon was wearing carnations in his lapel—pink and white carnations. He'd never worn flowers before, not even a boutonniere at our wedding.

As Simon bent to kiss Emily, she sniffed one of the pink carnations. "They're bee—oo—tiful, Daddy." She sniffed a white carnation as if the different colours might smell different.

Simon patted her head. "They're from Mr. Forbes's garden. It was nice of him to pick them for me."

"They're kind of puny-looking," I said and immediately regretted my words. Emily seldom saw flowers of any kind, other than weed-choked geraniums.

A gust of wind swirled through the parking lot, picking up grit and tossing it into our faces. "Come on," I said, hitching Norine higher on my hip. "Let's go inside."

Simon followed me, Emily helping him with the suitcase.

The aroma of cabbage rolls lingered in the lobby. It accompanied us up the stairs. But as we stepped into our apartment, I caught a whiff of something else. Cinnamon? Menthol? Aftershave? Simon never wore aftershave. I gave him a teasing grin, elbowing him in the ribs. "You smell like a cosmetics counter."

He made a fake-huffy face. "Thanks a lot. I'll have you know this aftershave cost me five dollars in the Dayspring Co-op."

"Five dollars!" Norine struggled in my arms and I set her down. "You spent *five dollars* on aftershave?" That was twenty-five percent of what I'd earned sewing all night.

"I was celebrating," Simon said, setting his suitcase on the floor.

My heart flopped like a fish. "You mean you got the job?"

"Not exactly." His tone was careful.

"So what happened?"

"I need to show you the numbers. Hang on. I'll go down to the car and get my notes."

"Numbers? So—" The phone jangled, making me jump. "That's probably Fayleen checking on whether we need more fabric. I'd better answer."

Simon nodded and grabbed Emily's hand. "Come on, Kiddo. Let's go down and get Daddy's briefcase."

As they headed for the door, I picked up the receiver. "Hello?"

Adeline's voice crackled over the phone line. "Susie!"

My world shrank, as it usually did when I heard her voice. "Mother Epp, what's up?"

CHAPTER 17

"I'm so happy," Adeline burbled. "I don't know where to leave myself."

"Oh, yeah?"

"You're moving to Dayspring."

"We are?" My mouth felt like it was full of straw. "So Simon got the job?"

"Of course he got the job if he'll just take it once. Ross loves him. The school board loves him. The fish farmers love—"

"I love Simon more than any of them do and I don't think he should—"

"You wouldn't hold him back, would you?"

I considered the question. As Simon's wife, I probably had enough influence to keep him in Sage City but at what price? He might regret the decision for the rest of his life...the rest of our lives.

"I naver before saw my boy so happy," Adeline burbled. "He's a different *bengyel* since the board offered him that *oabeit*."

Was Simon happier than he'd been on our wedding day? I wondered, switching the receiver from one ear to the other. Happier than when our daughters were born?

"Susie?"

"I'm still here." And here was where I wanted to stay, seven hundred miles away from Adeline. The sun through the freshly washed windows lent a magical glow to Norine's curls as she scooted across the floor.

"You'll love the house Ross has for you," Adeline gushed. "It's the old Janz place. Remember, we visited over by them once? You can see the lake from the bedrooms. But those rooms can get hot during afternoon. I'll order you some Venetian blinds. They should be fixed ready by the time you come."

I drew a jerky breath. "I hate Venetian blinds."

Silence.

"I mean I'd rather not have Venetians." Adeline was trying to help me, presumably.

"So, Susie." Her voice thinned. "What sort from blinds do you like?"

I didn't want blinds. I didn't want bedrooms with a lake view. I didn't want the house in Dayspring at all.

"Do you want curtains?"

67

I couldn't bring myself to answer.

"I can make you some wonderful-nice curtains. The Co-op has material."

I fumbled a tissue out of my pocket and blew my nose. "Why don't you leave the windows alone for now?" I wanted to tell Adeline to leave *me* alone but I couldn't. She was my mother-in-law.

A key rattled in the door. "There's Simon. I need to talk to him. We'll call you back."

CHAPTER 18

The school board wasn't as crazy about Simon as his mother had led me to believe. Since he didn't have a degree in education, they hired him on a trial basis until Christmas. If he didn't prove satisfactory, he'd be out. If he lasted until Christmas, they'd offer him a contract for the rest of the year.

Given the uncertainty around Simon's future, I decided not to move to Dayspring with him. I didn't like the prospect of my husband and I living apart. On the other hand, I didn't want to risk pulling up stakes in Sage City, only to discover that things weren't working out in Dayspring. Emily was in kindergarten. If I moved I'd need to uproot her. And I had things to do in Sage City. Fayleen was counting on me to make the dresses for her wedding. Also I needed to finish cleaning the apartment and then paint it.

Simon accepted my decision, reluctantly.

On his last evening at home, I put the girls to bed, then settled on the couch to mend a jacket he wanted to take along. I was almost done when Simon slouched out of our bedroom, where he'd been packing his suitcases. The corners of his mouth drooped.

"What's the matter?" I asked.

He studied an ink stain on the floor.

I pushed aside a jumble of the girls' toys to make room for him. "Come and sit on the couch?"

Simon came and slumped down beside me, aftershave and all. He'd worn that stupid aftershave ever since he'd returned from Dayspring a week earlier. I preferred his natural scent—apples and honey. I'd told him so but he stuck to cinnamon and menthol. I suspected he wore it to make a point of some kind but I couldn't figure out what that was.

I set my sewing basket on the floor and turned to look at him, expecting a kiss.

All I got was a wintery stare.

Something cold gripped my heart. I'd assumed we'd make love on our last evening together but Simon didn't seem interested. Did the prospect of moving by himself upset him more than I'd expected? I was his wife, his helpmate. I should probably move to Dayspring with him despite the uncertainty about his job. But it was too late to change now. Our plans were all made.

I sighed, picked up his jacket, and rose to hang it in the closet. As I stepped around the coffee table, my foot caught on Emily's stuffed turtle, which lay halfway underneath it. Simon grabbed my arm, steadying me.

"Thank you."

He didn't let go. Instead he took the jacket and tossed it onto the armchair. Then he drew me down into his lap. He kissed my forehead, my nose, my mouth. "Hang on," he said, his breath coming quick and hot. He rose and latched the living-room door, as we did when we didn't want the girls wandering in. Seconds later he was back beside me. He fumbled with the buttons of my blouse. Then his right hand slipped into my bra, his left pulling my skirt up. I helped him out of his trousers and underpants. We made slow gentle love, our bodies old friends, our feet bumping against our children's toys.

That night I lay awake for a long time listening to Simon breathe and recalling the delicious weight of his arms around me. I loved him. I was probably making a huge mistake by not going with him.

Early the next morning, I kissed my husband goodbye in the parking lot. He patted me on the backside, swung himself into the Volkswagen, and drove off with a jaunty wave.

CHAPTER 19

It was a challenge, carrying Norine down three flights of stairs while dragging her stroller behind us. Unfortunately I had no other choice. I couldn't leave a nine-month-old alone in the apartment while I walked Emily to kindergarten. Now that Simon had left, I had to do everything by myself.

"It's raining," Emily announced as we reached the lobby.

"Oh, shoot!" I yanked the stroller down the last step. "We didn't bring the umbrellas."

Emily bulged her eyes at me. "Daddy said, 'Make sure you bring the umbrellas.' I heard him."

I struggled to swallow my irritation. "If you were listening to Daddy so carefully, why didn't you remind me before we left the apartment?"

Emily flicked a glance up the stairs. "You can get the umbrellas, Mommy. Me and Norine will stay here. I'll keep care of her."

"I can't leave you kids alone," I said, settling Norine in her stroller. "Anyway we don't have time to get the umbrellas. We don't want to be late for kindergarten."

I opened the canopy of the stroller to keep the baby sort of dry. Then Emily and I pulled our jackets over our heads, hunched our shoulders, and dashed out into the rain. As we scurried along the sidewalk with the stroller, she peppered me with questions. "Does God have a sprinkler hose in heaven?"

"I doubt it."

"Will something bad happen if we step on the cracks?"

"Bad things happen but not because people step on cracks," I said, maneuvering the stroller around a slow-moving matron in a green raincoat.

Emily glanced over her shoulder. "Oma Epp has a coat like that."

"Yes, I think so."

"When are we gonna see her?"

"I don't know, Sweetheart. Daddy will see her tomorrow when he gets to Dayspring." I pictured his mother meeting him at the rental bungalow with a car-full of food and a mouthful of complaints about his wife and daughters not accompanying him.

Despite Adeline's *kvetching,* part of her would be thrilled to have her boy living alone only twelve miles from her. She could bake cakes for him, cook chicken soup. She could darn his socks, clean his windows, drive him crazy. She might even try to move in with him though Simon would probably draw the line at that.

"Mommy," Emily shrieked. "You're going past the school."

I jerked the stroller to a halt, making Norine whimper. My face burned with embarrassment as I turned the stroller around and joined the other parents who were shepherding their children toward the school building. They all carried umbrellas and/or wore raincoats, except for me and my daughter.

Emily gave me a rabbity look. "Bye, Mommy," she called and lolloped off to join her friends.

"Be a good girl," I called. I waved and smiled at the other parents, trying to look like a responsible mother with a good reason for letting her kid get wet. I wasn't usually so careless. Simon's departure had rattled me more than I'd expected. I was on my own for the first time in years, with no input from anyone except my bossy four-year-old. The situation unnerved me but there was something exhilarating about it too.

On our way home from the school, Norine and I stopped for groceries. "Kraft Dinner, fine," I said, dropping several boxes into the grocery bag that hung on the stroller. "You and Emily like it and it's an easy meal." Easier than the meals Simon preferred: meat, potatoes, and vegetables. Let his mother cook those for him.

Norine looked up with a slobbery grin and I noticed she had another tooth coming. I wheeled her over to the canned goods. "We'll get some sardines too. Your dad hates them but he isn't here to complain, is he?"

Back in our apartment building, I stowed the stroller in our locker on the main floor so I wouldn't need to drag it downstairs every time I took the girls out. Simon didn't want us keeping the stroller there. He was afraid someone might steal it but he wasn't home, was he? I was in charge. I could make my own rules.

CHAPTER 20

Two months after Simon moved to Dayspring, my friend Valerie phoned and invited me to meet her at the roller rink. She said she had a temporary part-time job for me. Something about costumes for a roller-skating production.

"Sorry," I said. "I'm afraid I don't have time."

"But you'd be ideal for the job. At least come and let me tell you about it."

Should I go and hear what she had to say? I wondered as I poured a glass of juice for Emily with my free hand. It would be an excuse to see Valerie. We hadn't managed coffee or lunch together since she'd started working for the city. "Okay, I'll see you there," I said.

After lunch the next day, I left the kids with a neighbour and took the bus to the roller rink. It was a beautiful afternoon, warm for October. The sky was berry blue with whipped-cream clouds. Bees buzzed among the wildflowers that grew outside the door of the rink. I entered the dimly lit foyer, stood blinking for a few seconds, and proceeded along the hallway as per Valerie's directions. My footsteps echoed on the wood floor. Photos of 1950s roller-skating champions lined the walls. Stale tobacco smoke hung in the air.

I found Valerie sitting at a Formica table in what looked like a former restaurant. "You look great," I said. My gaze flitted over her pink silk blouse and black trousers. "Nice threads."

"Thanks." Valerie fluffed up her scarf, a pink and purple paisley that flattered her olive complexion. "How're things?"

"Hectic." I took the chair across from her.

Valerie smiled; her front teeth protruded just enough to be cute. "I hope you can spare some time for this job."

"Maybe so if I can work at home. I already have a lot to do but I can probably squeeze in some time."

Valerie shook her head. "I don't think that would work. There wouldn't be room in your apartment."

"Why not? I sew in there now."

"Yes, but we need space for the volunteers."

"So you've got volunteers coming? Why do you need me?"

"You'd be their supervisor," Valerie said. "You'd keep them on task, answer their questions, and troubleshoot any problems."

I was flattered; I'd never supervised anybody other than my own kids. "So where do you plan on having the sewing done?"

Valerie glanced around. "Right here. The restaurant is closed but the city owns the whole building."

I scanned the turquoise walls, orange tile floor, and sparkling disco balls that hung from the ceiling. "It would be an interesting place to work. Tacky but interesting."

"So what do you think?" Valerie's eyebrows took a ride up and down. "It'll be fun. We'll have the sewing done in the evenings during rehearsals so you'll get to hear the music and meet the performers."

I ran a finger over a cigarette burn in the table. "How many evenings a week would you want me?"

"Two. Three at the most. You'll still have your days free."

I didn't need more work. Actually more work was the last thing I needed. But Valerie's job promised status, fun, adventure, camaraderie. "I could get here on the bus," I said. "But I'd need a babysitter. I don't think I could bring the kids."

"My mom could baby-sit." Valerie said this so quickly, I suspected she and her mother had already discussed it.

"That could work if I decide to take the job. I'd pay your mom of course."

"Sure. We can discuss it later."

I glanced around the room. "What about sewing machines?"

"We plan to rent some."

"Are there enough plug-ins?"

"Lots of plug-ins," a bass voice called from the kitchen. A beaded curtain clattered open and a tall young man in a cowboy shirt and jeans rattled out. "The circuits are fine too. I just checked them."

Cowboy shirt sauntered toward us. He was a long, loose-limbed guy. Valerie jerked her chin at him. "Susie, this is Florian Bouchard. He studies sculpture at the college and works part-time for the city. Florian, meet Susie Epp."

Florian was the most unusual yet beautiful young man I'd ever seen. He had blue-violet eyes, hair the colour of the sun, and a face that looked old-fashioned and modern at the same time. Classic might be the word for it. Florian's fingers were long and slim. When he shook my hand, I felt his elegant bones.

"Are you the girl who might be supervising the sewing?"

I grinned at Valerie. "Did you hear that? Florian called me a girl." I was twenty-five. He was probably a year or so younger.

Valerie gave him a backhanded slap on the arm. "No flirting with Susie. She's married with kids."

Florian winked at me and my scalp almost lifted off my head.

That was ridiculous. He meant nothing to me and should mean nothing.

As he strolled toward the cold-drink dispenser, Valerie pulled a sheaf of papers out of her briefcase. "Here, Susie." She thrust the papers at me. "This is what Florian and I thought the costumes could look like."

I took the papers from her but they blurred in front of my eyes. Every ounce of my consciousness was concentrated on Florian Bouchard. He was a magnet; I was an iron filing.

With an effort that felt superhuman, I forced myself to focus on the papers. They were mostly historical photos and drawings. Native people in animal hides decorated with colourful quillwork, fur-traders in buckskins, priests and nuns in black, Scottish settlers in kilts, Dutch women in white-winged caps. I glanced at Valerie, my scalp tingling with the knowledge that Florian was only a few feet away. "This looks like a lot of sewing. When do you need these costumes by?"

Florian ambled toward us, gulping root beer from a brown bottle. "Not until November." He lowered the bottle from his heart-stopping mouth. "And we don't need everything made from scratch. Some of the cast members already have clothes they can wear."

"Or they can borrow clothes," Valerie added. "We just need to make the hard-to-find items like caps for the Dutch settlers."

"What about kilts for the Scots?" I asked. "Making a kilt must be a lot of work. All those pleats."

Florian grinned. "But think of the fun you'll have with the fittings."

Valerie gave him another backhanded slap though her eyes glittered with amusement.

"Sorry." Florian glugged the last of his root beer. "I've gotta run. Gotta pick my dad up. We're going to drive down to Kelowna and look at fabrics."

"For the costumes?" I asked.

"No, for Dad's shop. He's a tailor."

"Interesting."

"We think so." Florian's gaze lingered on my face. "I'll see you later, I guess."

"Maybe." I attempted a Mona Lisa smile. "Maybe not." I shuffled the papers Valerie had given me. Pretending to examine them, I tried not to hear Florian's footsteps receding along the hallway.

Valerie checked her watch. "So, Susie, what do you think?" From her business-like tone, I gathered she was referring to the job, not Florian.

"I'm not sure."

Valerie took the papers from me and stowed them in her briefcase. "I'm paying five dollars an hour."

Five an hour! That was impressive but I remained silent, waiting for her to raise her offer. Bargaining came naturally to me. Valerie knew it. We had met at an outdoor market where she was selling handmade jewellery and hair ornaments.

"What's the job worth to you?" She took her calculator out of her briefcase and punched in some numbers. "I could go to five-ten."

"I don't know." I twisted a button on my blouse, wondering how much higher I could push her. "I've still gotta finish the dresses for the wedding, do some more cleaning, and paint the apartment."

"You'll have your days free, remember."

I examined my fingernails. Valerie's job was my sort of thing. I was already visualizing a pattern for the Dutch women's hats. As for Florian, my reaction was ludicrous. Flirting probably came naturally to him. A guy like that must be catnip to women. I glanced at Valerie. "I might do it for five-thirty an hour."

She consulted her calculator. "Five-twenty. That's as high as I can go."

I pushed my chair back. "I'll let you know. I should talk it over with Simon."

That evening I phoned Simon and told him about Valerie's offer.

He was impressed that the city would hire me as a supervisor, and especially that they'd pay five-twenty an hour. However, he didn't like the idea of me staying in Sage City until Valerie's job finished in mid-November or later. He wanted his wife and children in Dayspring with him, the sooner the better.

I missed my husband of course. So did our girls. But I still dreaded the prospect of living in Dayspring, so close to his mother. "How's your teaching going?" I asked. Part of me wanted it to go well. Another part hoped something would make him want to return to Sage City. Like flak from the school board, or annoying co-workers, or the realization that he needed his degree after all.

"My job's going great," Simon said. "Ross says I'm a natural teacher. He thinks the board would be crazy not to offer me a contract."

"But that wouldn't be until Christmas, right?"

"That's the deal."

"So the girls and I had better stay here. A lot can happen between now and Christmas."

"You might be right." Simon didn't sound convinced.

"What about Valerie's job? Maybe I should give it a try since I'm going to be here a few more months anyway."

"What about the wedding dresses, and painting the apartment?"

"I can hire people to help if I need to, with all the money I'll be making."

"I suppose so." Simon sounded like his throat needed clearing. "You'll do what you want no matter what I say."

I chose to take his words as reluctant agreement. The next morning I phoned Valerie and told her I'd be happy to accept her offer.

CHAPTER 21

During my days and free evenings, I made as much progress as I could on Fayleen's dresses. Whenever I was scheduled to be at the rink, Valerie's mom picked up the kids about four in the afternoon. She took them home for supper and the night.

Usually I arrived at the rink for my skating lesson by five o'clock. The lessons were a treat I allowed myself because I'd never learned to roller skate. The city offered free instruction to any employee who wanted it. Eight of us signed up. The skating coaches taught us. Sometimes Florian taught if his classes finished in time, and if he didn't need to drive his dad somewhere.

Whenever Florian showed up, he maneuvered himself into a position that made it seem natural for him to teach me. I should have maneuvered myself away from him. Sometimes I did. Other times I yielded to temptation.

Skating with Florian was like skating with a butterfly. He was so quick and light on his feet. With him I became a butterfly too. "That's it, Susie," he said, his young breath warm on my face. "Go with the natural rhythm. Your muscles flexing and relaxing. Flex. Relax. Gl-i-i-i-i-de." His right hand cradled my shoulder blade and his left rested on my waist. Our feet flew over the floor. We created a breeze that ruffled my hair and his. "You're doing fine," Florian said. "See? It's like dancing."

"I'll take your word for it." Dancing was a sin according to my Mennonite Brethren upbringing. It encouraged lustful thoughts and immoral behaviour. I'd always accepted that as fact. But now, skating with Florian, I began to think it might be too simple an assessment.

My lesson always finished too soon. At six o'clock I removed my skates and went to help the sewing volunteers get started. Soon the cast members arrived and the rehearsal began, the music competing with the whir of our sewing machines.

Florian's job was to provide advice on the visual aspects of the production including costume design. From time to time, he came to the former restaurant to check on the sewing volunteers and me, especially me. He gave me soulful looks and leaned against my desk, brushing my shoulder as if by accident.

His attentions were unrealistic, even ridiculous. At least that was what I told myself. Granted, I wasn't bad-looking. Having babies had improved my figure; I wasn't so scrawny anymore. My hair was shinier than when I was younger. My eyes were still slightly crossed but they were large and bright. "Mesmerizing," Florian said.

Why was he interested in me? There were other women and girls at the rink—younger, prettier, and more charming. I was married with children. Maybe Florian yearned for mothering, consciously or subconsciously. He and his dad and brothers had been on their own since his mother's death. That must have been difficult for a sensitive soul like Florian.

I understood emotionally sensitive. I'd spent my teenage years longing for friends my own age and afraid no suitable man would ever love me. Then Simon Epp had burst into my life and swept my fears away. I thanked God for Simon. At the same time, I suspected I'd married too young. If I'd waited longer, I might have met someone who communicated more directly with my heart. Like Florian.

I loved Simon but our marriage had a plodding feel to it. It seemed like something we needed to work on, not something that flowed naturally. Did all marriages get that way after a few years?

CHAPTER 22

When I worked at the roller rink, I usually returned to my apartment about nine o'clock in the evening. But the evening of the staff party, I came home early to give myself a facial. I stood in the bathroom peering into the mirror, spreading green mud on my face. The ads said it would make me look radiant. At that point it just made me look ridiculous with the left side of my face green and the right not. As I squeezed more guck from the tube, the phone rang.

I rinsed my hands, hurried into the bedroom, and grabbed the phone. "Hello?" I held the receiver to the mud-free side of my face.

"Hi, Sweetheart." Simon sounded buoyant. Boyish even.

"Hi yourself." My husband liked to phone from bed. It seemed more romantic. Also the rates were lower at night.

"Look out the window," he said. "Unless it's cloudy there, you should see the new moon in the old moon's arms."

I pulled the curtain aside. "Yes, it's beautiful, isn't it?" Florian had shown me the moon earlier, when he was arranging to pick me up for the staff party.

"How are things?" I asked, shutting the curtain.

"Great," Simon said. "I'm doing great."

"Your mother doesn't think so." I sank onto the bed. "You should have heard her on the phone yesterday: 'Poor Simon,' I said, imitating Adeline's *kvetching* voice. 'All day he has to learn the kids their science lessons at school. Then he has to go home and cook, wash dishes, wash clothes, try to learn himself to iron his shirts. He needs you, *Meyaalchye*.'"

My mother-in-law had recently started calling me *Meyaalchye*. It was a ridiculous nickname. I wasn't a little girl. I'd reminded her of that several times but she persisted.

"I do need you, Susie," Simon said. "I miss you."

"I miss you too, Darling." I was probably a terrible wife, refusing to move with Simon. Worse, I was fluttering around another man. A moth around a light bulb.

"How are the girls?" Simon asked.

"Fine. Norine's getting another tooth."

80

"How's Emily doing with her bike?"

"Good. Valerie's mom is teaching her." Simon would have loved to teach his daughter himself.

"Dayspring is a great place to ride bikes," Simon said. "There's so much to see along the trails. Wildflowers, meadowlarks, rabbits, gophers."

I grimaced as the mud tightened the left side of my forehead. What kind of a mother was I, keeping the girls from such a paradise? And from their father.

"Have you phoned any moving companies?" he asked.

"I think it's too soon." I still dreaded moving to Dayspring.

"You must be almost finished with those wedding dresses."

My left cheek twitched as the mud seized up. "I'm getting there but don't forget I've got commitments at the rink too."

"How's that going?"

"The rink's going good." I attempted a neutral tone of voice. "But the volunteers and I need to change the fur-traders' hats. Florian—" I gulped, wishing I hadn't mentioned his name. "The artistic adviser thinks they don't look authentic enough."

"I'm sure you'll handle it fine." Simon didn't sound interested.

"I guess so but it's frustrating." I was frustrated about the hats, sure. I was even more frustrated about my feelings for Florian. They were electrifying, spine-tingling, opening doors to possibilities I'd never been exposed to. They were also wrong, un-Christian, forbidden, *verboten*.

If Simon had been here, I might not have become infatuated with Florian. I was accustomed to love-making on a regular basis. I wasn't getting that now. "Our anniversary's coming up," I said. "I hope you'll be here." A few nights with Simon might break the Florian spell.

"I wish I could come up but—"

"I'll put the satin sheets on the bed." My voice rose with enthusiasm. "I'll make a dinner reservation at *L'Assiette*. We can have chicken cordon bleu, duchess potatoes, hearts of palm, and cherries jubilee. You wouldn't find a dinner like that in Dayspring."

Simon laughed. "Try overdone roast beef, mashed potatoes, and canned peas."

"So you'll come to Sage City?" Several flakes of dried mud fell off my face. I picked them off the bedspread and dropped them into the wastebasket.

"I don't think I can get away."

"You'd only be gone a few days. There must be substitute teachers even in that no-stoplight village of yours."

"We've got substitutes, sure, but I'm really busy right now. Ross wants me to develop a unit on fish farming for the grade elevens. It's taking longer than I expected. I need to collect more equipment, take pictures, interview fish farmers."

"Can't you do that some other time?" I asked. "The fish farmers aren't going to swim away."

"No, but a professor's coming from Saskatoon to give me some pointers. He's an expert in—"

"A professor is coming on our anniversary?"

A pause. "Not on the actual day."

Had Simon forgotten our anniversary? He'd always remembered before.

"Look," he said, "why don't you just pack up the girls and come here?"

"I don't have a car, remember?" My voice rasped with irritation.

"You could take the bus. Mother could pick you up in Davidson."

"It's a two-day trip. The kids are too young to ride on the bus for two days and a night."

"I guess so." Simon sighed. "Susie, it's hard on us both, trying to hold this marriage together with telephone wire. Why don't you move here right away? Just cut your threads in Sage City and move."

"I've got too much to do. Look, I've gotta go now. Busy day tomorrow." I needed to wash the dregs of this mud off my face and polish my high-heeled red sandals for the staff party.

CHAPTER 23

I didn't drink. Mennonites weren't supposed to drink. So why was I floating in this alcoholic fog, my sandals wobbling as Florian steered me into my apartment?

Oh, yes. Memories flickered toward me. The staff party at the country club. Music, balloons, laughter, dancing. A skinny woman in a turquoise turban saying, "Here, Susie. This is a good drink for you. It's like a milkshake with just a splash of brandy for flavour."

How many of those milkshakes had I drank...drunk...drunken? Four? Five?

A thumping sound made me jump. Must be the door shutting. Florian switched on a light. I flinched away from its brightness, my hand over my eyes. "Shwish it off. Please."

The light made me feel guilty. I shouldn't be here alone, drunk, with Florian. Or Florian shouldn't be here alone, not drunk, with me. Or something like that.

The light went off and I breathed a sigh of relief.

Florian took my elbow and steered me across the floor. We were going somewhere, me and Florian. Florian and me. Two musketeers, going somewhere. Moonlight gleamed through the windows onto something on my couch. Norine's teddy bear.

"Mmy kidsh." I dragged my mind up from the pit it was sinking into. "Wherrre are mmy kidsh?"

"I'm sure your kids are fine," Florian said. "They're with Valerie's mom, remember?" He set the teddy bear on the coffee table and helped me sit on the couch.

"Sho mmy kidsh arre okay?"

"Yes, they're okay."

My mind sank back into the pit. I hauled it up like a pail of water on a rope. "You and mmme, Florrrian, we sh-sh-shouldn't be alone here. Togetherrr." This was an important idea. I needed to hang onto it.

"Don't worry. I'll leave in a few minutes. I just want to make sure you're all right." He knelt on the rug and removed my sandals, his long fingers turning my insides to pudding. Vanilla pudding. I reached out to pet his hair, then pulled my hand back. "Florrrian, yyyou shouldn't be here."

"I said I'm leaving." His voice was crisp with impatience or efficiency; I couldn't tell which. "I'll just get you a glass of water first. It'll help clear your head." He switched on the floor lamp, went to the kitchen, and returned with the water.

My arm felt too heavy to lift the glass. Florian sat beside me, raising it to my lips. I gulped water like a child, my eyes on his. When the glass was empty, he set it on the coffee table and leaned closer to me. My eyes lost their focus and I saw two Florians. As I tried to decide which Florian was real, his lips met mine. My heart melted.

Gentle as a mother, Florian laid me back against the cushions.

I was tired. I wanted to rest beside Florian. But if I did, I might lose something. My self-respect, maybe more. Florian picked up my feet one at a time and set them on the couch.

What came next? Love-making. It would feel right but it wouldn't be right. I was a married woman. Dear God, help me. I gathered all my strength and pushed Florian away. "You gotta leavvve."

He sucked in a breath and blew it out through his mouth. "You're right. I gotta leave. I'm a gentleman."

I lurched to my feet, grabbing the lamp to steady myself. "Sho why don't you leavvve?"

He gave me a boyish grin, one eyebrow twitching. "I could leave. Or I could stay for breakfast."

I pictured Florian and me at the breakfast table. Toast, eggs, coffee, memories of lovemaking. It was a tempting picture. "Not a shance." I jerked my head in the general direction of the door. "Get out. Shhhcram."

CHAPTER 24

I groaned and rolled over. Somebody was pounding on the door of my apartment. Or maybe I was dreaming.

"Susie! Open up."

My mother-in-law. No. Please, no.

"Meyaalchye! Open this door."

I opened one eye and brought the alarm clock close to it. Six o'clock. Only six in the morning.

"Susie!"

What was that woman doing here? She belonged in Dayspring, seven hundred miles away. "Please, God, help me." My mouth tasted like copper pennies. "You've helped me before when I didn't deserve it. Please make Adeline go away. Either that or give me the strength to face her."

"MeYAALchye! Hurry yourself. Manfred's bringing the boxes already."

What boxes? What Manfred? Simon's brother Manfred? If Manfred was here, Simon must be too. My heart leapt at the prospect of seeing my husband. He'd scold me for being hung over. Then I'd apologize, careful to leave Florian out of my story. My husband would forgive me and I'd be safe, back in the bonds of matrimony.

"Susie!" Adeline shrieked.

"Hold on. I'm coming." I stumbled out of bed, threw my robe on, and tottered into the hallway. I ran my fingers through my stringy hair, prayed for strength, and opened the door.

"Susie!" Adeline spread her arms wide.

"Mother Epp!" I said out of the side of my mouth, hoping she wouldn't smell my breath.

She clutched me to her bosom. Thank God I hadn't let Florian stay overnight. My heart pounded at the thought of Adeline and Simon finding the beautiful man here.

"Come in, Mother Epp." I stepped aside to let her barge into my apartment. I wish you'd phoned before you came over. I'm not feeling well this morning."

Adeline pinched my cheek. "Your colour's not good. What's loose?"

"I'm mostly tired," I said, shutting the door behind her. "I'll feel better once I see Simon."

She tucked a stray curl under her hairnet. "Simon didn't come with."

"What?" My heart sagged into my slippers. "Why not?"

"Me and Manfred didn't tell him we were coming."

"Didn't tell...." I stared at her. She and Manfred had spent two days driving all the way from Dayspring, Saskatchewan through Alberta to Sage City, British Columbia without telling Simon? "Why wouldn't you tell him?"

Adeline laid a heavy hand on my shoulder. "We're making a surprise for him, for your anniversary."

"What kind of a surprise?" I was leery of my mother-in-law's surprises.

"We're going to...." Adeline's voice trailed off as heavy footsteps sounded in the hallway. "That'll be Manfred."

I opened the door and Simon's brother Manfred clumped in carrying an armful of flattened cardboard boxes. He was an older, stouter version of Simon with grey hair instead of sandy blond and a ruddier face.

"Hi, Manfred," I said, careful to keep my distance. He wasn't the hugging type.

"Hi, Girlie." He set the boxes on the floor, leaning them against the wall.

"What are the boxes for?" I asked.

Adeline squared her narrow shoulders. "Me and Manfred came to move you to Dayspring. You and the girls."

"What? You're joking, right?"

My mother-in-law crossed her arms. "You should live together with Simon. You're his wife."

"I can't leave Sage City yet." I gulped like a dying fish. "I miss him of course. So do the girls but I have too much to do here."

Manfred consulted his watch. "I'll go get the truck washed and gassed up."

"Truck?" I drew a jagged breath. "Surely you're not thinking of moving me in a truck." I'd pictured a proper moving van, when I was good and ready for it.

After Manfred left, Adeline grabbed my arm. "Come here once." She led me to a window in the living room. "Give a look." She jerked her head toward

Manfred's grain truck, which leered from the parking lot like a huge brown toad. "See how it's big? There's lots of room for your stuff."

That was probably true if I was moving but I wasn't. "I told you, Mother Epp. I can't move yet."

She dismissed my protest with a wave of her hand. "We brought a tarpaulin along with. We can throw it over your furniture, dishes, clothes, sewing machine...everything. It's got a lock. You won't need to worry yourself. Nothing will get wet or *jestolen*."

"I can't move yet."

Adeline lugged the armchair over to the window and thumped herself down into it. "This is the best time. The roads will get snowed in and icy if we wait longer."

She had a point. Winter came early in the mountains.

I sank onto the couch, my eyes burning with fatigue. "There wouldn't be room for all of us in the truck cab. The kids need their car seats."

"I brought my car along with," Adeline informed me. "It's at the motel."

I groaned. "You think of everything." I pictured her and Manfred motoring in tandem across the prairies, through the mountains, and down the Cutbank River to Sage City. The truck labouring up the slopes, guzzling gas. Adeline's ancient Chevy rocking like a boat.

I frowned at her. "I realize you and Manfred went to a lot of trouble and expense. I appreciate that but I can't move yet. I've got to finish Fayleen's dresses plus there's my job at the rink. People are counting on me."

"People will find somebody else. You're not the only girl in Sage City that knows from sewing."

I sighed. "It's a special kind of sewing, making those costumes. I've got it figured out better than anyone else."

"So explain it to some smart person."

"That wouldn't be easy. Besides, I have to paint this apartment. Otherwise Simon and I will need to pay back-rent."

Adeline pushed her hairnet higher on her forehead as if readying herself for action. "Me and Manfred will paint."

"But—"

"You wanted to marry my Simon." Her voice spiraled into a higher register. "You married him so you should live together with him. It's God's will.

My Isaac and I, we naver stayed apart one night from the day we married ourselves."

"That was different. Isaac always worked close to home."

Adeline shook her head. "Not at first. Not when me and him first outwandered from Russia. We landed up at my cousins' place near Herbert, Saskatchewan. We didn't have nothing, not even our own five dollars. Isaac hired himself out to a rich neighbour and I worked for my cousins. So much *oabeit* they made me do! Scrub the floors, milk the cows, mess out the barn, plough the potato field."

"I think your cousins took advantage of you." They must have been strong-minded cousins. Either that or Adeline's formidability index had risen since then.

She fetched the footstool from beside the couch and propped her feet up on it. "Sometimes in the evenings I was so tired, I didn't know where to leave myself. Then I'd lift my eyes up to the road and there would be Isaac, coming to me for night. Sometimes on a horse, sometimes by bicycle." Tears shone in Adeline's eyes. "I'd run to him, *Meyaalchye!* Even if I was so tired that my feet felt like made from stone, I'd run to my Isaac. I was so *verliebt* in him."

My heart bowed its head in awe. It must be wonderful to love a man that much. I did love Simon though probably not the way he deserved to be loved.

Adeline leaned toward me. "Life is hard for you in Sage City. I can easy see that. You've got no relatives to help you. Things will be different in Dayspring."

No kidding.

She glanced toward the bedrooms. "Aren't your kids out from bed yet?"

"They might be but they're not here. They stay with Valerie's mom when I'm working. Simon must have told you."

Adeline sniffed. "I naver left my kids with nobody else. I always kept care of them myself."

"You never held a paying job either."

"*Na yo.*" Adeline's mouth fell into a sulky line.

I scored a point for myself though the victory felt false. I hadn't been working the night before. I'd been at a party with Florian, getting drunk.

Adeline sprouted up from the armchair. "I can't hardly wait to see my grand-girls. Tell me where Valerie's mom lives and I'll get them."

I glanced at the clock. "It's not even seven yet. Too early to disturb her."

Adeline clicked her teeth together like she did when she was annoyed.

"I'll tell you what," I said. "Why don't you make us some breakfast while I take a shower and wash my hair? Then we'll go get the kids."

"Me and Manfred already ate," Adeline said, heading for the kitchen. "But we like second breakfast too." She pulled drawers open, pawing through them until she found an apron. "I can make pancakes." She tied the apron around her midsection. "Or muffins."

"How about muffins?" I said. They'd take longer. "The baking stuff is in the cupboard by the toaster."

Half an hour later, showered and dressed, I emerged from my bedroom feeling almost like a human being again.

Manfred was standing out on the balcony, leaning against the railing and drinking coffee. Adeline stood at the kitchen stove frying sausages and singing *Amazing Grace*.

While we were eating breakfast, a sudden thought struck me. "I almost forgot. Fayleen and her bridesmaids are coming for a fitting this morning." I glanced at the clock. "They'll be here in an hour."

"I'll help with the fitting once." Adeline refilled Manfred's coffee cup. "I know what looks nice."

I pictured her prodding Fayleen, telling her to stand up straight. Complaining about the dresses being un-Christian and insisting we make shawls to cover the girls' bare arms. I needed to lose my mother-in-law before Fayleen and company arrived. I gave Adeline a 150-watt smile. "There's no need for you to hang around the apartment. Why don't you and Manfred pick up the kids and take them downtown?"

Adeline forked a couple of sausages onto her plate. "You don't want I should help you? I'm good at sewing."

She was and I felt bad about rejecting her offer. However, the feeling passed. "No, I'll be fine. You go downtown and enjoy yourselves. Stroll around and see what's new. Let the kids take you to the playground. You could have a nice lunch downtown. The German restaurant serves sauerbraten now."

Adeline helped herself to a muffin, her gaze drifting into the distance. I could almost see pot roast in her eyes—in a brown sauce with red cabbage and tender little dumplings. Apple strudel for dessert. "Does it give a paint store downtown?"

"There's a hardware store," I admitted. "They sell paint."

"So me and Manfred can buy paint for your apartment."

"Please don't. I don't even know what colour."

"Cream-white, what else? Same like now. We should better start painting today. The sooner we paint, the sooner you can move."

"I told you. I'm not moving." I felt like a stuck record—the needle going around and around in the same groove, repeating the same sounds with irritating persistence.

"Your apartment needs painting anyways, *nicht?*"

I nodded.

"So we'll paint. Then we'll talk moving."

CHAPTER 25

After Fayleen and her bridesmaids left, I took advantage of my family's absence to take a nap.

When I woke, I sat up in bed, leaned against the headboard, and poured my heart out to God. I didn't want to move to Dayspring. My insides shriveled at the prospect of getting trapped in such a small place so close to Adeline.

But that might be my only option. I had let my feelings for Florian accelerate until they were like a runaway locomotive. If I stayed in Sage City, I'd almost certainly break my wedding vows.

God wanted me to move to Dayspring. Deep in my heart, I knew that. I should leave Sage City while Adeline and Manfred were here to help, and while the mountain roads were still passable.

I picked up the phone to call and tell Simon I was coming, then set it down again. Adeline and Manfred had gone to a lot of trouble to surprise him for our anniversary. It would be a pity to spoil their plans.

I went into the kitchen, made a cheese and onion sandwich, and brewed a pot of tea. As I ate, I started making the phone calls that would seal my fate. I arranged to have Fayleen pick up the dresses, pay me what she owed me, and find someone else to finish them. Next, I resigned from my job at the rink.

As I was discussing the apartment lease with the superintendent, Adeline trooped in with the girls. "We got the paint," she announced. "It was on sale yet. Manfred's bringing it in."

"Good, I guess," I said, helping Norine out of her jacket.

Adeline's gaze flitted around the living room. "We'll start here in the big room."

"Whatever you think. But the apartment is going to stink once we start painting. It won't be healthy to sleep in here."

Adeline dragged the armchair into the middle of the room. "The girls sleep by Valerie's mom's house anyways, *nicht?*"

"Some nights. I guess we could pay her to keep them every night. But what about me?"

"Maybe you could sleep by Valerie's mom too."

"She doesn't have space."

"So come to the motel and stay by me. My room has two beds, one empty."

"No, but thanks anyway." I forced a smile. "Maybe I could sleep in Valerie's apartment. She's in Seattle but I'll phone her and ask."

CHAPTER 26

On my second to last evening in Sage City, I took the bus to the roller rink. There, I said a reluctant goodbye to the sewing volunteers and other people I knew. I retrieved the personal belongings I'd left in my desk—measuring tape, thimbles, scissors, tailors chalk, notebook, and sweater. I stowed them in my shoulder bag, then watched the rehearsal for a while, hoping Florian Bouchard would show up so I could say goodbye to him.

We'd already said goodbye on the phone but I wanted to see him one more time. I needed one more Florian memory to carry into my new life.

I waited half an hour but there was still no sign of him. I swallowed my disappointment, shouldered my bag, and stepped out into the October twilight.

The Cutbank River was a shining ribbon curling through the city that had been my home for the past five years. Blue-violet shadows lay on the mountain slopes, almost the same colour as Florian's eyes.

My footsteps echoing, I headed along the street to Valerie's apartment, where I'd been sleeping while my apartment was being painted. I could have taken the bus but Valerie's building was only eleven blocks away. It was hardly worth waiting for the bus, which only came every forty minutes in the evenings.

I made my way past the lumberyard, the appliance store, and the make-your-own-wine shop. As I approached the flooring store, a vehicle growled up behind me. I expected it to pass but it stayed a car-length behind me, crawling along with its engine rumbling.

The hair on the back of my neck prickled. Who was in that vehicle? Maybe muggers or worse. Fighting the temptation to look back, I walked faster—shoulders squared, head up, chin out. If I looked strong and purposeful, whoever it was might decide I wasn't worth bothering with.

"Good evening." Florian's bass voice.

I stopped short, almost collapsing with relief. "Florian, what are you doing here? I expected to see you at the rink."

Florian cut the engine. "I had to pick my dad up at the airport. His flight was late." He leaned out through the car window, his hair bright in the fading light. "Susie, we need to talk."

I hardened my heart, or tried to. "We have nothing to talk about. I'm leaving in two days so all we can say is goodbye again. So goodbye." I gave him a Queen Elizabeth style wave. Hand vertical, wrist twisting.

Florian snorted. "That's not a proper goodbye." He nodded toward the passenger seat. "Get in. I'll drive you to Valerie's place."

I hitched my bag higher on my shoulder, my nerves feeling as tight as violin strings. "No, thanks. I prefer to walk." Riding with Florian would stir up feelings I had no right to.

"It's getting dark. It's not safe for you to walk alone."

It wasn't safe to ride with Florian either. "I'll be fine." I hugged my bag against my side.

He reached over and opened the passenger door. "Come on."

"I told you. I prefer to walk. It's only a few blocks."

"Susie, don't do this."

"What?"

"Don't pretend you don't care about us."

"I'm not pretending." This was a lie but what else could I say?

He parked the car, got out, locked it, and stepped toward me.

I backed away from him. "Florian, I'm a married woman."

"I realize that but can you honestly say you don't feel—"

"This isn't about feelings," I said.

"So what is it about?"

"It's about the wedding vows I took before God and the church."

Florian swallowed. "Could we go somewhere and talk? Just have a cup of coffee and talk?"

"I can't. I promised God I wouldn't go anywhere with you again."

"The art gallery on River Street has a new exhibit. Wood carvings from Quebec. It's open late tonight. Shall we go and take a look?"

"I'm sure it's very interesting," I said, "but I don't want to go." I set off again, my eyes fixed on the roof of Valerie's building. Only seven more blocks.

Florian fell into step beside me. "Did I tell you I got a B+ on my latest sculpture? My professor says my work shows promise."

"That's nice." I walked faster.

Florian matched my pace. "I'm planning to do a sculpture of Jesus next. Then one of the Virgin Mary."

"Really?" I slowed.

"Nope." He gave me a teasing grin. "I just said that because you're churchy."

"Churchy?" I gulped, trying to decide what to say. "I don't just attend church. I mean I'm not just religious. I—I have a personal relationship with Jesus Christ."

Florian smiled. "That's nice. How's it going?" He actually sounded interested.

"It wasn't going too well for a while but I've returned to the Lord. I promised I'd try to live in a way that pleases Him."

"You sound like my mom. She used to say things like that."

"Yeah?"

"She was a Catholic, devout."

I stopped walking, surprised. "Really?" We Mennonites disagreed with Catholics on many points, but we acknowledged that many were Christians under all their rituals and traditions.

"I was baptized as a baby...." Florian's voice wavered, then found its way. "So were my brothers. Mom took us to Mass almost every Sunday."

"She was a good mother, I guess."

"Yeah." He fiddled with a button on his jacket. "But things fell apart after she died."

"I'm sorry."

Florian dug a tissue out of his pocket and blew his nose. "We survived."

"Did your dad take you to church?"

"Him? No."

"Do you go on your own?"

Florian shrugged. "I drop in at the Cathedral from time to time."

"What for?"

"I like to see the sculptures and wood carvings."

"That's all?"

"Pretty much." He stuffed the tissue back into his pocket and offered me his arm. "Come on. Let's go to the gallery. Some of the carvings are religious."

Part of me wanted to go to the gallery with Florian. Another part said it was dangerous to go anywhere with him, even to see religious carvings. Even if I didn't take his arm.

He smiled. "Come on, Kid."

"I'm not a kid." I wished I were a kid, maybe nineteen years old. But I was twenty-five with a husband and two children. I should be thanking God for them, not playing with fire.

But Florian's soul reached out to me. I could let my soul reach out and meet his, or I could do the right thing.

I jumped as Florian touched my elbow. "Come on. Let's just go see the exhibit and talk for half an hour."

"I'm sorry." My voice broke under the strain of resisting temptation. "I can't." I stepped away from him and headed off like a homing pigeon, pointing myself toward Valerie's building.

Florian followed me. "Isn't our friendship worth half an hour?"

What could I say? Our friendship was worth a lifetime. I just didn't have a lifetime to give it.

"Okay," Florian said, "if you won't go to the gallery, let me at least walk you to Valerie's place."

"You can walk anywhere you like. This is a public sidewalk."

Florian ignored my sarcasm and fell into step beside me again. "I wish you were twins, identical twins. One of you could move to Dayspring. The other twin could stay here with me."

"I'm too ordinary for a guy like you." My voice came out flat. "You'd get bored with me."

"You don't give me much credit." He guided me past a manhole with an orange barrier around it. "With you by my side, I could be a good husband. And with you to inspire me, I might become a great sculptor."

"And what would I become?" Other than an adulteress.

"A dress designer," Florian said. "A famous designer specializing in first-communion dresses. Emily and Norine could be your models."

"We're not Catholic," I said as we passed the hedge outside Valerie's building. "Anyway Emily and Norine aren't just my kids. They're Simon's too." I trotted up the sidewalk toward the front door.

Florian followed me like a dog. "I wish you and I could have our own kids." He opened the door for me.

How many men would say that to a woman? I wondered, hurrying across the lobby with Florian at my elbow. How many twenty-three-year-old men? I pictured Florian and I living in a sprawling house near a park. Climbing trees with our kids, playing ball with them, taking them on trips to Quebec and France. Attending ceremonies where Florian received awards for his sculptures. It was a nice dream. Too nice. I shoved it out of my mind.

The elevator's UP button was shaped like a cougar's head. As I reached to push it, Florian took my hand. "Wait a minute, Susie. Please. Can you spare me another minute?" He reached into an inside pocket and took out a small blue box.

My breath thinned. Florian wouldn't— Surely not.

He held the box out to me. "I want you to have this."

I hesitated a moment, then took the box. My fingers shook as I lifted the lid. Inside was a mother-of-pearl heart nestled into white satin. Carved into the heart was an image of a spool of thread.

"It's a brooch." Florian showed me the pin on the back. "I made it for you." His eyes looked like a little boy's, timid and hopeful. "Do you like it?"

My head sailed off my body. "It's gorgeous, Florian. Thank you." I would have loved it even if it was ugly. I stood on tiptoe, kissed him on the mouth, and pushed the UP button.

The elevator pinged.

"I love you, Susie." Florian's voice vibrated against the swish of the door opening. "Be happy."

I stumbled into the elevator with my bag, letting the door swish shut between us.

CHAPTER 27

Adeline's Chevy was a 1949 green job with a three-speed manual transmission on the column. On our way to Dayspring, she and I took turns driving it, following Manfred's grain truck, which was loaded with all my worldly possessions. In the back seat of the Chevy, Emily and Norine squirmed, played, fought, cried, and whined. When they napped, Adeline sometimes rode with Manfred.

Our progress was slow through the mountains because there were so many curves and steep slopes. Then rain slowed us even more, and we spent a dreary night in a roadside motel that reeked of strawberry air freshener. However, after the town of Vegreville with its Easter egg sculpture, the sun came out. From there, it was blue-sky prairie all the way through the rest of Alberta and into Saskatchewan.

About four o'clock on the third day, we finally approached the turnoff for Dayspring. I was behind the wheel of the Chevy with the kids napping in the back. Manfred and Adeline were in the lead with the truck. Shivering with excitement and apprehension, I followed them into the village that would become my new home.

We passed the Dayspring Hotel with its faded sign, then followed the wide main street past an Esso Gas Station, Snusteads' Gift Store (closed for the season), Prairie-Pointe Gallery (closed until June 15, 1976), Flatlander Café (open), grocery store, post office, and village office. After the village office, I was surprised to see Manfred wheel his truck into the vacant lot beside Mahs' Café. I had expected us to drive straight through to Simon's house near the lake, but I pulled into a parking spot in front of the café.

Adeline cranked her window down. "Susie," she called, "you should go alone to Simon's house. It'll make a better surprise for him, *nicht*? Me and Manfred will keep care of the kids."

I leaned out my window. "Why don't we all go together?" This wasn't only about me. It was about the girls too. Simon would be thrilled to see them. Also, what would be the point of the surprise if Adeline and Manfred weren't there to witness it?

My mother-in-law heaved herself out of the truck and loped over to me. "No, *Meyaalchye*. You should go alone." She scurried around to the back door of the Chevy and unbuckled Norine's car seat.

The toddler's eyes flickered open. "Mommy." She reached for me.

I squeezed her warm little hand. "Did you have a nice nap, Dear? Are you ready to surprise Daddy?"

Norine smiled, showing the sweet little gap between her two front teeth. I smoothed her curls. "See, Mother Epp? She wants to come along."

Adeline lifted Norine out of her car seat. "No, it should be romantic. Just Simon and you."

What did she expect? That he and I would make wild passionate love the moment I walked in the door? That wasn't likely since I was having my period. Too messy. "Are you saying children aren't romantic?"

"No, they're not." She scooted around to the other side of the car. "Come on, Sweetie." She unbuckled Emily. "We'll go in the café once and eat ice cream while Mommy surprises Daddy."

I groaned.

"What's loose with you, Susie?" Adeline asked. "Don't you want to see my Simon?"

"Of course I do. It's just that—" What could I say? Her pushiness was sapping all the excitement and spontaneity out of the occasion.

Adeline hitched Norine up on her hip and brought the girls around to my window. "Maybe your nerves are breaking down like your mom's."

"There's nothing wrong with my nerves." Nothing that spending the rest of my life away from my mother-in-law wouldn't cure.

Emily tugged at her grandmother's arm. "Can me and Norine have cherry ice cream?"

"Please?" Adeline prompted.

"Please?" Emily said.

Norine bounced in Adeline's arms. "Ikeem, ikeem."

I filled my lungs with prairie air, blew it out, and turned the key in the Chevy's ignition. "Okay," I said, "just give me an hour with Simon and then bring the girls out." I waved to my daughters. "Be good. I'll see you soon."

As I navigated the car along the wide main street, Florian's words echoed in my mind: "I love you, Susie. Be happy."

Those words would live in my memory forever. But now I needed to shift gears, forget Florian, and readjust myself to my marriage and real life.

I turned left at the railway station, followed Railway Avenue past a row of houses, and crossed the tracks, praying for joy in living at Dayspring. I passed the cemetery with its high iron gate, praying for happiness and long life for Simon and for Florian.

Along the gravel road that led to Simon's house, I caught glimpses of Knutson Lake—cobalt-blue between hills so low they could hardly be called hills. They wouldn't qualify in Sage City. On my left, harvested fields stretched toward a flat-line horizon. Unassuming prairie scenery.

As I nosed the car into my husband's driveway, I wondered what he was doing. He'd probably be home from school by now. Maybe he was ironing his shirts, wishing I was there to take over. Maybe he was standing in front of his refrigerator, wondering what to have for his lonely dinner.

I parked Adeline's Chevrolet beside Simon's Volkswagen, then powdered my nose and reapplied my lipstick. I got out of the car, brushed a bit of lint off my slacks, breathed a prayer for courage, and ventured up to the house. It was a long brown bungalow that looked like a train with the locomotive heading straight toward me.

I knocked on the door of the lean-to porch.

No answer.

I tried again.

No footsteps, no voice calling. But I heard faint sounds from farther along in the house. Music. Violins. An oboe. A tenor voice singing something from an opera, maybe Italian. That was weird. Simon didn't like opera. Maybe he'd fallen asleep with the radio on.

I knocked again, more forcefully.

No answer, just music blowing on the wind. I followed the sound around the west side of the bungalow. As I picked my way past a thorny rosebush, a baritone joined the tenor, the two voices interweaving.

The voices seemed to come from the second-last window. That would be the master bedroom according to the drawing Simon had sent me. I detoured around several clay pots, some with shrubs growing in them, and approached the window. "Hello?"

No response.

"Hello, Simon?"

Nothing.

I stood on my tiptoes, straining to see through the window. Too high. I got one of the empty clay pots, turned it upside down, stepped onto it, and peered inside.

The bedroom was large, with a green linoleum floor. A stepladder partly blocked the door of what must be a closet. On the lowest rung of the ladder stood a mountain of a man with a grin on his ruddy face and a wallpaper roller in his hand. Ross Forbes, school principal, based on the pictures Simon had sent me.

On top of the stepladder lay a roll of wallpaper like what covered parts of the walls. The pattern was composed of purple triangles intersecting with green circles. It was too geometric and hard-edged for my tastes but I didn't spend much time thinking about it. I was too busy staring at the large grey parrot that sat on Ross's shoulder.

The parrot was shredding a length of wallpaper, producing ragged strips and tossing them into Ross's hair. Some strips clung to his auburn waves. Others fluttered down onto his coveralls.

On the bed near the opera-blaring radio lay my husband, shirtless and laughing like a baboon. "Hoo, haw, whoo," he shrieked with excitement. I'd never heard Simon laugh like that. He sounded like a stranger, not my husband.

CHAPTER 28

What was going on in that bedroom? I wondered, stumbling down off the clay pot. Why didn't Simon have a shirt on? Maybe he'd been changing into an older one, planning to help Ross wallpaper.

If so, why was he lying on the bed laughing like a maniac? Granted, the parrot's antics were amusing. They'd entertain someone who liked that sort of thing. But laughter like my husband's didn't seem normal.

The two men appeared to be at ease in the bedroom together, Simon comfortable half-naked in Ross's presence. Maybe Simon and Ross—no, I couldn't go there.

A chorus of operatic voices swelled through the window. The voices belted out a few lines accompanied by drums and brass instruments. Then a soprano took over, singing four or five words and repeating them with irritating persistence.

The chorus erupted again, but this time a louder sound overwhelmed it. A truck rumbled up the driveway, its horn blaring. That would be Manfred and company.

The music stopped in a buzz of static.

I stepped back up onto the clay pot and peered through the window. The bed was empty, the blankets rumpled. Nobody stood on the stepladder. A ragged strip of wallpaper dangled from the top rung.

I left the window and hurried around to the lean-to at the front of the house. I knocked on the door, glancing over my shoulder at Manfred's truck passing the vegetable garden. "Simon?" My voice cracked with apprehension.

No answer.

I knocked again, raising my voice. "Simon?"

The sound of hurrying footsteps came from inside. The door opened and there stood my husband with his shirt partly buttoned, his hair wild, his cheeks flushed. Was that shame I saw on his face, or embarrassment, or just surprise?

"Susie, Darling." He hurried out onto the porch and threw his arms around me. "What are you doing here?" He kissed me, his lips thick and warm.

"Your mother." I jerked a nod at the truck as Manfred backed it toward the storage shed. "She wanted to surprise you."

"I'm surprised all right." His eyes searched my face. "I feel like I'm dreaming. Are you here to stay or just visiting?"

I tried to smile. "Our children and all my worldly goods are in that truck."

"That's great, really great." He laughed like a little boy. "I was beginning to wonder if you'd deserted me. I thought maybe you'd moved without telling me. The last couple of times I tried to phone you, the operator said your number was no longer in service. I hoped it was a mistake but—"

"I'm sorry. I had the phone disconnected before we left the apartment. I should have told you but your mother didn't want me spoiling the surprise."

"You're here now. That's what counts." He pulled me into a tighter hug, his heart thumping against mine.

As Simon released me, Adeline swanned over from the truck with Emily and Norine. Then there were more hugs and kisses, Simon exclaiming over how much the girls had grown.

"*Na yo,* Simon," Adeline said. "We sure surprised you, *nicht?*"

"You sure did, Mother. I'm still surprised."

She beamed at me. "Did he show you the inside from the house yet? Have you seen how nice it's painted and wallpapered?"

"No." I slid a sidelong look at Simon. "He didn't hear me knocking when I first arrived."

"I'm sorry, Sweetheart." Simon laid a hand on my shoulder. "Ross and I had the radio on loud."

"I noticed," I said. "I didn't know you liked opera."

Adeline snorted. "Opera! Who can understand that?" She jerked her chin toward the lean-to. "Let's go into the house once." She barged inside, herding the girls ahead of her. Simon and I followed.

As Adeline maneuvered the kids past the bookshelves that dominated the lean-to, Emily pulled away from her and darted into the hallway that led to the kitchen. "This is where we're going to live, right?" She burst through the door into the kitchen, then came running out, reaching for Adeline's hand. "Oma, there's a man in there. He's got a bird on his shoulder."

"That's Uncle Ross," Simon said, leading the way into the kitchen. "You don't need to be afraid of him."

"Hello, Emily," Ross boomed. "Hello, Norine." He turned to me. "Susie, it's great to meet you at last." He offered me his hand, his face as innocent and friendly as a Saint Bernard dog's.

I shook Ross's hand, wondering what to think about the scene in the bedroom. Were he and Simon just friends enjoying each other's company? Or something else?

As I withdrew my hand from Ross's, the parrot on his shoulder let out a screech.

I backed away, almost bumping into Adeline.

"Don't mind Callum," Ross said. "He won't hurt you."

"I guess not," I said, "but I'm not accustomed to having birds in the house." The parrot scared me though I didn't want to admit it.

The bird stared at me, his yellow eyes looking a hundred years old. "Hello, Sugar." His voice sounded tinny, like it came from an old-fashioned record player. "Give us a little kiss."

I glanced at Ross. "He's interesting," I managed to say. "But I wonder, do you have a cage for him?" I pictured Callum flapping around the kitchen releasing foul-smelling droppings and perching on my children's heads, maybe pecking at their foreheads.

"Sure," Ross said. "I can put him away." He limped into the living room and returned with a wire cage. Emily and Norine watched with dinner-plate eyes as Ross transferred the parrot from his shoulder to his hand and then into the cage. When he shut the door, Callum let out a piercing scream.

Emily yelped and ran over to Adeline, who was rooting around in the refrigerator. "Oma, is Callum nice?"

Adeline set a pound of lard on the counter. "I've seen nicer birds." She took a carton of eggs from the refrigerator. "But he talks good anyways."

"What are you doing, Mother Epp?" I asked as she took a mixing bowl out of the cupboard.

"Making an onion cake for our supper."

Our supper? Were she and Manfred staying for supper? I wished they wouldn't. I wanted to be alone with Simon, just the two of us and our girls in our new home.

Summoning all my courage, I pulled the mixing bowl out of my mother-in-law's hands.

She stared at me. "What's loose with you?"

"I don't want you making an onion cake." This was my kitchen. The sooner we clarified that, the better.

She clicked her teeth together. "My sons love my *sippel kuchen*. Ross will like it too, for sure."

"I'm sorry." Ross limped toward the door with his parrot. "I can't stay."

The girls followed him. "What happened to your leg?" Emily asked.

"Emily, that's rude," I told her.

"No," Ross said, "it's a fair question. A car hit me when I was a kid. I was running across a street after a ball."

Emily frowned at him. "You should have looked where you were going."

"You're right," Ross said. "I'm sure you would have been more careful."

He transferred the cage from one hand to the other. "I'd better shove off. I'll come back later and finish the wallpapering."

"Don't bother," I mumbled. I didn't like the purple and green wallpaper. More important, I didn't want Ross in our bedroom. The house belonged to him but that room should be out of bounds for anyone but Simon and me.

Adeline opened the refrigerator and glommed at its contents. "It doesn't give much to eat in here. Better I should make an onion cake."

"Better you and Manfred should go home," I said, surprised at my own boldness.

The kids' eyes widened. They weren't accustomed to hearing me speak so bluntly to their grandmother. But I needed to defend my territory.

Simon headed for the door. "I'll go help Manfred unload the truck."

I followed. "It doesn't need to be unloaded tonight. Your mother and Manfred can come back tomorrow."

Adeline turned on her son, her eyes full of accusation. "Your wife doesn't want me here, after everything I did for her yet."

I sighed. "I appreciate your help, Mother Epp. I wouldn't be here if it wasn't for you and Manfred. But I need to run my own show now. Please try to understand."

Her chin quivered. "I was just trying to be a good mother-law."

"I realize that but I don't…. I can't…."

"Mother," Simon said, "you and Manfred should probably run along. It's getting dark anyway."

"*Na yo,*" she said, frowning at me like I was a bug in a flour barrel.

After she and Manfred left, I rummaged through the refrigerator and found half a loaf of raisin bread. "We'll have raisin toast and scrambled eggs for supper," I announced.

Emily narrowed her eyes. "Oma was going to make onion cake."

I sighed. "I'm sorry. We'll ask her it to make it another time, okay?"

Simon took plates out of the cupboard and started setting the table, his face thoughtful.

The girls rushed to help him.

"Wash your hands first," I said in my automatic-Mommy voice.

"Where, Mommy?" Emily asked.

Norine grinned, showing her new teeth. She was our sunshine—too young to feel the tension in the room.

She and Emily grabbed Simon's hands. He herded them toward the bathroom. I was glad to see the girls and their father together again. On the other hand, I suspected that life in Dayspring would be even more challenging than I'd expected.

CHAPTER 29

It was the evening of our fifth anniversary. I lay in bed with my head on Simon's chest, gazing at the moon through the window.

"It's a great view, isn't it?" Simon murmured, stroking my hair. The moonlight made a silver path across the lake.

"It's beautiful. Not many people have a water view from their bedroom."

"We're among the lucky few." Simon ran a finger around the outside edge of my ear.

Our daughters were in bed in their room down the hall. Now, according to the standard script for anniversaries, we should make love. But I was still having my period. We never had sex when that was happening. Also the lack of a window-covering made me nervous. "Doesn't it bother you," I asked, "knowing that anybody can look in anytime?"

He snorted. "Who's going to look in? We're a mile from the nearest neighbour."

"Still—"

"I like seeing the sky at night. I like watching the owls hunt. Bats flitting around."

"Doesn't the moonlight bother you?" I asked.

"I close my eyes when I sleep. Sometimes I wear a sleep-mask."

"I don't think that would work for me. I'm going to find some curtains, or make some. As soon as I get a chance."

"Whatever you think," Simon said, "as long as we can open your curtains when there's a thunderstorm. Or an eclipse of the moon or a UFO landing."

I laughed. "We can open them anytime you like, within reason." I paused. "But there's something else."

"Yeah?"

"That wallpaper. It's got to go." The purple triangles and green circles were too garish and hard-edged for a bedroom. More to the point, Ross had hung them there.

Simon pulled away from me. "That paper is excellent quality, better than the cheap stuff underneath."

"Did Ross buy it?" I couldn't picture Simon shopping for wallpaper.

"He ordered it from Toronto. He thought it would look nice in the foyer of his château."

"Foyer? Château? Aren't we fancy?"

Simon shrugged. "Ross has a beautiful house and he's proud of it. What's wrong with that?"

"Nothing but why try to impose his taste on us?"

Simon blew out an irritated breath. "He ordered too much paper so he offered to hang the rest in here rather than let it go to waste."

"Well." I heaved myself into a sitting position, "I don't like it."

"Right. I'll tell Ross it doesn't meet with your ladyship's approval. But this house belongs to him, don't forget. He can decorate it any way he likes, strictly speaking."

"Against his tenants' wishes?"

"I don't know but I guess he'll understand if you want to paper over it. He's a reasonable man."

Reasonable and what else? Honourable? Was he a principled principal who wouldn't steal someone's husband? Was I being paranoid, even asking myself such a question? Probably. Simon wouldn't be attracted to Ross, not in that way. He wasn't the type. He was married. We had sex. He enjoyed it.

On the other hand, I'd been attracted to Florian Bouchard despite being married and enjoying sex with my husband. Thankfully I'd left Sage City before that situation spun out of control.

CHAPTER 30

On Thanksgiving Sunday, bouquets of ripe wheat sat on the organ in the country Mennonite church near my mother-in-law's house. Baskets of home-grown carrots, beets, potatoes, and cabbages decorated the steps leading up to the pulpit.

Vases of white clematis sat on the windowsills. Their sweet aroma accompanied Simon and me and our children as we proceeded up the aisle to the pew where his mother sat.

My footsteps dragged. I was tired from unpacking. I had suggested to Simon that we attend the Lutheran church in town; it was only ten minutes from our house. But his mother, Adeline, had insisted we come to her Mennonite church for Thanksgiving, *Erntedankfest*.

But Adeline. But Adeline. These words galloped through my mind as Simon, the girls, and I sat down with her. I felt like a show horse jumping over hurdle after hurdle, all of them marked *But Adeline*.

On the wall behind the pulpit hung a wooden cross, shiny with varnish. I focused on it, trying to see Adeline through Jesus' eyes. He died for both of us. He loved us both so we should love each other too. As I prayed for the grace to love my mother-in-law, Norine scrambled off my lap and onto Adeline's. Emily slipped past me to sit beside her grandmother.

I heaved a sigh of resignation, determined not to let jealousy sour my good intentions. Of course Adeline must seem comforting to a child. She was big and soft, and always sure of what was right and wrong. It must be nice to go through life like that. No doubts, no second guesses.

Pastor Warkentin stepped up to the pulpit, darkly handsome in a black suit and striped tie. "Let's begin by singing hymn number 251: *Now thank we all our God*."

I rose with the rest of the congregation, accepting my half of the hymnbook Simon held out to me. It felt good to stand beside him again, feeling the pleasantly irritating prickle of his grey tweed suit against my shoulder. His tenor voice soared above, around, and under the other voices including my sparrow-like soprano. It made me proud to be his wife.

A violinist and two guitarists in their twenties stood near the organ, accompanying the singing. The violinist wore a sage-green dress whose neckline featured interlocking slits that flattered her ample bosom without showing too much. The skirt hugged her slender hips while still maintaining modesty. That shade of sage-green was perfect on the young woman. It made her alabaster skin glow and complemented her crisply curling black hair.

The longer I watched her, the more familiar she seemed. Where had I seen those oval eyes before, that dimpled chin with the saucy lift to it? I let the hymn forge on without me while I rummaged through my memories.

Simon's yearbooks—high school and teacher's college. Of course. I'd seen that face in all of them, younger versions of it. In some, the photo was autographed *Love, Bethany*.

The lovely violinist was Simon's former girlfriend, the wealthy widow Adeline had wanted him to marry. What was she doing here? As the last notes of the hymn died away, I prodded him with my elbow, whispering, "I thought Bethany Banman moved to Regina."

He shrugged his tweed shoulders. "She moved back."

"Why?"

"I don't know," he whispered as we sat down. "Maybe she missed her fish farm." Simon didn't appear to care one way or the other.

After the morning service, the men retreated to the parking lot to loosen their ties and swap farming stories. Most of the women descended to the basement to put the food on the tables for the noon meal. Many of them wore polyester dresses. Practical dresses that washed well, with gathered or pleated skirts—easy to walk in.

As I followed the other women, herding Emily and Norine down the stairs, I noticed a different kind of skirt outside one of the basement windows. It was a slim sage-green skirt. Alabaster legs descended from it, ending in high heels. As the girls and I reached the bottom of the stairs, a pair of grey tweed trouser legs approached the sage-green skirt. One alabaster leg shifted. One of the tweed legs mimicked the motion.

What were my husband and Bethany Banman doing out there? Discussing fish farming? Sharing school memories? Simply gazing into each other's eyes?

Maybe my imagination was running away with me. Simon and Bethany had known each other for years. Obviously they'd have things to talk about.

"Susie," Adeline called, barreling toward me. "You can put the pickles in dishes." She indicated several jars of dill pickles that sat on a table near the refrigerator. "Use the white bowls. They're in the cupboard the plates beside." She whisked herself away, sweeping Emily and Norine ahead of her. "Come along with, girls. The Sunday School teachers are playing games with the children. I'll show to you where."

My mother-in-law was a whirlwind; I was a breeze. Wondering how I could make myself more dynamic, I twisted the top off a jar of pickles. I was forking them into a dish when Bethany came down the stairs, her high heels tapping. She approached me, smelling of wind and citrus cologne. "You must be Simon's wife." She smiled. "He said you were the pretty one in the pink dress."

"My husband's a flatterer," I said.

"I'm Bethany Banman." She offered me her hand. "Simon said you have a sewing and knitting business."

"Not anymore." I shook her hand with its long cool fingers. "That was in Sage City."

"But you're going to start again, right?"

"I might," I said. "I don't know."

"I'm looking for somebody to knit some sweaters for me. I know a good knitter in Regina but I'd rather work with someone local."

"I'm local," I said, pursuing another pickle, "as of last Thursday."

Bethany's smile accentuated the dimple in her chin. "It'll be nice to have another transplanted city girl around."

I captured the pickle and forked it into the dish. "I wouldn't have let myself get transplanted so soon but Simon begged me to move to Dayspring." I gave her a long level look. "My husband missed me like crazy." There. I'd told Bethany how things stood between Simon and me. Hopefully she'd caught the message.

CHAPTER 31

The tables for the noon meal were made of sheets of plywood laid on sawhorses. Each table was covered with a tablecloth that hung almost to the floor. I sat across from Simon at a blue-draped table. Emily sat beside me, then Adeline with Norine on her knee. Bethany sat several tables away but her elegant presence made me feel like staking a stronger claim on my husband. I slipped my right shoe off. Then, under the cloth, I ran my stocking foot up his tweed-suited leg.

A corner of his mouth twitched.

We hadn't made love since I'd arrived in Dayspring because it had been the wrong time of the month. But it was the right time now. I eased my foot up my husband's thigh, then eased my toes under the napkin that he'd tucked into his belt. "Simon, what do you think?" I said in an offhand tone. "Shall we go home for dessert?"

"Home?" Adeline shrieked. "They're having children's stories this afternoon." She threw an arm around Emily. "You want to hear stories, *nicht?*"

Emily rounded her eyes at me. "Can we stay, Mommy, please?"

I slid my toes into Simon's crotch.

"I wonder, Mother...." His voice turned husky. "Could the kids stay here with you this afternoon? You could bring them home later."

Adeline scowled. "What's loose with you?" She glommed around at the congregants around us. "People will gossip if you leave now."

I forced a yawn. "If anybody asks, tell them I'm tired from unpacking."

She gave me an exasperated eye-roll and hugged my children closer.

Simon and I drove home in record time, the tires of the Volkswagen spurting gravel as we roared up to the storage shed. We rooted through my boxes until we found the orange curtains I'd brought from Sage City, raced to the house, and hung them in our bedroom. They were too long and they looked terrible with the purple and green wallpaper, but that didn't matter.

We made wild crazy love. Then we slept in each other's arms for a while and made love again. Afterwards, I drifted into a contented doze, barely aware of Simon tiptoeing out of the room.

I woke to late-afternoon sunlight. It glowed through my orange curtains, giving the room a magical look. I stretched like a cat. Maybe life at Dayspring wasn't going to be so bad after all. Maybe I just needed to make some adjustments, like shorten my curtains and cover that ugly wallpaper. I might be able to find orange wallpaper to go with the curtains. The stores in Dayspring had no wallpaper of any kind but I could drive to Moose Jaw or Saskatoon.

I rolled onto my back, wishing I had a friend to drive to the city with. Someone like Valerie to eat lunch with in some foofy city restaurant. I missed her.

I missed Florian too, but that chapter of my life was over. The book was closed. Not even a bookmark remained.

CHAPTER 32

"Ross invited us over for supper," Simon announced on Monday afternoon when he arrived home from teaching.

I lifted a stack of plates out of the box I was unpacking. "Tonight?"

"Why not?" My husband looked smart in a navy jacket, red tie, grey trousers, and the white shirt I'd ironed that morning. I was glad he dressed well for work, especially since the school board still hadn't decided whether to offer him a permanent position.

I set my plates on the table. "Couldn't we stay home tonight? Why rush out to visit someone I hardly know?" Simon was obligated to spend time with Ross at work, but that shouldn't mean we needed to socialize with him in the evenings.

Simon shuffled his feet. "I guess I could phone Ross and tell him we can't make it. But he's going to a lot of trouble for us. He's making fish stew and baking his down-east brown bread."

"Ross bakes bread?" I was impressed. I hadn't mastered the art myself though Adeline threatened to teach me.

"He does. He went home at noon to get the dough started, left once this afternoon to punch it down, and left again to put it in the pans."

"So if you knew at noon that we were invited, why didn't you tell me?" I might have been more enthusiastic if I'd had time to prepare. Like take a nap, wash my hair, iron a nice blouse. Look like a vital, attractive wife.

"I phoned you," Simon said. "I didn't get an answer."

"You must have phoned while the kids and I were downtown." I grimaced. "If you can call one straggly street a downtown."

Simon sank onto a kitchen chair. "I wish you wouldn't badmouth this place. I need to make a go of it here. This is my big chance. You should encourage me."

I wanted him to do well though I wasn't sure he could without a degree. "Look, Simon. I'm trying to encourage you. I tried to get groceries so I could cook you a nice supper but the store was locked with the blinds down. Why didn't somebody tell me everything's shut tight on Mondays?"

He shifted on his chair. "It never occurred to me."

"Why didn't your mother say something? I went looking for food and came back with nothing, not even a stalk of celery."

"All the more reason to eat at Ross's tonight."

I pictured the kind of supper we'd have at home. Toast, canned beans, ham out of a can. Simon giving me reproachful looks. Emily complaining because we'd eaten the same meal too many times already.

"You'll like Ross's house," Simon said. "It's one of a kind."

How often had my husband been there? Alone or with other people?

"How about it, Susie?"

I sucked a frustrated breath through my teeth. "Okay, if you really want to."

At a quarter to five, we set off across the pasture toward Ross's house. Emily scampered ahead. Simon and I followed with Norine riding on his shoulders. Late-autumn grass crunched under our feet.

The yeasty aroma of baking bread greeted us as we approached Ross's 'château.' My mouth watered despite my misgivings. Ross—in a black turtleneck, jeans, and a denim apron—ushered us into a foyer with a high ceiling. Late-afternoon light shone through the leaded-glass windows, glinting off a white piano near a green loveseat. The floor was white marble with green veining.

The wallpaper was the same as in our bedroom but the purple triangles and green circles looked appropriate in this setting, even good. I wished I'd found time to iron my silk blouse.

Ross hung our jackets in the closet. "Supper isn't quite ready. Shall we go and say hello to my birds?"

I didn't really like birds. I loved animals but anything with wings and a beak gave me the creeps. On the other hand, I didn't want to seem like a party-pooper. I accompanied the others along a hallway lined with pictures of ships and rocky shorelines.

We heard Ross's birds before we saw them. Their twittering and shrieking grew louder as we neared the end of the hallway. Ross opened the door, and the kids and I stared into a huge room like nothing we'd ever encountered before. Wire shelving lined all four walls of the room. Plants sat on some of the shelves but most held cages in which canaries, budgies, parakeets, parrots, and other birds fluttered, pecked, and preened themselves in front of tiny mirrors. Skylights dominated the ceiling. Some were shuttered. Others showed rectangles of fading light.

I lingered in the doorway while Ross and Simon took the girls inside. Callum, the parrot we'd met earlier, occupied a place of honour near a fake-leather armchair and a tiled table. He burbled something. Emily's eyes widened. She left her father's side and darted toward him. "Hi, Callum." Two feet short of his cage, she stopped, hesitated a moment, and then scurried back to Simon. "Daddy, is Callum nice?"

"He can be quite nice," Simon said, leading her and Norine to the parrot's cage. As they approached, Callum cocked his grey head, looking wise.

"See," Simon said, "he remembers you."

Emily extended a cautious finger toward the bird, then jerked it back.

Ross took a tin off a shelf and took out an unshelled peanut. "Shall we give him a treat?" He handed the peanut to Simon.

Simon held it so Callum could see it. "Can you sing for us?"

The parrot stared past Simon's left ear.

"Harken, harken," Simon sang in his mellow tenor, "music sounds a-far!"

Harken? Was that from a hymn? Or maybe opera.

Simon held the peanut almost within Callum's reach. "Sing, and I'll give you your treat." He sang the prompt again: "Harken, harken, music sounds a-far!"

Callum pecked at a bar of his cage.

Emily's shoulders sagged. "Why doesn't he sing?"

"Maybe too many people around," Simon said. "He's not used to so much company."

Who was usually here when Callum sang? Just Simon and Ross? That must be cozy.

As Emily's attention wandered toward the canary cages, an eerie sound emerged from Callum's nose holes. "Harken, harken, music sounds a-far!" The voice was Simon's but it sounded thin and scratchy, like an old recording. "Harken, harken, with a happy heart!" The parrot stopped and smirked, then delivered the punchline: *"Funiculì, funiculà, funiculì, funiculà!"*

"Mommy," Emily called, "did you hear? Callum sang like Daddy."

Ross gave me a thumbs-up, beaming as if Callum were his talented son instead of a bird. I wasn't sure how impressed I should be. I knew almost nothing about birds.

The parrot fixed his yellow eyes on Emily. "Give us a little kiss."

She clamped her hand over her mouth. "Yuck! I don't kiss birds."

"Well, I do." Simon pressed his face against the bars of Callum's cage.

The parrot brushed Simon's lips with his beak, making a kissing sound—smoooooch.

Emily wrinkled her nose in disgust.

Simon set the peanut in Callum's beak. "Here's your treat."

As the parrot shelled the peanut, Ross limped back to where I stood in the doorway. "I had Callum for twenty years but he never sang for me. Simon taught him in a month."

"Is that true or are you just flattering my husband?"

"I'm serious," Ross said. "Simon is amazing."

"You really think so?"

"Really."

I was practical enough to admit that Simon didn't strike many people as amazing. He hadn't achieved a lot in his thirty-one years. He'd spent too much time flitting from one possible career to another.

But maybe he was coming into his own here in Dayspring. I hoped so; I loved him. We suited each other—Susie the wallflower and Simon the late-bloomer. However, I suspected I had a rival for my husband's affection. Maybe Bethany. More likely Ross. Or was I chasing a straw dog?

"Be not afraid," the Bible said. Right. That was easier said than done. I should pray for courage. I should also pray for discernment. If Ross or Bethany posed a threat to my marriage, I should know. But if I knew, what would I do? Ignore the threat, hoping it would go away? Stand up and fight? How? My fighting experience was limited; I was a Mennonite—a pacifist, and a timid one at that.

CHAPTER 33

Ross had a purple and green tablecloth on his dining table, with plaid napkins in the same shades. The plates were white with purple and green borders. The effect was lively yet elegant though I wasn't crazy about the colour scheme.

I set Norine in the highchair Ross had borrowed from a neighbour, put her bib on her, and tucked Emily's napkin into the neck of her blouse.

As we seated ourselves, Ross raised an eyebrow at me. "Would one of the girls like to say grace?"

Was he a believer? I hoped so. A believer would be less likely to lead Simon astray.

Emily raised her hand, waving it in the air. "I'll say it." Hardly pausing for breath, she plunged in: "Come, Lord Jesus." Norine murmured an accompaniment. "Be our guest. And let this food to us be blessed."

"Amen." Ross glanced toward the bird room, flapping his arms like wings. "Callum can say grace in Gaelic if he's in the mood. Shall we try him?"

"Maybe another time," Simon said. "I think the girls are hungry."

"Right. I'll get the stew." Ross rose and limped toward the kitchen, then paused in the doorway. "Susie? Simon? What would you like to drink? How about Perrier?"

"Perrier would be nice," Simon, said, tossing the word off in a worldly-wise tone.

"Is it alcoholic?" I asked, glancing at my husband. "Mennonites don't drink. They're not supposed to anyway."

Simon curled his lip in embarrassment or maybe disgust. "Susie, it's just sparkling water."

"Oh," I said, feeling like a hick. "Sure, I'll try some Perrier."

The Perrier was bubbly with a hint of lemon. It soothed the lump that was forming in my throat. Maybe the stew would help too. Steam rose from the pot as Ross ladled it out.

I mashed Norine's fish and vegetables, put her spoon in her hand, and turned my attention to my own bowl. The heat felt good on my throat but the lump persisted.

What was wrong with me? Probably too much had happened too quickly. I had moved to Dayspring to join my supposedly lonely husband, only to discover that he wasn't lonely at all. He was blossoming in the company of a wealthy, cultured mentor who broadened his horizons in ways I couldn't match and probably didn't even understand.

Norine's chin needed wiping. I found a tissue in my pocket and took care of it. Then I buttered a piece of bread for her, and one for Emily.

As I helped myself to the cabbage salad, Ross rose from the table, stepped over to the sideboard, and put a tape into his tape-player. A moment later, opera music soared out, accompanied by a chorus of canaries or what sounded like canaries.

"Are those real birds?" Emily asked, her eyes bulging.

"You bet," Ross said. "This is a Performing Birds tape. My canaries are pretty good at singing with it." He limped down the hall to the bird room. When he opened the door, we heard his canaries chirping along with those on the tape. Their timing wasn't perfect but it wasn't bad. Ross shut the door on the birds and returned to the table. "This next bit of tape is fascinating."

A deep-voiced trainer and a parrot named Delilah were discussing colours and shapes. But instead of using spoken words, they sang their questions and answers.

> Trainer: "What's this?"
> Delilah (the parrot): "Red triangle."
> Trainer: "Good. What's this?"
> Delilah: "Blue."
> Trainer: "Blue what?"
> Long silence, then: "Blue square."

Ross shut off the tape-player and beamed around the table. "Isn't that great?"

"It's interesting," I said, wondering if the taped parrot was real or fake.

Ross poured more Perrier into my glass. "I think Callum could learn to do that."

"Really?"

"He could if Simon taught him."

Whoa. "Why wouldn't you teach Callum yourself?" I didn't want Ross leading my husband even farther along the path of parrot-focused togetherness.

"Like I said before," Ross said, ladling a little more stew into Emily's bowl, "Callum doesn't learn from me like he does from your husband. Simon could probably have him ready to go on tour if they start right away."

"On tour?"

Norine was whining in the highchair. I lifted her out and set her on my lap.

"Some of the students and teachers and I do a variety show every spring," Ross said. "We present it in Dayspring first. Then we take our show to Central Butte, Davidson, and Outlook. We might even get invited to Moose Jaw next spring."

"And you're thinking of taking birds along?" Bizarre. Would birds even survive a trip like that?

"We took a xylophone-playing crow last year," Ross said. "She was a hit. A parrot singing about geometry would be even better."

"I suppose so," I said, trying to picture a xylophone-playing crow. "But Simon doesn't have time to train Callum."

There it was. I'd spoken my mind almost as forthrightly as Adeline or Aunt Frieda would have.

Simon kicked me under the table.

I ignored him and barged ahead. "My husband is too busy teaching school and helping the fish farmers. If he was tutoring Callum too, he'd hardly have any time for the girls and me. We need his attention—" I broke off, realizing that I'd made Simon's family sound like a handicap. We shouldn't be. We should be an encouragement and a support.

Ross ran his finger over the handle of his knife. "I didn't mean to upset you, Susie, but your husband has rare talents. It would be a pity not to develop them."

Norine grabbed a piece of bread off my plate and threw it on the floor.

Simon leaned over and picked up the bread. "Tutoring Callum would improve my chances with the school board. They're leery about offering me a permanent position but they're crazy about this variety show. If I was a key player, they wouldn't want to risk losing me."

"I suppose not," I said, wondering what was really motivating Simon. Obviously this was a matter he and I needed to discuss in private.

Emily's napkin slipped onto the floor. I retrieved it. "Is this plaid a family tartan?" I asked in a changing-the-subject tone of voice.

"Right," Ross said. "It's one of the Forbes tartans."

Simon twisted his wedding band on his finger. "Ross is researching his family tree. He thinks one of his ancestors was the Alexander Forbes that Forbes Point, Nova Scotia is named after."

"That's intriguing." I ate another spoonful of stew. "So, Ross, are you from Nova Scotia?"

"From Saskatchewan originally. I was born here."

Simon sipped his Perrier. "Ross's mother taught in a couple of country schools near Dayspring, and then in town."

"Of course. Miss Forbes." I'd heard her name but hadn't made the connection. I glanced from Simon to Ross. "So did you two know each other, growing up?"

Ross shook his head. "My mom took me to Halifax and left me with my grandparents when I was a year old. They raised me."

"So how did you get back to Dayspring?" I wished he hadn't.

Ross shrugged. "The school board offered me the principal's job and I accepted."

"You must miss Nova Scotia."

"Sure, but I'm pleased to have the opportunity to spend time with my mom after all our years apart."

"Ross and his mother built this house together," Simon informed me. "She lives upstairs."

Ross glanced toward the stairway. "I'd invite her down to meet you but she's not home. She went to play the piano for a ladies' meeting at the United Church."

"Interesting." I hoped a mother who played the piano for church ladies would be a positive influence on her son.

Emily twisted a lock of her hair around her finger. "Where's your daddy?"

Ross gave her a wry smile. "I don't know, Sweetheart. Because I don't know who my daddy is." He heaved himself to his feet. "I'll get the pie and make tea."

Emily watched him disappear into the kitchen, biting her lower lip. She knew who her daddy was. There'd never been any question about that. Ross's situation was different.

I wondered what his life had been like, growing up with an absent mother and a missing father. Hopefully his grandparents had been good to him. I felt more sympathetic toward Ross now that I'd heard some of his story. But I still didn't know how far I could trust him around my husband.

CHAPTER 34

The bungalow we rented from Ross had a backroom with windows on three sides. It offered great views of the lake, the sandhills, and farmers' fields. Simon used that room to store his filing cabinets, which were stuffed full of papers and science journals. However, he didn't spend much time in the room because a young man had killed himself in there—a schoolmate of Simon's who'd put a bullet through his brain.

Being in the backroom didn't bother me. It probably would have if I'd known the young man. Since I didn't mind the room and Simon did, it became my refuge. I installed an old green armchair, positioning it so it faced the lake. In the afternoons while the girls napped, I often sat in that chair drinking tea, working on a sweater Bethany had hired me to knit for her boyfriend, and brooding about my marriage.

Simon's and my relationship had blurred after he'd moved to Dayspring. He had changed in ways I couldn't understand or relate to. I myself had blurred our relationship by becoming infatuated with Florian and hiding my infatuation from Simon.

But my 'fling' with Florian was tame compared with the secrets Simon might be hiding. I couldn't wrap my mind around the idea of my husband falling for another man.

During our five years of marriage, I'd never suspected anything of the kind until two weeks ago. Etched into my mind was the sight of a mountain-like man balancing a paper-shredding parrot on his shoulder while Simon lay on the bed half-naked and laughing like an ape.

The scene had struck me as wrong when I'd stumbled on it.

Or maybe I'd misread it. Maybe Ross Forbes was nothing more than Simon's boss, co-worker, friend, and mentor.

I could ask Simon—come right out and ask him. What might happen if I did? I wrote a list of arguments for and against confrontation. I hoped that committing them to paper would help clarify them in my mind.

Arguments for confrontation

–If Simon is using me as a smokescreen for a romance with Ross, I should know. (So I can do what?)

–Simon loves me. He must. Otherwise, why did he want me to move to Dayspring? Why does he sleep with me? He wouldn't involve himself in a relationship that could destroy ours, would he? If I confront him, he'll reassure me, hopefully.

–I'm a responsible grown woman. I should try to defend and preserve my marriage, even if doing so causes discomfort to myself and others. If I confront Simon, we may be able to work this out and move on.

–I owe it to my children to confront Simon and clarify the situation. Emily and Norine will be happier with a mother who isn't bogged down with suspicion and indecision.

–I'm not as crazy about Simon as I once was. I wouldn't be devastated if I confronted him and lost him (and Adeline). If we got a divorce, he'd probably pay child support. Also, I could get a job, maybe parttime at first. Emily and Norine would miss their dad of course. I'd miss him too, and I'd miss being married.

Arguments against confrontation

–Many wives find themselves in worse situations than mine. Many suffer from physical abuse or abandonment, or have husbands who are addicted to alcohol or drugs. That's never been the case with Simon, thank God. Maybe I should keep my mouth shut and count my blessings.

–My family's livelihood depends on Ross. If I alienate him by bringing this matter to a head, Simon might lose his job. We might lose our home.

–If I force the issue, I might push Simon into doing something he wouldn't otherwise do, like leave me for Ross. A partly committed husband may be better than none at all.

–If I insist that Simon disclose his romantic and sexual feelings, it would be only fair for me to tell him about Florian. I doubt that I could do that.

–When I pray about the situation, God doesn't seem to indicate whether I should voice my suspicions or not. So maybe I should keep quiet for now. Maybe Simon's and Ross's relationship will blow over if it even exists.

When I woke at night, which was often, I pondered my arguments. Several times, I considered talking things over with my friend Valerie in Sage City but I always rejected the idea. Valerie had never been crazy about Simon. She considered him too stodgy. If she came up with a plan, it would be something over-the-top like hiring a detective to follow him. That wouldn't be my style. Anyway I couldn't afford a detective.

I could ask Pastor Warkentin for advice but I hardly knew him. And raising the matter with my mother-in-law was out of the question. She'd go ballistic and probably make things worse.

In the end, I decided to do nothing for the time being. Confronting Simon might be premature. I'd only moved to Dayspring a few days ago. I should probably sit tight, watch, wait, and hope for the best.

CHAPTER 35

Needing a project to take my mind off my anxieties, I devoted my energy to transforming the backroom into a sewing room. I moved Simon's filing cabinets and their contents out of there and into the lean-to. I pulled a table into the backroom and set my sewing machine on it. I built brick-and-board shelves, unpacked my sewing stuff, and arranged it in labeled boxes. Patterns in one box, thread in another, elastic and seam binding in a third, and so on. I got the kids busy sorting my buttons according to colour.

Simon didn't object to my taking over the backroom. It was a trade-off since he had installed Ross's parrot, Callum, in our living room. This was Ross's idea. He wanted to make it easier for Simon to tutor the bird in the finer points of singing about geometry and colours.

I wasn't keen on having Callum in our house. He was a noisy bird, became bored easily, and needed a lot of care and attention. Despite that, I preferred his presence to the alternative—Simon spending hours and hours at Ross's house doing heaven knows what besides tutoring Callum.

Despite my suspicions, Simon's and my married life proceeded smoothly, at least on the surface. We were good at routines. The rhythms of everyday life kept our relationship going. He kissed me goodbye when he left for school, hello when he returned, and good night after we went to bed. We made love on Friday evenings and sometimes on Saturdays.

Most Sunday mornings found our little family in church. Sometimes we attended the Lutheran church, where Simon occasionally led the choir or sang solos. Sometimes we drove out to the country Mennonite church, where we sat with his mother. We ate lunch at her house afterwards.

Simon usually invited Ross to our place one evening a week. I didn't see how I could object without accusing my husband of improper ideas or—perish the thought—improper activities. I wasn't willing to do that, not yet anyway. Also Ross's parrot, Callum, lived with us. It seemed only fair that Ross should have a weekly opportunity to visit him.

As I became better acquainted with Ross, I admitted to myself that he was a pleasant person to be around—jovial, urbane, and quick-witted. Over time, I developed a rapport with him, chummy on the surface though uneasy underneath.

CHAPTER 36

One Saturday evening in late November, we were relaxing after supper at our house. I sat on the couch working on the sweater for Bethany's boyfriend. Simon and the kids sat on the floor building a castle out of plastic blocks. Ross stood near Callum's cage, winking at the parrot and trying to get him to wink back. When Callum didn't oblige, Ross turned and winked at me. "I generally don't like accordion music. But I guess it's all *accordion* to the way it's played."

Ross enjoyed punning. I enjoyed trying to match him.

"I hear the Drylander Band got a drum," I said, picking up stitches around one of the armholes in the sweater. "Can you *beat* that?"

"Good one." Ross gave me a thumbs-up. "I went to a Scottish opera in Saskatoon. Do you know how I knew it was Scottish?"

"How?" I asked.

"Everybody was *kilt* at the end."

Simon scowled up at us. "That's awful. It's in bad taste and it's not even funny." My husband generally disapproved of our puns, clever or not. That was part of the three-way relationship between him, Ross, and me.

"Simon is right," I said. "I don't have a scrap of *symphony* for a joke like that."

An outside observer might have sensed an emotional bond between Ross and me. Something like that did exist but I sensed a deeper one running between Ross and my husband.

Callum rattled his beak against the bars of his cage. "Red bead, blue bead," he chanted. "Crash, smash. Red, blue, yellow, purple bead."

Emily scrambled up from the floor. "I think Callum wants his abacus." She found it in his toybox and put it in his cage.

The parrot began pecking at the abacus. Ross watched for a few moments, then eased himself down into the armchair.

Simon raised an eyebrow at Emily. "Could you please get the footstool for Uncle Ross?"

She dragged it over to him.

Ross smiled. "Thanks, Alberta."

She shook her head, her ponytail skimming her narrow shoulders. "My name isn't Alberta. It's Emily."

"Oh, sorry. I keep forgetting." Forgetting Emily's name was one of Ross's many ways of teasing her.

He hoisted his bad leg onto the footstool. "You're good at singing, Alberta—I mean Emily. Do you know a song about Isobel?"

"Isobel?"

Ross sang in his rich baritone. "Isobel that builds the boat. And Isobel that sails her. Isobel that catches the fish. And brings them home to Liza."

Norine gave him a toothy grin but Emily frowned at him. "That's not how that song goes."

Ross shrugged. "That's how I sing it."

Emily did an exasperated eye-roll. "I'll show you how it really goes." She planted herself in front of Ross. "I'se the b'y that builds the boat," she sang in a strong clear voice, only slightly off-key. "And I'se the b'y that sails her. I'se the b'y that catches the fish. And brings them home to Liza."

"That's the Newfoundland version," Ross said. "I like the Isobel one better."

"Well, I don't." Emily glanced at the parrot, who was flinging the abacus beads back and forth with maniacal energy. "Can we teach it to Callum? The right way?"

"Maybe your daddy can," Ross said. "Your mommy and I have to do something in the sewing room."

I was making a Santa Claus suit for Ross. We were ready for a fitting.

"There's a hockey game at the rink," Simon said. "I'll take Emily and Norine over there for a while."

After they left, Ross followed me into the sewing room, where I handed him the fuzzy red trousers I'd basted together.

He pulled them on over his jeans, groaning as he maneuvered his lame leg into position.

I stepped back to assess my handiwork. "You'll need some stuffing." I took a cushion off the armchair and tossed it to him. He tucked it into his waistband.

I handed him the jacket.

He put it on over the cushion, and I marked a few adjustments.

"Red green bead!" Callum shrieked from the living room. "Isobel, bell, bell!"

As Ross removed the jacket, a wistful look crept into his eyes. "Callum used to talk about Isobel a lot. She was one of his favourite people."

"Who was she?" I asked, taking the jacket from him.

"My girlfriend."

"Your girlfriend?" I hadn't figured Ross for the type of person who'd have a girlfriend. "Where is she?"

"Halifax." Bitter laugh. "A friend stole her from me."

"Oh, Ross, I'm so sorry." I laid a hand on his arm. "That's terrible."

"It is," he said, struggling to remove the Santa Claus trousers.

I pulled a chair out from the table for him. "What's she like?"

He sat and pulled the trousers off, one laborious leg at a time. "She's Black, bright, beautiful, busty, smells like guavas. An opera-singer."

"Not Isobel Sealy?" I didn't follow opera but I'd heard of her.

"That's her married name." He gave the trousers a shake and handed them to me. "Should be Forbes."

"Sad."

"I'll get over her eventually." He eased himself off the chair and limped out to the lean-to, where his outdoor jacket hung.

I followed. "How long has it been?"

"Three years since I got the Dear John letter." He pulled his jacket on. "I moved to Dayspring soon after. Trying to run away from my feelings."

"I'm sure that hasn't been easy." I drew a cautious breath, afraid to ask my next question. "Has there been anyone since Isobel?" Like Simon?

"There's a woman in Outlook, a nurse at the hospital. We see each other a couple times a month. Nothing serious." Ross stepped into his boots. "Thanks for supper." He gave me a little wave and limped out into the night.

As I tidied the kitchen that evening, I pondered what Ross had said. Maybe—lonely after losing Isobel—he had recognized a kindred spirit in my husband and made an effort to cultivate his friendship. But what about Simon? Did he have romantic feelings for Ross? If so, did Ross know? Had the men discussed the situation or just let it slide?

Or maybe Ross's stories about Isobel and the nurse in Outlook were inventions intended to steer me away from what was really happening.

On second thought, they couldn't be. Those stories would be too easy to check. Isobel Sealy was a public figure, and there were only six or seven nurses at the hospital in Outlook.

CHAPTER 37

I needed to look good for the Christmas luncheon. It would be the first staff function I would attend with Simon. I wanted him to be proud of me. Also, I wanted to help him make a good impression on the school board so they'd be more inclined to offer him a contract.

The nicest outfit I owned was a green velvet suit with gold trim. It needed dry cleaning so I took it to the grocery store. That was what people did in Dayspring. The grocer sent their clothes to a dry-cleaning company in Moose Jaw, seventy-five miles away. The company cleaned them and returned them to the store. It was a complicated system but it seemed to work. I sent my suit two weeks before the luncheon, expecting to receive it back in three or four days.

Eleven days later, my suit still wasn't at the store. I phoned the dry cleaner and discovered that they'd mistakenly sent it to a D. Epp in Birsay. They apologized, promising to retrieve the suit and deliver it to Dayspring by nine AM on the day of the luncheon.

By ten-fifteen on the big day, my suit still hadn't shown up. The luncheon started at eleven-thirty. Choking back tears of frustration, I hurried home and got my mauve wool dress out of the closet. It was ordinary-looking compared with the suit, and too big because I'd lost eight pounds since my move to Dayspring. But the mauve dress was the best alternative. I put it on, tightening the belt to make it fit better.

The clock was ticking away—ten minutes to eleven—and I still needed jewelry. I'd worn my gold chain and earrings with this dress before, but they looked too timid that day. I tried my mauve ceramic locket. Not the right mauve.

"What's the holdup?" Simon called from the kitchen. "I took the kids to the babysitter twenty minutes ago." My husband was as nervous about the luncheon as I.

"Coming." I grabbed my pearl earrings and necklace; they went with everything. I jabbed the earrings into my ears, clasped the necklace around my neck, and yanked on my strappy black shoes. "Oh, no!" I groaned as one of the straps broke.

"It's five after eleven," Simon called in a steel-edged voice.

"I said I'm coming." I searched the closet for another suitable pair of shoes. What about my white pumps? They were out of season. Stylish women didn't wear white shoes in the winter. Unfortunately they were the only half-appropriate shoes I had. They sort of complemented my pearls. I stepped into them and grabbed my purse, then changed my mind and left the purse on the dresser. It was black, didn't go with the shoes.

As I teetered into the kitchen, Simon's nostrils flared. "You're wearing that? Didn't you see I had my mauve shirt on?"

I would have cried if we'd had more time. I had wanted to look smashing and now I didn't even look acceptable according to my husband. "It's okay if we both wear mauve," I said. He wasn't exactly an arbiter of fashion. "We're on the same team, aren't we?"

"Sure, but we'll look like a couple of insecure kids. Now I've gotta go and change."

"Don't be silly. That shirt goes great with your suit." His grey tweed suit made him look strong and reliable. The mauve shirt added just the right touch of whimsy.

Simon grunted and disappeared into the bedroom. A few minutes later, he barged out wearing a white shirt with a blue tie. We threw our coats on, dashed to the car, and roared downtown to Mahs' Café.

Dayspringers had a habit of arriving early for social events. Their over-the-top promptness was part of the local culture. By the time Simon and I bolted into the café, the tables were almost full.

Only two empty chairs remained. One was at a long red-draped table between mathematics teacher Judy Medby and school secretary Crystal Patterson. The other was at the gold-draped head table between the wall-eyed Muriel Beasley and school principal Ross Forbes.

Simon frowned. "If you hadn't made us late—"

"*I* made us late? You were the one who insisted on changing." I glanced around at the assembled guests: teachers, school secretary, part-time librarian, janitor, some spouses, other guests. Maybe someone would offer to move so I could sit with my husband.

People smiled and nodded at us. Some said hello but they all sat tight.

"Simon," Ross called from the head table. "Over here."

What? The rookie teacher was being invited to sit with the bigwigs—mayor, councillors, members of the school board. That was peachy for Simon but what about me? Why hadn't Ross saved a chair for me?

"Come on." I grabbed Simon's arm. "Let's go and ask Ross if we can both sit with him. Maybe somebody wouldn't mind moving."

Simon pulled away from me. "It would be rude to ask them to move. Anyway they're too high-powered."

"Right." They were high-powered and I wasn't. They were top dogs in the community. I wasn't. Most had more education than I did, especially Muriel with her PhD in psychiatry.

But I was Simon's wife.

"Please don't make a scene," my husband whispered. "Everybody's watching us."

I was embarrassing Simon. That wouldn't gain him any points with the school board. I hesitated a moment, then allowed myself to be escorted to the chair between Judy and Crystal. Simon pulled it out for me. "You'll be fine here, Susie. I'm sure you and these ladies will find lots to talk about."

We probably would. Judy and Crystal had both been friendly whenever I'd happened to see them around town. But I resented Ross's lack of consideration, especially since I had sewed the Santa Claus suit he wore.

Trying to swallow my resentment, I seated myself between Judy and Crystal, holding my head high like Elizabeth II, Queen of England. That was a little trick I'd learned: When you're in an awkward social situation, pretend you're the Queen of England. Nothing fazes her. With a regal smile, I watched my husband make his way to the head table and take his place beside the man I suspected him of being in love with.

CHAPTER 38

The hum of conversation in the café died down as Ross hauled himself to his feet. His Santa Claus suit looked good, including the beard I had created from a string mop. "Welcome, everyone." He ran a hand over the beard. "The chef tells me our buffet will be ready in a few minutes. In the meantime our newest teacher, Simon Epp, will lead us in singing grace."

Singing grace was standard procedure at public meals in Dayspring. Everyone knew the words and tune. Even a cat or dog could have led the prayer, but my husband was the chosen one today. Simon started and everyone joined in, except for the usual agnostic hold-outs.

> Be present at our table, Lord.
> Be here and everywhere adored.
> These mercies bless and grant that we
> May feast in paradise with Thee.

As the Amen faded away, Ross beamed around at the crowd. "Simon will lead us in more singing later. We look forward to that. He brought a wonderful musical talent with him from Sage City, British Columbia."

Polite applause. Did some people smirk or was that my imagination?

Ross turned and brushed something off his sleeve. I hoped his beard wasn't shedding. "Simon also brought his lovely wife, Susie, from Sage City. Susie, would you please stand?"

Surprised and embarrassed, I rose in my too-big dress and acknowledged the applause with a Queen Elizabeth-like tilt of my head. It was thoughtful of Ross to introduce me but why hadn't he saved me a seat beside my husband?

"All right," Ross continued, "the chef just gave me the signal. Our buffet is ready. Please help yourselves. I don't think we need to line up in any particular order."

After a polite pause several people scraped their chairs back and made their way toward the bins of food arranged on a steam table near the kitchen. My companions Crystal and Judy motioned for me to go ahead but I waved them forward. "I think I'll wait a few minutes." Hopefully my husband would come and escort me. I looked at the head table, hoping to catch his eye, but Simon had his back turned to me. He seemed to be deep in conversation with Ross and the wall-eyed Muriel.

Why was my husband acting like I didn't exist? A bolder wife would have gone and tapped Simon on the shoulder. She would have swept all three eggheads with her to the buffet, laughing and joking on the way. Sadly I wasn't that kind of a woman.

Snowflakes were swirling past the windows. I felt a draft from the side door, especially on my feet. Muriel wore suede boots with what looked like fur trim. Most of the other women also wore winter boots. Meanwhile I suffered in my out-of-season white pumps.

Usually when my feet got cold, I needed to visit the washroom. This time was no exception. I slipped away from the table, hurried around the buffet line, and followed the hallway past the pay-phones to the washrooms.

As I emerged from the ladies' room a few minutes later, I almost bumped into a fox-faced young man who was tinkering with one of the phones. He bowed and smiled, showing spooky white teeth. "It's an honour to meet the lovely wife from Sage City."

I matched his formal tone. "Whom do I have the pleasure of meeting?"

He took a business card from his pocket, bowed again, and presented it as if it was made of gold. "Borya Palko at your service."

"Charmed, I'm sure." The words on the card were small and crowded: *Borya Palko, Box 131, Dayspring, Sask., Bachelor of Science. Beekeeper, meteorological observer, water-witcher, and substitute teacher.*

I reached for my purse to put Borya's card away. Then, remembering that I didn't have my purse, I handed the card back to him. "You keep busy, evidently."

"I do what I can." He cracked the knuckles of one freckled hand, then the other. "I'd be a fulltime teacher if it wasn't for Shuffletoesy."

"Shuffletoesy?"

"Ross the boss. He's the turkey who convinced the board to hire your husband instead of me." Borya's syrup-colored eyes widened. "Does that seem fair to you? I'm better qualified. Simon doesn't even have a degree."

My feet wobbled in my too-big shoes. "I'm sorry you didn't get the job." I really was. If the board had hired Borya, Simon and I would still be in Sage City. He might never have met Ross the boss.

But I needed to stick up for Simon; I was his wife. "My husband may not have a degree," I said in a prim Queen-Elizabeth-minus-the-accent voice. "But he brings a unique perspective to the teaching of science. As I'm sure you know, he worked in a veterinary clinic for a number of years."

Borya narrowed his eyes. "And what else?"

A flush warmed my face. "Simon knows a lot about fish; he has most of a degree in marine biology. And he's good with the students." I couldn't imagine Borya Palko getting along well with teenagers. He was too weird.

Borya's upper lip curled around his spooky teeth. Were those teeth real? They looked too white. "And how else does Sweet Simon endear himself to the principal?"

I stood up straighter. "I'm not sure where you're headed with this conversation but I don't think I like it."

"Whether you like it or not, you should know there's gossip about Simon and Shuffletoesy. Some folks say there's hanky-panky going on between them. Or at least hanky." Borya laughed a harsh, coughing laugh.

My heart seized up, the tightness spreading to my arms. "You're just trying to stir up trouble." I hoped that was the case. "You're jealous of my husband."

"You're wrong, Susie. The word is out. Once it spreads, Simon's job will be burnt toast. Maybe Ross's too." Borya laid a hand on my arm. "I'm sorry for you. I really am. You're a pretty woman, a nice woman. You deserve somebody better than Simon."

I yanked my arm away from him. "That's not the sort of thing a gentleman says to a married woman." I turned and marched back into the dining area, my back straight, my mind ping-ponging between rejecting Borya's innuendo and suspecting there might be something to it.

CHAPTER 39

By the time I'd helped myself at the buffet and carried my plate to the table, my companions Judy and Crystal had finished eating. They talked while I ate, showing me pictures of their children and telling me about their plans for Christmas.

I nodded and smiled though my mind was on Simon, who was eating chop suey and almond chicken at the head table with his back turned to me. He inclined his head toward Ross, looked at Muriel, and then leaned toward Ross in an *I'm all ears* posture.

Borya Palko kept glancing at me from the far end of my table. Was he the one who'd started the rumours about Simon and Ross, if such rumours even existed? How seriously did people take Borya?

"Borya Palko seems like quite a character," I said, trying for a whimsical tone of voice.

Judy laughed. "He's a hot-blooded Slav with an eye for a pretty woman." She smiled and waggled her fingers at him.

Borya flashed us a creepy smile.

Crystal giggled. "I think he likes you." She winked at me. "Are you interested?"

"Of course not. I'm a happily married woman." This was debatable but I didn't want to fuel suspicion. "I was just wondering if...."

My voice trailed off as Ross rose to his feet, adjusting the cushion under his red suit. "All right, people, Santa Claus is going to give out the gifts now." He nodded toward two teachers who were rolling wheelbarrows of wrapped parcels in through the side door. "But Santa doesn't walk too well so he's going to enlist the help of one of his favourite elves, Simon Epp."

Favourite elf? No, Ross, please. Didn't he realize how people might interpret words like that? Some applauded. Borya half stood and gave a wolf whistle.

Simon stared down at the tablecloth. Were his ears reddening?

My face felt hot. My head swam. Nausea crept up my throat. I couldn't stay in this café, couldn't witness any more of Simon and Ross's revolting togetherness. I pushed back from the table in un-Queen-Elizabeth-like haste. "I'm sorry, Judy, Crystal. I have to go. It's been nice talking to you."

I fled to the coat rack, threw my coat on, and stumbled toward the front door.

Borya beat me to it. "Allow me." He opened the door with a princely sweep of his arm.

Simon hurried toward us. "Susie, where are you going?"

"Home." I choked on the word.

Simon shouldered Borya aside. "I'll handle this."

Borya stepped back, leering. "No need to get touchy. I was just trying to be a gentleman."

Simon took my arm. "What do you think you're doing?" he whispered. "Everybody's watching you."

I scanned the crowd. People were flicking glances in our direction while pretending to listen to Ross mouth platitudes about how plans can unexpectedly change.

I jerked my arm out of Simon's grasp and bolted out the door onto the icy sidewalk.

Simon followed. "Hang on a minute, Susie. I'll get my coat."

Not waiting for him, I darted to the car, planning to roar away before he caught up with me.

Of course I couldn't get into the car because I didn't have my key. No purse. With tears of frustration blurring my eyes, I set off on foot. As I tottered along the sidewalk in my stupid white shoes, I heard footsteps come up behind me. Simon's.

"What's the matter, Susie? Are you sick?"

"Yes, I'm sick. Definitely sick." I walked faster, skidding, losing my balance and catching it again. "Sick of you and Ross making fools of yourselves." The wind whistled around the corner of the post office, tossing a flurry of snow pellets into my face.

Simon grabbed my arm. "What's that supposed to mean?"

I wheeled around to face him. "If you don't know, you're a fool. You and Ross, a couple of damned fools." I sucked in a breath, shocked at my own profanity.

"Get into the car." Simon half-pulled, half-led me to the Volkswagen. "People are staring."

I glanced around. "I don't see anybody staring. Anyway, if you care so much what people think, why were you acting like such an idiot in the café?"

He opened the passenger door for me. "I don't know what you mean." His voice sounded as hard as the sidewalk.

"You looked like a lovesick sheep, hanging on Ross's every word." I flounced into the car. I realizing I was overstating the case but I had a point to make.

Simon went around and slid into the driver's seat, a muscle in his jaw twitching.

"I can just hear the gossip," I said. "'There's gotta be hanky-panky going on between Simon and Ross. Did you see them making eyes at each other?'"

Simon twisted the key in the ignition. "I'm sorry you viewed our interaction in that way." His tone was cold with a frosting of sarcasm. "Ross and I were discussing the variety show with Muriel Beasley."

"What's Muriel got to do with anything?"

The tires squealed as Simon roared into a side street and parked in front of a vacant lot. "Muriel's an adviser to the school board."

"Since when?"

"Since yesterday. Ross just found out. That's why he wanted me to sit with her. He thinks if we impress her with my musical and leadership abilities, she'll encourage the board to offer me a permanent job."

That sounded believable, I had to admit. But what about the rumours Borya said were swirling around Ross and Simon? What would happen when they reached the ears of the board? "Simon, you and I need to talk."

He shrugged. "Go ahead. Talk."

"Not here." I massaged my right foot, trying to restore some feeling to it. "Let's go home."

He frowned at his watch. "I can take you home if you like, but then I'll need to get back to the café. I'm supposed to lead the carol-singing."

"Forget the singing," I snapped. "You're not the only wonderfully talented song-leader in this burg. Both of us need to go home, now."

My husband gave me a baleful stare. "You want me to go with you?"

"What do you have for brains? Icicles? I can't talk here. My feet are freezing."

"You should have worn your boots."

"They're in the trunk. I would have asked you to get them if you'd been paying any attention to me."

"Pardon me for being too busy advancing my career. I'll get your blessed boots now if you want."

"Don't bother." I massaged my left foot. "I just want to go home."

"Shall we pick up the kids?"

"No, they'll be okay at the babysitter's place for a while. Let's go."

CHAPTER 40

At home, I escaped into the bedroom, and put on socks and slippers. Then I took a few deep breaths and ventured into the living room, bracing myself for the showdown with Simon. My insides quaked with fear. But now that I'd broken open the subject of his and Ross's relationship, I needed to press on until I had some answers.

Simon sat broomstick-straight in the armchair watching hockey on TV and drinking red wine from a water-glass.

Wine? I almost stumbled on the carpet. Simon never drank wine or any other alcoholic beverage. Drinking was a sin according to our Mennonite Brethren church. The bottle stood on the table beside him, its green and yellow label depicting vineyards on a sunny hillside. A neighbour had given us the wine. I had hidden it in the back of a cupboard, planning to give it away.

I opened my mouth to deliver a lecture on sobriety, then closed it. I had a bigger issue to tackle.

I shut off the TV.

"No," Ross's parrot screamed. "No, no, no. He shoots, he scores."

I threw the cover over the bird's cage, carried him into my sewing room, and turned the radio on for him. Classical music, loud. I didn't want Callum hearing and maybe repeating whatever Simon and I were about to say to each other.

By the time I got back to the living room, my husband's glass was empty.

He picked up the bottle. As he poured a wobbly stream into his glass, I blurted out the question I should have asked weeks ago. "Are you in love with Ross Forbes?"

Simon's hand jerked, sloshing wine onto his shirt and tie. Red splotches seeped toward his trousers. "Shit!" He slammed the bottle down and stomped into the kitchen. "Shit, shit, shit!"

I followed him. "Leave those," I said as he scrubbed at the wine stains with a towel. "You can't get them out that way." I grabbed the towel from him and threw it in the sink. "Answer me. Are you in love with Ross Forbes?"

Simon peered down at his shirt. "I'm wet." His lower lip pouched out like a child's.

"So go and change your clothes."

He slunk into the bedroom, latching the door behind him like a maiden aunt.

I seethed for a few minutes, then went and knocked on the bedroom door. "Come out of there and face me like a man."

Nothing.

"I said come out of there. I need an answer."

The latch rattled. Simon shambled out wearing jeans and a mis-buttoned denim shirt, his hair sticking up at odd angles. "Ross Forbes is making a success of me," my husband said, sagging into the armchair. "Thanks to Ross, I've got a good job, a house, and a future."

"But you could lose all that." I clenched my fists, digging my fingernails into my palms. "People are gossiping about you and him."

"You think so?"

"Borya Palko says so."

Simon forced a laugh. "Borya! That clown is one of a kind. Bee-keeper, water-witcher, mad scientist, pain in the butt. Did he tell you about his tooth-whitening experiments?"

"No but from the looks of his teeth, he went too far." I crossed my arms, determined not to get sidetracked. "And you and Ross went too far too. The way you acted in the café must be fueling rumours. If enough people believe them, they won't want you teaching their children anymore."

His face reddening, Simon grabbed the wine bottle. As he tilted it toward his glass, I snatched it out of his hand. "You don't need more wine. You need to tell me what's going on between you and Ross. Don't you have anything to say?"

"Not at the moment." Simon sounded like he had a poker up his spine. "But I'll consider your allegations and get back to you."

"You sound like a lawyer, not my husband."

He glanced at the clock. "Would you look at the time?" He lurched out of the armchair. "I've gotta get to Central Butte."

"Now? It's four-thirty already. What do you want in Butte? You didn't tell me you were going."

He swayed on his feet. "I need some stuff. Gotta get to Butte before the stores close."

"What about the kids?"

"I'll pick them up and take them along. We'll have supper in the café."

"You're drunk." My voice sounded like it had splinters in it. "I don't want the kids riding in the car with you." I blocked his path, raising the bottle like a weapon.

He wrenched it out of my hand. "I'm fine. Get out of my way."

"Simon, please." I clutched at his arm. "We both need to calm down. Maybe we could pray about this."

"Go ahead and pray." He pushed past me, barging out into the lean-to.

I followed. "There's no way you're taking the girls in the car. You're in no condition to drive." I wasn't sure about that. I had zero experience with drinking, or almost zero.

He grunted. "I'll leave them with the babysitter and pick them up on my way back."

"Still too risky." I wasn't sure how long it took for alcohol to wear off. "I'll phone the sitter and ask her to bring them over."

"Suit yourself." Simon shrugged his jacket on and went out.

After he left, I collapsed onto the couch with tears streaming down my face. I'd taken a risk in confronting Simon. I'd hoped for a definite response. He could have thrown his arms around me, scoffed at the idea of Ross as his lover, and told me he loved me, only me.

Or he could have told me he loved Ross, and was leaving me for Ross. Or that he loved both Ross and me, and knew that was wrong, and wanted me to pray for him.

Instead of something understandable like that, the confrontation had only raised more questions. How did Simon feel about Ross? Was he trying to deny his feelings? Did he even know what they were? Dear God, what should I do? Pack up the kids and run away? Who would I run to? Valerie in Sage City? Bethany on her fish farm? My monster-in-law? I almost laughed.

Did Florian Bouchard still love me? It was two months since we'd said goodbye to each other, only two months. The mother-of-pearl brooch he'd made for me was hidden under my patterns in the sewing room. I stumbled into that room and shut off the radio, which was still blaring—a news broadcast. I didn't want to hear the news. I had enough troubles of my own.

The parrot grumbled, his voice muffled under his cover, and then fell silent. He tended to be slow and dozy in the evenings, thank goodness.

I carried him into the living room, hung his cage up, and went into the bedroom, where Simon's wine-stained clothes lay on the bed. I opened the door of the closet, threw them in, and gave them a kick. Let him send them to the cleaners if he wanted to. I sure wasn't going to.

I wasn't going to sleep with Simon either. I cringed at the thought of lying in bed beside His Royal Coldness, hearing him breathe and feeling the warmth of his body while shrinking away from his frosty soul.

Please, no. I went to the hall closet, dragged out some bedding and a foam mattress, schlepped them into the sewing room, and made a floor-bed. I fetched my nightgown, housecoat, and slippers from the bedroom and threw them on top of it. Then I phoned the babysitter.

A few minutes later, the sitter arrived with Emily and Norine. She'd already fed the kids so I put them to bed. Then I hauled myself into the kitchen to find something to eat. I dumped leftovers onto a plate. I was microwaving them when tires squeaked on the snowy driveway outside.

Simon! I didn't want to see him. I grabbed my plate from the microwave, grabbed cutlery, and scurried along the hall to the sewing room. Safe in my lair, I locked the door, doused the light, and stood gasping for breath. Let Simon think I'd gone to bed or let him think whatever. I didn't care. I didn't want anything to do with him. Feeling my way through the shadows, I set my plate and cutlery on the table, pulled up a chair, and thrust my fork into my lukewarm meal. It tasted like tears and sawdust.

CHAPTER 41

I lay awake a long time that night, crying, worrying, and praying. About four o'clock in the morning, I dropped off and slept like a stone. I woke with a start, surprised to see it was eight-thirty already. That was good in a way. I wouldn't need to see Simon; he'd be at school. Hopefully he had fed the girls before he left.

I hoisted myself off my floor-bed, visited the bathroom, and put yesterday's clothes on. As I carried last night's dishes along the hall toward the kitchen, I noticed that Simon had left our bedroom door shut. We usually kept it open in the daytime but today I was glad to see it shut. It hid the bed where we'd made love and the lake view we'd enjoyed together.

Callum the parrot screamed from the living room. "Goodbye. Hello. What's up? Red circle. Purple square."

Had Simon remembered to feed him? I'd better check after I put the dishes in the kitchen. Callum was hard to like, at least for me, but he was only a bird after all. Nothing was his fault.

I opened the kitchen door and stopped short. The girls were sitting at the table in their pyjamas, their hair frowzy, their eyes sludgy with sleep. A bowl of puffed wheat sat between them, no milk.

"Mommy!" Emily blurted. "Where were you?"

"I slept in the sewing room last night," I said, setting my dishes in the sink. "Did Daddy make breakfast for you?"

Norine shook her head no, her curls glinting in the morning light.

"We called you," Emily said. "You didn't answer. Then we called Daddy. He didn't answer."

I put my arm around her. "You poor dears. I was in the sewing room so I didn't hear you but Daddy should have."

Emily bulged her eyes at me. "We knocked on the bedroom door. Loud. Nobody came." The girls had been trained not to enter our room without being invited.

"Mommy's here now," I said in my in-charge voice. "Here, let me fix your cereal." I divided it into two bowls, got the milk from the refrigerator, and poured some into each bowl. "Shall I slice a banana—"

The phone jangled. I grabbed the receiver. "Hello?"

"Good morning, Susie. It's Crystal at the school."

"Good morning, Crystal." My stomach twisted at the memory of the scene in the café. What had she and the others thought of my sudden departure?

"Do you know where Simon is?"

"Isn't he at school?"

"No," Crystal said. "He planned to come in early with some papers to photocopy but he hasn't arrived yet."

"I haven't seen him this morning. I slept in. But I'll look for him and call you back."

Maybe Simon was still in the bedroom. If he was, why hadn't he heard the girls knocking? Maybe there was something wrong with him. He didn't have the strongest heart in the world. My own heart started stampeding as I hurried along the hall toward our room.

Emily and Norine darted after me.

I shooed them away. "Go back to the kitchen. Please go and shut the door."

Outside the bedroom door, I hesitated a moment, then opened the door and reeled back, repelled by a stench like rotten apples and vinegar. Simon lay on the bed in his jeans and mis-buttoned denim shirt. His chest rose and fell in breathing rhythm, thank God, but he must be very drunk. A couple of empty wine bottles lay on the floor, along with three empty beer bottles. He must have stocked up in Central Butte.

Simon looked disgusting. Disgusting and pitiful. Maybe I shouldn't have been so harsh when I confronted him about Ross. If I'd known he'd react like this, I'd have tried to be more diplomatic.

I got a quilt from the closet and laid it over him. His forehead twitched; I leaned over and kissed it. There was something so essentially—Simon—about him. My heart reached out to him, sympathy over-riding my disgust.

I tiptoed out of the bedroom and back to the kitchen. "Daddy doesn't feel good," I told the girls. "We need to keep quiet."

I sliced a banana onto their puffed wheat and then phoned Crystal. "I'm afraid Simon's not well. He won't be at school today."

"Has he got the flu? It's going around."

"Something like that." It was none of her business but this was Dayspring.

"Are you okay yourself?"

"So far so good." My life had turned upside-down and inside-out. Otherwise, I was fine.

"I'm glad to hear that. Some of us wondered why you left the café in such a hurry."

"I felt queasy all of a sudden," I said, "but the feeling passed." Maybe people suspected I was pregnant. That wasn't likely given the complications surrounding Norine's birth, but it wouldn't hurt to let them speculate. Gossip about a pregnancy might distract the locals from the rumours about Simon and Ross, if they existed.

"Tell Simon not to worry about his classes," Crystal said. "I'll find someone to substitute for him. Probably Borya."

"Isn't there anybody else?" I could just hear Borya bad-mouthing Simon to the students: *Is that what Mr. Epp said? Well, he was mistaken. My research shows, blah, blah, blah.*

"Sorry," Crystal said. "I don't think anybody else is available. Thora's got the flu."

"Okay, I just thought I'd ask."

After I hung up, I ate breakfast, then dressed the girls, fed Callum, and took a tray into the bedroom for Simon. He was still asleep, drooling onto the pillow. I left the tray and tiptoed out into the living room, where the girls were chatting with Callum.

"Come on," I whispered. "Let's go into the sewing room so it's quieter here for Daddy." I lifted Callum's cage off its hook. As I carried it along the hall, the kids followed me like I was the Pied Piper.

In the sewing room I handed out paper, paste, crayons, and scraps of fabric. While the kids created works of art and entertained Callum, I started making the quilt the local real-estate office had commissioned. They wanted it to feature the historic buildings of Dayspring. The old bank building. The sod house and museum. The old brick school. The high-spired Lutheran church—the tallest structure in the village, besides the grain elevators.

As usual, quilting helped me forget my problems. I even smiled as I cut out maroon and cream-colored shapes for the bank building. The fabrics looked wonderful in the morning light. They were only remnants but the colours sang together.

About one o'clock that afternoon, I left my Sangri-la, made lunch, and brought it back to the girls. After we'd eaten, I took another tray to Simon. He was still asleep, his eyelids twitching, his breakfast untouched. I put Emily and Norine down for their nap, then went to clean up the kitchen. I was washing dishes when I heard Simon stomping around in the bedroom.

Good. The alcohol must have worn off. Maybe we could talk.

A few minutes later, he clumped into the kitchen wearing a clean T-shirt and jeans. His hair was combed though he needed a shave and smelled like vomit.

"Feeling better?" I asked.

"No." He grabbed his gloves off the shelf by the door, gave me a hard stare, and headed for the lean-to.

I followed him, my hands dripping dishwater. "Where are you going?"

"Out."

"You're not going to school, are you? You'd better not. Borya's substituting for you."

"I'll bet." Simon shouldered himself into his parka.

"When will you be back?"

"I haven't got a clue." He went out, slamming the door behind him.

I returned to the sink and hunched over it, watching a tear plop into the dishwater. Two plops, three, four, then a steady stream. Dear God, what should I do?

CHAPTER 42

By suppertime Simon still wasn't home but the girls and I needed to eat. I put some leftovers into the microwave. As I opened a can of corn, I heard the front door open. I hurried into the lean-to and met my husband coming in carrying two liquor-store bags.

"How could you?" I hissed, keeping my voice down because of the kids. "You already drank yourself stupid last night." I paused, telling myself to be diplomatic. "I mean I don't think it's wise for you—"

"It's my own business." Simon pushed past me and headed for the bedroom.

"Please." I followed, catching him by the hood of his parka. "Don't do this to yourself and us." I glanced toward the kitchen, where Emily and Norine were setting the table. "I don't think God wants you to—"

"I'm not perfect like you." He yanked his hood out of my grasp, barged into the bedroom, and slammed the door behind him. The latch rattled into the metal eyelet.

I leaned against the wall outside the bedroom, tears in my eyes. "Drinking isn't going to make our problems go away," I said through the door. "Can't we talk? I was too emotional yesterday. I'm calmer now."

No answer.

"You can't keep ignoring me. I'm your wife. Say something."

Nothing.

I buried my face in my hands. Dear God, please show me what to do.

"Mommy," Emily called from the kitchen, "the microwave beeped."

"Right. I'm coming." I wiped my eyes and returned to the kitchen.

A few minutes later I called Simon for supper though I didn't expect him to come.

He emerged from the bedroom walking like a zombie and smelling like alcohol. As he scraped his chair up to the table, Emily slid him a sidelong look. "What's wrong, Daddy?"

He grunted.

I managed a smile. "I told you, Emily," I said, setting the leftover scalloped potatoes on the table. "Daddy doesn't feel good."

"Oh," she said, her face tight with anxiety.

"Oh," Norine echoed.

I brought the corn and leftover trout to the table, then sat down.

Emily and Norine bowed their heads to say grace.

"Why don't you say the one you learned in Sunday School?" I said. I hoped it would strike a chord with Simon.

Emily started and Norine chimed in.

> You feed the owl and waterfowl.
> The spotted frog and prairie dog.
> Thank you, God. You feed us too.
> Help us to love and follow you.

I joined the girls in the Amen but Simon remained silent, his face stiff. As he spooned scalloped potatoes onto Emily's plate, she bulged her eyes at him. "Me and Norine saw a bird playing in the snow."

"It was a big bird," Norine offered.

Usually remarks like these were guaranteed to start a conversation with Simon the science teacher. He just gave the girls a curt nod.

We ate in silence. The only sounds were our cutlery scraping against our plates and Callum muttering at a TV game show in the living room. "Atlantic Ocean. Botswana. Fifty points. Thank you. Tashkent."

Emily tried again. "The radio said some people have the flu."

"The flu is no fun," Simon said. "I hope you girls don't catch it."

"We'll try not to," Emily said, fiddling with the sleeve of her sweater.

Norine beamed at her father, cheeks dimpling. She was a sweet-as-sugar child who looked a lot like Simon, at least when he was himself.

He returned her smile but his looked mechanical.

After the girls had excused themselves and retreated to their room, Simon pushed his chair back from the table.

"There's no need to rush away," I said. "I can make tea or coffee."

"No, thanks." He rose and shambled toward our bedroom.

I followed. "Getting drunk is a sin. You know that."

With a poisonous look, he lurched into the bedroom, latching the door behind him.

That evening Emily and Norine included Daddy's flu in their prayers. I hoped God heard them. They also asked the Lord to bless their Uncle Ross, as they were in the habit of doing. I couldn't bring myself to agree with them on that point. Ross was the turkey who'd landed us in this mess.

I tucked the girls in and returned to the kitchen, where I busied myself washing dishes, rearranging the mugs in the cupboard, and alphabetizing the herbs and spices. Anything to take my mind off the damage Simon was doing to himself in the bedroom. As I took the racks out of the oven to clean them, I heard a knock at the outside door. Surprised, I left the racks and went to the door, flipping lights on along the way. "Who's there?"

"Ross."

The man of the hour. "What do you want?"

"I made some chicken noodle soup. It's supposed to be good for the flu."

I gathered all my strength, yanked the door open, and slapped Ross's face as hard as I could.

He staggered back. "What'd you do that for?" His nostrils oozed blood. "I'm just trying to help."

"I don't want your stupid soup." I grabbed the kettle from him, barged onto the porch, and hurled it into the yard. Yellowish liquid splashed into the snow, the noodles looking like worms in the glow from the porch light.

Ross pulled a tissue out of his pocket and dabbed at his nose. "What's gotten into you, Susie?"

"You stole—" My voice creaked. "You stole my husband away from me."

"What do you mean?" The porch light flickered, and for an instant I saw Ross's skull under his skin. I saw what he'd look like dead.

"I think you know." I swatted tears out of my eyes. "My husband—Simon is in love with you."

Ross's eyebrows shot up toward his hairline. "That's preposterous." He sucked in a breath. "I can't believe—" another breath "—you would— Simon and I are friends, not lovers."

"I don't believe that." Shivering, I wrapped my arms around myself. Why hadn't I grabbed a jacket on my way to the door?

Ross fixed me with a level stare. "Are you calling me a liar?"

"Yes."

"You're wrong. Ross Ian Forbes may be a lot of things but he's not a liar."

"Prove it." I threw the words at him.

His face working, Ross limped off the porch and retrieved his soup kettle. "Let me explain," he said in his teacher voice. "Your husband is a gifted man."

I narrowed my eyes. "So?"

Ross set the kettle on the porch beside the door. "He has a way of holding students spellbound. I've never seen anything like it. And Simon's musical gifts are phenomenal. But he has the type of personality that needs a manager. I'm trying to fulfill that role in his life." Ross paused. "Do you understand what I'm saying?"

"I'm not stupid," I mumbled, "even if I don't have a university degree."

"I didn't call you stupid." Ross jiggled his lame leg. "I'm just saying Simon won't achieve his full potential unless he feels someone is firmly in charge."

Like Ross or Adeline, not like me. "Maybe so but who put you in charge of my husband?"

"I'm the principal."

"Shouldn't a principal treat all the teachers alike? It doesn't seem right, you paying more attention to Simon."

"Simon needs it more and he has more potential. He could achieve more than any of them, but not without proper management." Ross leaned against the doorframe. "I'm just trying to help your husband, as well as you and the children. But if you want me to back off, I will."

"I wish you would. It doesn't look good, you favouring him over the rest of the staff." The wind was cold. I backed into the lean-to, away from it.

Ross followed. "I don't get the impression anyone's upset about that."

I took a deep breath, like a diver on a high board. "People say there's hanky-panky going on between you and Simon."

Ross's face darkened. "Who says that?"

"Borya Palko." I gulped. "And other people."

"What other people?"

As I racked my brain for an answer, I heard footsteps behind me. I wheeled around and saw my drunken husband stagger into the lean-to, his face mottled, his hair wild, his belly protruding from his half-buttoned pyjama top.

Part of me was glad to have Ross see his protégé look so disgusting. A bigger part was mortified.

Simon wobbled toward us, bumping against the bookcase on the way. "Rosh." His voice was thick. "Why are you shtanding out here?" He threw me an accusing look. "Didn't the grouchy little woman invite you in?"

With an effort, I restrained myself from slapping my husband. "Ross just stopped in for a couple of minutes," I said. "He's leaving now. He's gotta go home to his birds."

"His birdsh are fine." Simon waved an unsteady arm. "I'm sure they're fine. Rosh, come in. Have a drink."

"I think I'd better run along."

"Ross can't stay," I said. "He needs to work tomorrow." Simon should go to work too but the chances of that happening were zilch.

My husband squinted at Ross. "Shuzie'sh a killjoy. She doeshn't like sheeing people have fun." He wavered on his feet, reached out to steady himself on the bookcase, missed, and toppled to the floor, his head thumping against the bottom shelf.

I hurried to him, kneeling on the floor beside him. "Simon, are you all right?"

"I'm fine, fine, fine," Simon said. "Nnnever been better. Jusht taking a little resht."

I grabbed him by the shoulders. "Come on. Let's get you to bed." I tried to pull him to his feet but he just lay there like a sack of rotten apples.

I glanced up at Ross. "Could you help me put him to bed?"

"Sure." Ross knelt and hung one of Simon's arms around his neck, then motioned for me to do the same on the other side. With a heave-ho, we lifted him into a more or less vertical position.

We were a lopsided team, Ross and I, one towering over the other but we managed to half-carry half-walk our sweetheart into the bedroom. Was Simon really Ross Forbes's sweetheart? If what Ross said was true, he wasn't. Maybe Simon wished he and Ross were sweethearts.

"It's pitiful to see him like that," Ross said after we'd laid the drunken sod on the bed and pulled the bedding up over him.

"Life in Dayspring hasn't been good to Simon," I said as Ross and I returned to the lean-to.

"I've tried to make it good. I've tried hard."

"You had good intentions, I guess, but things aren't turning out well."

"Maybe I can do something about that." Ross opened the outside door, stepped onto the porch, and picked up his soup kettle. "Let me think about it."

After he left I wandered back into the kitchen, thinking maybe Simon and I and our girls should leave Dayspring. We could make a fresh start somewhere else, away from Ross and Adeline. But where would we go? What would we do? We couldn't work for Simon's brother Wally in Davidson even if we wanted to. Wally had taken a teaching position at the university in Saskatoon. He and Myrtlemay and her parents had bought a house in the city. They planned to move there soon.

CHAPTER 43

The following morning, I was in the kitchen brooding over the previous evening's events when Adeline's Chevy pulled into the driveway. I allowed myself a bleak smile. She was in for a surprise. Simon would be in rough shape by now. He hadn't eaten breakfast, and he'd been clinking his bottles in the bedroom for an hour or more.

I answered Adeline's knock with a mixture of anxiety and hope. Anxiety as I braced myself for her reaction to the state Simon was in. Hope because I thought maybe she could help. She might be able to get through to him where I hadn't. She was his mother; they shared a bunch of genes and a long history.

"How's by my son?" Adeline bustled in carrying a big blue soup pot. "I heard he caught the flu."

"Something like that." Bottle-flu.

Adeline jostled me into my kitchen and thrust her pot at me. "I brought you some chicken noodle soup."

"That was good of you." I cleared a space in the refrigerator. "It might fit in there." I stepped aside and let her wrestle it in.

"That's a lot of soup," I said, managing to shut the refrigerator door on the pot. "We'll be growing feathers before we finish it."

Adeline ignored my attempt at humour. "I brought Simon some cough drops. Russian ones." She rummaged in her purse and pulled out a red tin the size of a sardine can. "They're stronger than that sweet Canadian junk."

"Oma!" Emily darted out of the sewing room with Norine at her heels. "Come and hear. We learned Callum to sing *I'se the bye that builds the boat*." She bounced on her feet. "We learned it to him the right way, not Uncle Ross's way."

A smile lit Norine's face. "We're making a boat."

"For Callum," Emily said. "A paper boat. Oma, come and see."

"Later," Adeline said. "I need to first give your daddy his cough drops." As she opened the tin, I caught a whiff of turpentine and camphor. Adeline extracted a couple of lozenges the size of horse pills, each wrapped in a twist of brown paper.

Emily reached for them. "Can me and Norine have one?"

I pulled my daughter's hand back. "They're too strong for you."

"We like strong."

"Let's see how they work for your dad first," I said. "You girls go to the sewing room and keep Callum company." The encounter between Adeline and her drunken son was bound to be dramatic. I didn't want the girls witnessing it.

Norine ambled toward the sewing room but Emily stood her ground, feet planted apart. "I want to see Daddy."

"Not now," I said. "Oma and I need to be alone with him."

Adeline grabbed Emily by the back of her T-shirt. "Go already." She steered the child into the sewing room. After shutting the door on her and Norine, she bustled back along the hall to the bedroom door. "Simon!" she called, pounding on the door.

No answer.

Maybe he'd heard his mother arrive, and escaped through the window.

"Simon, son."

He coughed. Bedsprings creaked.

Adeline tried the door. The latch rattled in its metal eyelet. "I need to see you once." Her voice vibrated with concern.

Nothing.

She raised an eyebrow at me. "He's maybe too sick to open the door."

I shrugged. Let her do her own research.

"I wonder me...can we break that lock?" She backed away from the door, beckoning me to follow. "I'll say *eins, zwei, drei*. Then we'll run." She counted. We ran and hurled ourselves against the door. The latch screeched out of its screws and clattered to the floor. Adeline shot into the room. "Simon!" she gasped. "For shame!" She pounced on him where he lay on the bed in his rumpled pyjamas with a wine bottle in his hand. "Drunkenness is a sin. You know that." She yanked the bottle out his hand.

"Gimme that." Simon reached for it but Adeline was too quick for her befuddled son. She swung the bottle away from him, scurried around me, and rocketed out of the bedroom.

"I'll spill this where it belongs," she called from the kitchen. Simon's face paled at the sound of liquid running down the drain. Glug, glug, glug.

Good for her. Three cheers for sweet Adeline.

"She'sh got no rrright to do that," Simon muttered.

"I'm glad she did," I said, plucking an empty beer bottle off the floor. "You deserve it."

Adeline loped back into the bedroom and grabbed Simon by the collar of his pyjamas. "Why are you *bedrunken?*" "What's loose with you?"

"You wouldn't undershtand."

She glowered around the room. "Does it give more bottles in here? Susie, help me look." She hustled over to the dresser, yanked a drawer open, and rummaged through it.

My mother-in-law and I were allies all of a sudden. That gave me sort of a good feeling. I hurried into the closet and searched among the blankets and pillows on the shelf. A wine bottle tumbled out, almost bonking me on the head. I checked inside the boots on the floor and found a bottle of beer in each of them.

I emerged from the closet and looked in the wastebasket, then behind the curtains. Adeline pawed through the bedding. Simon stood beside the bed leaning against a night table, stinking of alcohol. He didn't try to stop his mother or me. Didn't seem to have any fight in him. We had the moral advantage.

Between Adeline and myself, we found ten bottles, some full, some part-full. We carried them into the kitchen, where she poured the contents down the drain. I made no attempt to stop her.

When all the bottles were empty, lined up on the counter, she barged back into the bedroom. "Simon," his mother barked, "get yourself dressed once."

He gave her a hangdog look and shuffled toward the closet. Adeline and I returned to the kitchen, where she started scrubbing the sink with bleach and detergent. "When did my boy start drinking?"

"After the teachers' Christmas luncheon," I said, blinking. The bleach was making my eyes water.

"Why?"

"We had a fight." I blinked again. "He left. Drove down to Central Butte and bought liquor."

"What did my Simon and you fight about?"

For a moment I felt like spilling the whole story. It would be a relief. However, I wasn't sure I could trust Adeline to that extent. "I'm sorry," I said. "It's a private matter."

She stopped scrubbing and gave me one of her search-light looks. "I'll pray for you, Susie. You and Simon."

"Thank you," I said. I meant it.

"Now let's make for Simon what to eat. A bowl of soup. And maybe a sandwich from cheese. And maybe a *shtick* cake. And coffee. Lots of coffee. Then I'll take him to Pester Warkentin."

"Pastor Warkentin?" I stared at her. "What will the pastor think?"

"It doesn't matter what Pester Warkentin thinks. "My boy needs to get right with God."

CHAPTER 44

It was a slow-moving, watery-eyed Simon who returned with his mother that afternoon. "He's fixed up now," she announced as I hurried out onto the porch to meet them. "He confessed his sins, asked the dear God to forgive him, and promised never to drink again."

"That's good," I said, wishing Adeline had let Simon tell me about his transformation himself. It might have settled the matter more firmly in his mind.

As he wandered into the side yard, where Emily and Norine were making snow angels, Adeline glanced toward the kitchen. "Does it give any tea in your house, Susie?"

That was my signal to invite her in but I didn't feel like it. I wished she'd leave so I could talk to my fixed-up husband. On the other hand, I realized I should be grateful to her. She had apparently accomplished a lot with Pastor Warkentin's help. "Come in. I'll put the kettle on."

As I set out cups and saucers, Adeline refilled my cookie jar from a bag in her purse.

"Thank you," I said, only slightly resentful of her interference. I was becoming accustomed to it after two months in Dayspring. I even appreciated its advantages. It would be a while before I needed to bake cookies.

The girls' voices filtered in through the window. "That's a funny angel, Daddy. How did you make it? Do it again." The girls had regained their real father, hopefully. I prayed he wouldn't revert to the sullen, alcohol-soaked clod of the past few days.

"Susie, you need to make sure Simon keeps his promise," Adeline said over the whistling of the kettle. "If he starts drinking again, right away call Pester Warkentin."

"I suppose I could," I said, silencing the kettle. I wasn't sure how much influence the pastor would have if Adeline wasn't there. Anyway shouldn't it be Simon himself who decided to stay sober and developed the backbone to do that?

Adeline carried the freshly filled cookie jar to the table, plunked herself onto a chair, and selected a date turnover. "And try to keep my *benjel* away from people that drink."

I finished making the tea and brought the pot to the table. "That wouldn't be easy," I said, pulling up a chair. Social drinking was accepted in Dayspring, even by some Lutherans, though not by most Mennonites.

"The Christmas holidays are soon here," Adeline announced. "You and Simon and the girls could come and stay by me for a few days."

"I guess we could," I said slowly. We had arranged to spend Christmas and Boxing Day with relatives on Simon's father's side of the family. Other than that, we didn't have holiday plans.

Adeline poured cream into her tea. "You could bring Callum along to my house. A parrot can ride in a car, *nicht?*"

"I believe so if we keep him warm enough. But Ross's mother offered to take care of him over the holidays."

Adeline helped herself to another date turnover. "Why wouldn't Ross keep care of his own parrot?"

"Ross won't be here. He's going to fly to Halifax for a cousin's wedding."

Adeline blew on her tea. "His mother isn't going with?"

"No, she's staying home to take care of the house and Ross's birds."

"She'll be busy but you can have a nice peaceful holiday by me." Adeline reached across the table and took my hand. "Come for sure, Susie. You need rest; you look tired."

CHAPTER 45

I wished the fixed-up Simon and I could discuss our problems and clear the air. During the week before Christmas, I kept trying to start the dialogue but he either clammed up or changed the subject. Our conversations shrank to practicalities such as:

"Could you pick up the mail on your way home?"

"Did you turn the thermostat down?"

"Do you know where Norine's slippers are?"

After five years and two months of marriage, he seemed more like an acquaintance than my spouse.

Simon and I didn't sleep together. I camped on the floor of my sewing room. He had the bedroom. He didn't drink in there or anywhere else as far as I knew. That was a relief but I wondered how long his sobriety would last if we didn't dig out the roots of our problems.

When we arrived at Adeline's house the day after Boxing Day, she settled Emily and Norine in their usual bedroom, a small upstairs room papered with pink geraniums.

Down the hall from it was the room designated for Simon and me. It contained an oak dresser, a chair, and a double bed with a white chenille bedspread. The bed sagged in the middle. Despite that, it had sort of worked for us during previous overnight visits. It wouldn't work this time. We wouldn't be able to avoid rolling together. With our marriage on thin ice, that would be awkward.

During our first evening at Adeline's house, I put the girls to bed, then accompanied Simon to our room. While he was down the hall showering, I changed into my pyjamas, grabbed a pillow and blanket off the bed, and took a sheet and quilt from the closet.

I laid the quilt on the floor near the closet and arranged the sheet, blanket, and pillow on top. By the time Simon came in, I was settled in my floor-bed. I pretended to be asleep, taking slow regular breaths.

Simon stood beside the floor-bed for a long moment, then grunted and climbed into the double bed.

I didn't sleep well that night. With nothing but the quilt and sheet between me and the floor, I couldn't find a comfortable position.

When I woke in the morning, Simon wasn't in the room. I got up and peeked out into the landing.

No sign of life there though I smelled coffee and heard someone banging pots and pans. Adeline must be in her kitchen creating something 'healthy' for breakfast, like doughnuts or pastries with lots of icing. Emily's voice fluted up the stairs. "Oma, you should let us do it ourselves. We can do it. Mommy lets us."

I didn't hear Simon but as I continued to monitor the landing, the bathroom door opened. My husband emerged carrying his shaving kit and wearing the blue robe that matched his eyes. I was tempted to go and throw my arms around him. His warm solid body would feel good against mine.

I resisted the temptation, reluctant to make the first move. What if he rejected my overture?

Without a word, Simon pushed past me into our bedroom.

I took my turn in the bathroom. After I heard him go downstairs, I slipped into our room and got dressed.

During breakfast (freshly fried doughnuts, eggs, bacon, oranges, and toast), my half-estranged husband gave me several inquiring looks.

I squirmed in my chair, my hips sore from trying to sleep on the floor.

That afternoon, Adeline stayed home to start a batch of bread while Simon and I and our girls walked the mile and a half to her bachelor son Manfred's place. He lived in a wood-frame cabin with moose antlers above the door. The inside was cozy with a wood fire in the stove, hooked rugs on the floor, and windows overlooking a sea of snow-covered prairie.

Simon and Manfred watched hockey on TV while the girls played with Manfred's dogs. I sat in the rocking chair fighting sleep. Finally I gave up. "I need a nap," I told the men. "I'm going back to the house."

The outdoor air made me feel better. Snow crystals glittered along the trail as I crunched toward Adeline's house. I passed the one-room school Simon had attended. The place had been closed for years but I could still read the sign: *Coyote Junction School No. 1612.*

I pictured Simon copying his ABCs from the blackboard, warming his hands at the coal stove, singing solos at Christmas concerts. He was a musical prodigy though his brothers said he'd had trouble fitting in with his classmates. Too dreamy, and not allowed to participate in sports because of his heart. Poor boy.

Back at Adeline's house, I found her in the kitchen punching down bread dough. The bedding I had used was draped over a chair in the middle of the room.

Adeline gave her dough a couple of extra-hard punches, then turned and glared at me. "I found that badding on the dirty floor in your room."

"That floor isn't dirty." No floor in Adeline's house was dirty.

She yanked a stack of loaf pans out of a cupboard. "What was my nice clean badding doing on the floor?"

I stood taller, my hands on my sore hips. "What were *you* doing in our room?"

"Airing it." Adeline snatched a pan from the stack and banged it down on the counter. "I think you slept on the floor last night. Or Simon did." She greased the pan with a gob of lard. "Why?"

She banged another pan down on the counter. "Why didn't you sleep by the nice bad I fixed ready for you?" She greased a second pan. "Is something loose with it?"

"The mattress sags." I paused. "And I've been a restless sleeper lately. I didn't want to disturb Simon."

"Husbands and wives should sleep together with each other," Adeline said, greasing another pan. "It's God's will."

"Where's that in the Bible?"

"I don't know but I'm sure it stands somewhere in the *Biebel*." Adeline floured a bake-board and dumped her dough out onto it. "I can understand not sleeping together with a drunken person." She grabbed a butcher knife and began cutting the dough into chunks. "But Simon's not drinking now."

"No, thank God." I clasped my hands behind my back, crossing my fingers. "Maybe he and I just need time to get used to sleeping together again."

Adeline shaped a loaf and plopped it into a pan. "Maybe." She didn't sound convinced. "But nobody sleeps on the floor in my house. I'll pull the couch out in the living room and make for you a decent bad."

"Thank you." It was a kinder response than I'd expected.

CHAPTER 46

Adeline's living room was large, with a high ceiling. Her Christmas tree was decorated with crocheted stars, gingerbread angels, and woven-wheat wreaths. A manger scene sat on the pump-organ—donkeys, cows, Mary in blue, Joseph in brown, baby Jesus in white.

I appreciated Adeline letting me sleep in that room but it was too bright for my taste. Light from the moon and the yard-light reflected off the snow outside, slanting through the Venetian blinds.

I tied a scarf over my eyes. Then I stuffed cotton batting into my ears to mute the howling of coyotes from the south pasture. I hadn't noticed it in the bedroom.

Having sufficiently blinded and deafened myself, I settled into the pull-out bed Adeline had fixed for me. The sheets and pillowcases smelled like fresh air and ironing. After a drowsy attempt at prayer, I let the fog of sleep roll over me. The outside world receded and I dreamed about an old-fashioned boy in overalls and a blue jacket. He skated across a frying pan slick with lard. I wanted to skate too but my feet wouldn't move. The boy nudged me, his face a blur.

Panic rose in my throat as I realized that the blue-jacketed boy's face wasn't just a blur. He had no face at all.

The fog of sleep thinned and lifted. Had someone touched me or was that in the dream?

I rolled over and let sleep drift in again, then felt another touch on my shoulder. I rolled away from it.

A moment later the bed tilted as someone climbed in beside me. Too heavy to be Emily or Norine. "Simon?" I said, pulling the scarf off my eyes.

He whispered something in my ear.

I couldn't grasp what he said.

Simon whispered again, his breath tickling my cheek.

I took the cotton batting out of my ears. "What was that?"

"I said I can't sleep. I'm too lonesome."

"I'm sorry you're lonesome," I whispered, "but it's your own fault."

Simon ran a tentative hand up my arm, his eyes big in the moonlight. "I'm sorry."

Sorry? He hadn't said that word since our quarrel after the Christmas luncheon. "Sorry for what?" I whispered. We both knew but I wanted him to spit it out.

"For making you jealous. And for drinking."

"You quit drinking as far as I know. I'm glad but I'm still worried about you and Ross. I'm your wife. I have a right to know what's going on." I'd heard Ross's version but I wanted Simon's.

"Ross is strong. I'm not. He broadens my horizons and gives me new opportunities."

"Why? Is he in love with you?"

"No." Simon pulled the bedding up around our necks, then pushed it down. "I don't know."

I braced myself to ask the million-dollar question. "Have you and Ross had sex?" I edged away from Simon, afraid of his answer.

"Of course not," he whispered, his body stiffening.

Long silence. "Do you think about having sex with Ross?" I asked as gently as I could.

No answer.

My husband's silence was a curtain falling between us. I struggled to sit up. "We need to get away from that man."

"We can't. My future depends on him."

"Your future depends on God more than Ross Forbes." I glanced at Jesus, Mary, and Joseph in the manger scene. "You believe that, don't you?"

"I suppose so. Pray for me, Susie."

"I do. I will."

"And please don't keep freezing me out. You're supposed to be my friend. How can I sort my life out if you keep acting like my enemy?"

"I haven't been." I had tried to be understanding and diplomatic. When that didn't work, I retreated to a Cold-War stance.

My husband ran a hand up my spine. "It's time to thaw out, Sweetheart."

"I want to." I loved him despite whatever he had or hadn't done. "But I can't keep sharing you with dreams of Ross."

"I'll try to do better," Simon said, pulling me down into his arms.

I replaced the scarf on my eyes and fell asleep in Simon's arms. That was how Adeline and the girls found us in the morning.

CHAPTER 47

That morning, Simon and I cleaned up the kitchen after breakfast. I washed the dishes. He dried them. "Mother," he said, reaching around me to set a stack of bowls in the cupboard, "did you say you have a wallpaper book?"

Adeline looked up from tearing bread into little pieces for goose dressing. "Yes, Ruby Fehr borrowed it to me. What do you need with it?"

Simon glanced at me. "Susie and I are thinking of changing the wallpaper in our bedroom at home."

That was news to me. Simon knew I disliked the wallpaper Ross had hung but we hadn't discussed it lately.

"Why would you want to change?" Adeline asked. "Your bedroom is mostly papered real nice. You just need to finish it yet."

"That paper doesn't go with my orange curtains," I said, wiping the kitchen counter.

Adeline shrugged. "So make some new curtains already. You're a good sewer. The Co-op has material."

Simon hung up the tea towel. "We'd rather change the paper."

He was sticking up for me. Nice.

Adeline hauled herself to her feet. "I'll get the book once but I don't think it has orange paper."

"It wouldn't need to be orange," I said. "Just something that goes with orange."

She clumped upstairs and returned with the book, Emily and Norine trooping along behind her. "Is that book for us to colour in?" Emily asked as her Oma set it on the table.

"No, Sweetie," Adeline said. "It's just for looking at."

Simon flipped through a few pages of textured paper in neutral tones. "Not oatmeal. I don't want oatmeal on my walls."

Emily grinned at him. "You could eat it for breakfast."

Simon tweaked her nose. "I like real oatmeal like Mommy makes. She's a top-notch oatmeal-maker."

He turned a few more pages and happened upon the pink geranium wallpaper Adeline had used in the girls' room. "That's our flowers," Norine shouted.

Adeline beamed at her. "That's right. I ordered that paper from Winnipeg. Me and your Uncle Manfred pasted it on the walls."

Simon flipped through several more flower patterns. "I'd rather not have flowers." He turned a couple more pages, then stopped at a pattern of silver-green branches. "What's this?"

Adeline peered at it. "That's Mannonite wallpaper."

"Really?" I said. "I never heard of that."

"A Mannonite from Schteinbach made it." Adeline flipped to the back of the book. "Let's look the writing on. Yes, that's him, Dwayne Schellenberg. He writes that those are olive branches. They stand for peace. Mannonites don't hold any weapons. Good Mannonites don't anyway. They work for peace, not war."

"We learned that in Sunday School," Emily said.

Simon smiled at her and then at me, the blue of his eyes deepening. Hopefully he and I were on the road to peace between ourselves.

"Is this paper still available?" I asked Adeline.

"I'll ask Ruby."

"Please do," Simon said. "It might be just the thing for our bedroom."

CHAPTER 48

Our Christmas holiday at Adeline's house turned out better than I'd expected. My mother-in-law was irritating, overbearing, and bizarre but she cared about me or at least accepted me. Spending time in her presence made me feel less alone with my problems, even though I hadn't shared them with her.

I especially appreciated her letting me sleep on the couch in her living room. Simon visited me there from time to time, the possibility of being discovered lending an exciting edge to our lovemaking.

He and I and our girls arrived home in Dayspring one blustery afternoon in early January. The wind was snarling in from the north-east. Blowing snow swirled around the house, the flakes sparkling on our ice-covered porch.

I hurried Emily and Norine inside and turned up the thermostat. After settling the girls down for their nap, I went to help Simon bring in the boxes of food his mother had sent home with us—buns, sausages, pickles, jams, pies, and more. We were in the kitchen unpacking them when we heard a knock on the lean-to door.

Simon went to answer it. "Ross! How was your holiday?" My husband's voice sounded overly hearty. Maybe he was trying to make up for the disgusting condition he'd been in last time Ross saw him.

"My holiday was great," Ross boomed, following Simon into the kitchen.

"Hi, Ross," I said, giving him an embarrassed smile.

Ross's high spirits soared above my embarrassment. "I had a nice surprise waiting for me when I got home."

"Yeah?" Simon said. "What was that?"

"One of my budgies laid some eggs."

I laughed. "I don't think you need more birds, Ross."

"I'm delighted, actually. I just wish I was going to be here to see those eggs hatch."

"Why wouldn't you be?" Simon asked, offering him a chair.

Ross eased himself onto the chair. "I'll be in Halifax."

"Halifax?" I looked up from taking an apple pie out of one of Adeline's boxes. "You just came from Halifax."

"Yes, but I'm going again. To stay." Ross's eyes shone. "I've accepted a teaching position at the Maritime Conservatory of Performing Arts."

I gasped, almost dropping the pie. I had asked Ross to butt out of our lives but I hadn't expected anything that extreme.

Simon stared at him. "You're leaving Dayspring?"

"Yup. It's time to move on."

My husband gripped the back of a chair, his knuckles whitening. "You can't just walk away from your principal's job. People don't do that."

Ross tossed a lock of auburn hair off his forehead. His hair curled down over his collar, longer than I'd ever seen it. "Ian Glazebrook is taking over as principal. He'll do fine. We've already cleared it with the school board."

A muscle in Simon's left cheek twitched. "But why would you want to leave Dayspring?"

Ross glanced at me. "I believe it's time for a change. It'll be better for all concerned."

I telegraphed him a grateful look though I couldn't help feeling sorry for my husband.

Simon fumbled a chair out from the table and sat. "I realize it's an honour to teach at the Conservatory. But your job here is important too. And you have a history in Dayspring."

"I have more history in Nova Scotia. Uncles, aunts, nieces, nephews, cousins, second-cousins. There's nobody like a relative. I realized that at my cousin's wedding."

Simon leaned forward, his chair creaking. "Your mother is a relative if anybody is. What will she do if you move away?"

That was a good question though Virginia Forbes would probably get along fine without Ross. She was an independent soul, unlike my husband. What would Simon do if Ross left? Maybe he'd sink into a depression and start drinking again. He might even lose his job without Ross here to stick up for him.

Ross jiggled his lame leg. "Mom is willing to move to Halifax. She'll join me as soon as she packs things up and sells the house."

"What about your birds?" Simon asked.

"I'll leave them with Mom for now. We'll move them later, once we figure out the best way to do it."

I took a jar of beet pickles out of one of Adeline's boxes and set it in the cupboard. "Where do you plan on living in Halifax?"

Ross's eyes lit up. "I'm going to look for a big house with a verandah, a view of the ocean, and blueberry bushes in the garden. I grew up in a house like that."

"That sounds lovely." I admired Ross's courage and optimism. More to the point, I was glad he had decided to remove himself from our lives.

After he left, Simon slouched toward the bedroom like an old man. His shoulders drooped. His eyes drooped. Even his ears drooped.

"Are you okay?" I asked.

"Sure, fine." He sounded like he had a knife stuck in his chest.

"I know you'll miss Ross. I will too." Not so much actually. "But things will work out okay. You'll see."

Simon tottered into the bedroom.

I followed. "You should prepare some lessons. There's school tomorrow, you know." Simon needed to try harder if he hoped to keep his job. He'd already missed several days because of being too drunk to teach, or too hung over.

He stifled what sounded like a sob. "I don't know what's happening in my classes anymore."

"You could phone your substitute and ask."

"Ha!" Simon scowled down at his shoes. "Knowing Borya, he'll have everything screwed up."

I tried to smile. "You'll just have to unscrew things."

Simon shambled to the closet, pulled out his briefcase, flipped through some papers, threw everything on the floor, and kicked it under the bed. "I don't feel like teaching anymore."

"You will once you get started." I prayed he would.

CHAPTER 49

Simon moped around the house for three days. Every day, I phoned the school and reported his excuses. "He has a headache." (A heartache was more likely.) "He's dizzy." (Hard to prove.) "He's still dizzy."

At least he wasn't drinking anymore. But I was worried about what the new principal, Ian Glazebrook, would think of my husband's continued absence. His job wasn't rock-solid to begin with.

On the fourth day, Simon got up early, phoned Crystal to say he wouldn't need a substitute, and left for school, thank God. As soon as his car pulled out of the driveway, I phoned Ross Forbes and told him Simon was gone. Within minutes, Ross arrived at our door carrying a cloth-covered cage attached to a wooden box.

"Come in." I led him into the living room, where Emily and Norine were watching *The Friendly Giant* on TV.

The girls bounced off the couch. "Who's in the cage, Uncle Ross? Is it Callum?"

They'd been lonesome for the parrot, who had been living with Ross's mother since before Christmas. I hadn't missed Callum. I also wasn't keen on the birds in this cage. However, I had agreed to accept them for my daughters' sake.

I silenced the TV, then fetched some newspapers and laid them on the table by the armchair.

"Smells like Callum," Emily said as Ross set the cage on the table. I didn't detect the parrot's fried-food odour. Maybe she did.

Norine tapped on the cage. "Callum?"

We didn't hear any Callum-style shrieking or whistling. No ranting about shapes and colours. No opera. Just a faint chirping that sounded anemic by comparison.

Emily squinted up at Ross. "It's not Callum, is it?"

"No, it isn't. Sorry. I'm taking Callum to Halifax. Didn't Mommy tell you?"

"She told us," Emily said in a pained voice, "but we tried not to listen."

Ross patted her shoulder. "Callum will miss you and Norine. So will I. We'll miss your mommy and daddy too. But it's time for us to move on."

I couldn't have agreed more. I liked Ross better than I ever had. On the other hand, I could hardly wait to see the back of him.

Emily planted her fists on her narrow hips. "You can't take Callum away. Daddy's teaching him shapes and colours."

"Emily," I said, "don't you remember? We talked about that. Callum learned so much from Daddy that we think it's okay to stop his lessons now." Actually the lessons had stopped three weeks ago and never re-started. First Simon was too drunk to teach anybody anything. Then Callum was living with Ross's mom.

Ross quirked an eyebrow at the girls. "Who do you think is in the cage?"

"Another parrot?" Norine asked.

Emily elbowed her in the ribs. "No, Silly. Parrots are loud."

Ross raised an eyebrow at me. "Why don't we ask Mommy to show us?"

Emily and Norine watched, wide-eyed, as I grasped the top of the cloth and paused for effect. "Ta da!" I lifted it with a flourish.

"Budgies!" Emily shouted.

Norine tugged at my arm. "Mommy, look."

In the cage, two snub-nosed little birds pecked at seeds in a dish. One of the birds was bright green, the other yellow and blue.

"Have they got names?" Emily's voice was hushed, as if she'd witnessed a miracle.

"The green one is Budge," Ross said. "Her husband is Buntie."

"Birds aren't married." Emily glanced at me. "Are they, Mommy?"

I'd never considered the question. "Maybe they are in a way. They have babies anyway."

"Babies!" Norine hollered. "Where's the babies?"

"They haven't hatched yet," Ross said. "Budge just laid her eggs a few days ago."

"Where's the eggs?" Norine asked.

Ross limped around to the back of the wooden box that was attached to the cage, and unlocked a small door. After he'd opened it, we peered in at tiny white eggs nestled in a bed of straw.

"They're beautiful," Emily whispered.

"How many eggs, Norine?" Ross asked. "Can you count them?"

"One, two, free—"

"Four," Emily said. "There's gonna be four babies."

"When will they hatch?" I asked. Not that I was looking forward to it.

Ross closed the door on the nest. "About fifteen days from now."

"That soon?" Presumably we'd need to provide food for the chicks. Also they might need a bigger cage once there were six birds instead of two. I pictured a long road of bird responsibilities and expenses ahead of us.

Maybe Budge sensed my dim view of the situation. Probably not. In any case, she left the seed dish, hopped over to the wooden box, gawked around a bit, and slipped into the box.

Emily frowned. "Why did she go in there?"

"She's going to sit on the eggs," Ross said. "She needs to keep them warm. If they get too cool, they won't hatch."

Emily scooted around to the back of the box. "Can you open the door, Uncle Ross? We want to see Budge keep the eggs warm."

"I'd better not. If we bother her too much, she might not spend enough time sitting on them."

Personally, I wouldn't mind bothering Budge enough to keep her from hatching her eggs but I needed to consider my girls' feelings. They were thrilled with the budgies. Simon would enjoy them too. I just hoped their presence wouldn't slow his transition to a Ross-free life.

CHAPTER 50

After Ross Forbes moved to Halifax, Simon hardly ever mentioned him except with respect to paying the rent on our house, which Ross still owned. My husband's silence regarding Ross worried me but I didn't say much about it. I tried to focus on the future.

I moved back into our bedroom though I felt like the Biblical character who built a house on sand. Simon and I made love. The Mennonite wallpaper arrived in the mail and we pasted it over Ross's green and purple paper. We fed and watered the budgies with the children's help and checked their eggs every day.

We heard the baby budgies before we saw them—a faint peeping from inside the shells. The first shell cracked one Sunday morning just as we were leaving for church. By the time we got home, the first little bird was out. It looked like a red rubber worm with an oversized head. The kids were delighted with it. "Isn't it sweet, Mommy?"

"I guess so." The proximity of birds made me nervous. A crow had divebombed me when I was four years old. I'd never forgotten how terrified I felt.

Norine's eyes caressed the tiny bird. "What's its name going to be?"

I glanced at Simon. "Do we know if it's a girl or a boy?"

He peered into what passed for the creature's face. "It's hard to tell at this age but I'd say a boy, judging by the colour of the nostrils."

"Can we call him Laurence?" Emily asked. Laurence was a character in one of the girls' picture books.

"Sure," Simon said, "that's a good name. Laurence of Dayspring."

The girls and their father spent all afternoon in the living room with the birds, waiting for more eggs to hatch. As I sliced tomatoes to go with hamburgers for supper, Emily burst into the kitchen to tell me that a second egg had cracked. I followed her into the living room, where we watched another big-headed worm struggle out into the world. This one looked even more ridiculous than the first, having a jagged piece of shell on its head. Simon and the girls were thrilled with the new arrival, who was probably female according to Simon. The girls named her Shelley.

By Monday morning we had two more babies, these smaller than the first two. Simon and the girls dubbed them Cheepie and Cheekie.

For some reason Budge and Buntie didn't seem interested in feeding their offspring. Their little worm-babies cheeped and squeaked in vain.

"We'll need to feed them ourselves," Simon announced on Monday afternoon when the girls and I returned from a doctor's appointment in Davidson.

Emily's forehead wrinkled. "How can we? We're not birds."

"We'll use this little spoon." Simon showed her. "See, I bent the end so it fits in their beaks."

Emily raised an eyebrow. "What do they eat?"

"I made them some porridge." Simon gestured toward a pot on the stove. "I made it thin so it's easy to swallow."

"Let's do it," Norine shouted.

"The sooner the better," Simon said. "We should probably start with Shelley. She's the loudest. That may mean she's the hungriest."

He spooned a bit of porridge into a small bowl, then picked Shelley up in his left hand. I shuddered to think what her rubbery body must feel like. Simon held her head between his thumb and forefinger, dipped the spoon into the porridge, and brought it to her beak.

She didn't open her mouth.

"She hasn't got the idea yet," Simon said, tapping her beak.

"It's open," Norine announced a moment later.

Simon rolled a drop of porridge off the spoon into Shelley's mouth. She swallowed. He gave her another drop. As he continued to feed her, a gross-looking lump formed on the front of her chest. "See, her crop is full," Simon said. "That means she's eaten enough."

Emily reached for the spoon. "Can I feed Laurence?"

"Okay," Simon said. "But first we'll wash the spoon and get another bowl of porridge. We don't want the birds catching each other's germs."

When he'd reorganized the equipment, he placed Laurence in Emily's left hand. "Hold him gently, no squeezing." He handed her the spoon with a little porridge in it. "Keep your hand steady. That's it. Steady, steady."

After Laurence's crop was full, Simon helped the girls feed Cheepie and Cheekie. I admired my husband's patience and compassion. He had a gift for nurturing. Sadly I didn't seem to bring that out in him anymore. I had when I was a scrawny twenty-year-old. However, we'd both changed since then. I was stronger and hopefully wiser. Maybe he didn't think I needed nurturing anymore.

For the next few weeks, Simon fed the baby budgies on a regular schedule with help from our girls and from a couple of his biology students. He was happier than he'd been for months. Spots of colour burned in his cheeks, the way they sometimes had when he and I worked together in the veterinary clinic.

CHAPTER 51

One snowy afternoon about a month after the budgies had hatched, Simon slouched into my sewing room looking as serious as an oatmeal sausage.

I set my fabric and scissors on the table. "What's the matter?"

"I lost half my job."

"What do you mean?"

Simon sagged onto my floor-bed. "Borya Palko complained about me teaching without a degree. So the teachers' union forced the school board to cut me back to half time."

"That's terrible."

"It is. They cut my salary in half, of course."

"How can they do that?" I left my chair and went to sit beside him on the floor-bed. "You're a good teacher." I put my arm around him. "And we've got a family to feed."

Simon stared down at the quilt. "The board suggested I find a second job."

"Like what?"

"They offered me a spot in the bus-driving schedule. Or there's janitorial work at the school. Evenings."

"One of those might not be too bad."

Simon fiddled with the zipper on his sweater. "Ross had another idea."

"Ross!" I jerked my arm off Simon's shoulders. "You're still in touch with Ross?" I had assumed, apparently naively, that Ross had disappeared from our lives.

Simon folded his arms, defiant. "I phoned him. Why wouldn't I? He's the guy who got me the teaching job in the first place."

I sighed.

"Ross has a solution, better than the board's. He'll pay me ten dollars an hour to feed his birds, water them, and keep them company for a few hours every day."

"His mother could do that."

"Not anymore apparently. She's too busy packing and trying to sell the house."

"Babysitting Ross's birds is a make-work job, Simon. He only offered because he feels sorry for you."

"Ross feels sorry for all of us." My husband's voice rasped. "Us and our kids. I wouldn't have lost half my job if you hadn't chased him away. He would have found a way to protect me."

"*I* chased Ross away?" I had but I didn't like to admit it.

"Of course." Simon stretched his feet on the bed. Wide Dutch-German feet in grey socks darned by his mother. "If you hadn't been so insanely jealous, he wouldn't have moved to Halifax."

"He left because he got a better job in Halifax plus he wanted to live near his relatives." I gulped. "And leaving Dayspring was a handy way of escaping the gossip about you and him."

Simon lurched up off the floor-bed. "I don't need to stay here and listen to your drivel."

"People were gossiping, whether you believe it or not."

"Says who?" Simon asked.

"Borya Palko."

"Puh! Nobody takes Borya seriously."

"Oh?" I bolted to my feet. "The teachers' union took him seriously enough to make the board demote you."

Simon sighed like a balloon losing air. "That had nothing to do with your so-called gossip. The board downgraded me because Borya has a teaching degree. I don't."

"I assume he got the other half of your job."

My husband nodded. "I pity the students. He's a terrible teacher." Simon slumped against the wall. "Why can't life be fair?"

Simon's lack of a degree wasn't life's fault. It was his own for not staying in college. I could have reminded him of that, but there was no point in rehashing the past. "If you finished your degree, you could get a proper job with a more secure future."

Simon massaged his left temple. "The board suggested I finish it by correspondence."

"Is that possible?"

"Apparently. I just need to contact the university in Saskatoon, fill out some forms, and pay a fee. The university mails out the assignments. I complete them and mail them back for marking."

"Do you have the address?"

He pulled a piece of paper out of his pocket and gave it to me.

"So let's send for the forms."

"Where would we get the money?"

"It can't be that much," I said. "We'll find it somehow."

"We could try," he said slowly. "But how am I going to find time for correspondence lessons plus teaching plus whatever other job you'll let me take?"

"Simon, please. It isn't a matter of me allowing. Why can't we discuss this like reasonable adults?"

"Okay, let's discuss. I don't want to drive a bus and I don't want to scrub toilets." He raised two fingers. "So that's two possibilities down the drain."

"What about working for a fish farmer? I hear some of them are short-handed."

"My cousins at Birsay are," Simon said, "but it's too far to drive and I don't like the way they run their place."

"What about Bethany Banman? She needs help." Bethany had married her boyfriend, a young doctor from Regina. They were busy setting up a medical practice in Central Butte, besides running her fish farm.

"Yeah," Simon said, "Bethany would probably hire me but it would mean commuting."

"That wouldn't kill you."

"No, but it would be ridiculous when I can just walk across the pasture to Ross's house. I could work on my correspondence lessons while I keep the birds company."

"I don't want you spending hours and hours in Ross's house. It'll just stir up feelings you should—"

Simon reeled away from me. "I wish you'd quit telling me what to do. I'm responsible for supporting this family and I'll do it my own way." He headed for the door. "Now if you'll excuse me, I'll go and shovel the driveway."

I could have helped him; we had two shovels. I didn't feel like it.

CHAPTER 52

Simon peered down at a flurry of footprints beside the trail that led from Adeline's house to her son Manfred's. "Looks like an owl fancied muskrat for breakfast."

Emily squinted at the footprints, her red toque slipping low on her forehead. "How do you know, Daddy?"

"See, that's where the owl flapped its wings." He swept his arm around, mimicking the swooping lines in the snow.

Norine flapped her arms. "Like this?"

He laughed. "Yeah, something like that."

Adeline shifted the bags of sausages and cookies she was carrying. "Can you girls see the owl's feet-prints? They look like chicken tracks."

"There," Emily shouted. "That's them." Her cheeks were pink with cold and forced gaiety. She and Norine had learned to take advantage of times when their dad was sober. He was a wise attentive father then. Today he was sober in honour of his mother, who had invited us to join her on a hike to Manfred's cabin. We were going to cook and eat in the cabin—sort of a winter picnic. Manfred was in Arizona but Adeline had a key to his cabin.

Norine's nose was dripping.

I tucked my bag of salad under my arm and found a tissue in my pocket. "Can you girls see the muskrat tracks?" I asked, wiping Norine's nose.

"There?" Emily pointed.

"Right," Simon said. "They look like little hands." He pointed. "That's where the muskrat ran, trying to get away from the owl. See its prints cross the owl's? Once, twice, three times. Then poof, they disappear."

Emily gazed up at him, the sad truth dawning in her eyes. "That's when the owl ate the muskrat?"

"Probably not right here. It probably flew away with its meal."

Norine's lower lip quivered. "Poor muskrat."

Simon patted her shoulder. "Yes, it was sad for the little animal."

Emily pushed her toque higher on her forehead. "But the owl needed to eat, right, Daddy? It was very, very hungry."

"Right. The owl probably hadn't eaten for a while."

"Like us," Adeline said. "Come on once. Let's go make our food ready."

Simon glanced at his watch. "It's not even eleven yet. We could hike to the marsh and look at the muskrat lodge."

"You and the girls go," Adeline said. "Me and Susie should start cooking."

I reached for the bag of potatoes Simon was carrying. "Here, let me take that."

"Simon learns the girls interesting things," Adeline said as she and I set out for Manfred's cabin. "He's a good father."

"He is when he's having a good day," I replied.

She raised her eyebrows. "What do you mean?"

"Not every day is the same." Simon didn't drink when he was teaching or bird-sitting, or on Sunday mornings, when we went to church. The rest of the time, he was drunk to one extent or another. I drew a breath to break the news to his mother, then decided against it. "We all have our good and bad days."

Adeline tightened the red and purple babushka she wore on her head. "I know he feels *schlajcht* about losing half his school job but his bird job is going good, *nicht?*"

I kicked at a clod of ice in the snow. "Yes, but he's going to lose it in a week. Ross's mother sold the house. She's leaving for Halifax next Saturday, with Ross's birds."

"So soon?" Adeline squawked as we made our way past Manfred's clotheslines. "It's winter yet." She clumped onto Manfred's porch, took the key out of her pocket, and unlocked the door. "It's too cold to move birds."

"Apparently it's possible," I said, following her inside. The cabin smelled of bleach and furniture polish. Adeline had taken advantage of Manfred's absence to do a little cleaning.

She set her bags of food on the kitchen table. "Simon's going to miss those *foageln*."

He'd miss the birds, sure. More to the point, he'd miss their connection with Ross. I didn't tell Adeline that. She'd go ballistic at the mere suggestion that her son harboured romantic feelings for a man.

She grabbed a wooden spoon from the crock on the table. "Simon should be lucky he has the budgies yet. He and the kids love them."

I didn't. Sometimes I was tempted to take their cage outside, leave the door open, and let them flutter off to wherever their tiny hearts desired. I didn't tell Adeline that either. She wouldn't understand. I wasn't a cruel person at heart. I just didn't like being near birds. They gave me the creeps.

I changed the subject. "Emily's doing well in kindergarten."

The new principal had started a kindergarten above the bank. I was grateful for the educational and social opportunities it offered my daughter. Also I was glad it got her out of the house three days a week. Our home wasn't a happy place when Simon was drinking. He often stayed in the bedroom for hours, his depression seeping through the walls like poison gas. Or he stumbled around the house, knocking things over and barking at me and the girls if we dared to speak to him.

What long-term effects were Simon's depression and drinking having on our children? I wondered as I went to the stove to start a fire. Emily had started biting her fingernails—she'd never done it before. Norine had developed a fear of being flushed down the toilet. Both girls thought there were monsters in their closet.

Adeline opened the bag of potatoes. "Emily's smart. She takes after my side of the family."

"Good for her, I guess." I laid kindling on the grate and arranged firewood on top. Was Emily smart enough not to tell her teacher how her dad sometimes acted at home? I'd told her not to. I made excuses for Simon, saying he didn't feel well. But Emily was old enough to connect his bottles with his bad moods.

Adeline grabbed a frying pan off a hook. "Simon is more like his dad," she said, plunking a dollop of lard into the pan.

I struck a match and held it to the kindling. "Oh, yeah?" I'd never met Simon's late father but people said he wasn't much of a talker. *Stelle Isaak,* the local Mennonites called him. Quiet Isaac. "What do you mean?"

"Simon is a better talker than Isaac but he has his dad's dither-head. He needs managing."

Adeline had been an uber-manager of Isaac, according to Simon's brothers. She'd told her husband which tractor to buy, which crops to plant, and even what to say if the pastor asked him to pray aloud in church.

Simon evidently needed management too—more than what I could provide. Maybe he needed professional help but where would I find that in or near Dayspring? More important, how would I get Simon to accept help?

It would be a relief to share my problems with Adeline. I would have if she hadn't been such an overbearing woman. Her anti-drinking tactics hadn't worked last time. They had driven Simon's feelings underground.

Anyway Adeline wasn't going to be around for a while. Wally and Myrtlemay were moving to Saskatoon, along with Myrtlemay's parents. Adeline had volunteered to lend a hand. Simon and I would be alone with our problems.

CHAPTER 53

A couple of days after the picnic in Manfred's cabin, I received a letter from my friend Valerie in Sage City. It came as a pleasant surprise since she wasn't much of a correspondent. I made a pot of tea and settled at the kitchen table with my prize. Lunchtime had come and gone but I didn't feel like eating. Simon was drunk and snoring in the bedroom. Emily was at kindergarten, and Norine seemed happy under the table, running her toy train around my feet and up my legs.

Valerie's letter, written on pink paper, started with predictable pleasantries. Then she sprang some exciting news on me.

> I've got a new job! I work at Tod College now, helping to coordinate the classes. My boss wants to offer some sewing courses like quilting, garment construction, and basic fashion design. You'd be an ideal teacher. Is there any chance of you and Simon moving back here?

I pictured Simon, me, and our girls back in Sage City. Art galleries, concerts in the parks, ski slopes within driving distance. Trendy shops, a fabric store, choice of restaurants. Mennonite church close to home. Even a shopping mall.

Our life in Dayspring wasn't going well. Simon was only teaching half-time, and his bird-sitting gig would end in five days. Could I persuade him to move back to Sage City? He had no relatives there and no job prospects, but he might enjoy a change of scene. It might help him stop drinking. If I was teaching at the college, I could support us until he found work. Or he could focus all his energy on finishing his degree.

"Mommy." Norine tugged at my pant leg. "I'm hungry."

I got up and made her a peanut butter and cracker sandwich—her latest fad. After pouring her a cup of milk, I set her in the highchair and returned to Valerie's letter.

> I miss you. So does my mom. Give my love to the girls and Simon.
> I enclose a newspaper clipping you might find interesting.

As I unfolded the clipping, my heart jumped at the sight of the name in the headline. Florian Bouchard—the beautiful young man I'd left five months earlier.

I sucked in a breath and read on.

> Three works by Sage City sculptor Florian Bouchard were chosen for the *Emerging artists of British Columbia* exhibition set to tour the province during the next few months.
>
> Hermione Gaudet, an art professor at Tod College in Kamloops, said, "Many of Bouchard's works portray women. His touring sculptures are depictions of Rapunzel, Helen of Troy, and Cleopatra. Remarkably, all of Bouchard's women share one distinctive feature. They all have slightly crossed eyes that seem to follow the viewer around the room. This illusion of movement is difficult to achieve in sculpture.
>
> "When I questioned Bouchard about the characteristic eyes, he said, 'They were inspired by the first woman I ever loved. Our ill-fated romance soon ended, but she remains in my heart, my quintessential woman.'

Had Florian meant me? Surely not. I peered at the photo that accompanied the article. The sculptured woman didn't look like me. She had a round face, longer hair, and an old-fashioned dress. However, the eyes were mine—large, too close together, and slightly crossed.

My heart caught me by surprise, howling with longing for Florian. I ordered it to be quiet and returned to the article, half afraid of what I might read next.

> "Bouchard wouldn't reveal the identity of his quintessential woman but the memory of their star-crossed love gives the young sculptor an air of romantic longing.
>
> "What's in the future for Bouchard? He said, 'I was forced to put my education on hold when my father became ill. I currently work

in pottery sales. My job doesn't leave much time for sculpting. However, I hope to finish college eventually and become a full-time sculptor or an art curator.'"

I bit my lower lip. Florian—smart, charming, and talented—had been reduced to selling pottery, probably made by other people. That didn't sound like a very exciting or lucrative career. Just the same, I'd be more than happy to share it if I could. I could help Florian with sales, keep records, cook for him, wake up in the mornings with his loose-jointed body curled around mine.

But I was married to the snorer in the bedroom. Even if I wasn't somebody else's wife, Florian probably wouldn't be interested in me anymore. Maybe, having taught himself to sculpt those distinctive eyes, he had developed the quintessential-woman story as an explanation for using them again and again. Lost love fascinates people.

Florian's and my love was lost from the start. My relationship with Simon was more logical and reliable. At least it had been. Simon and I had enjoyed five good years together. Nobody could take those away from me. They'd remain in my memory forever.

But sadly, my husband seemed to have lost the will to move on with his life. He drifted in the shallows. Parttime teacher, parttime temporary birdsitter, parttime husband and father, parttime slave of the bottle. The correspondence lessons from the university might have nudged him forward, but they sat on a shelf in the lean-to, unopened.

By contrast, Florian seemed to do okay despite setbacks and holdups. There must be a way for Simon to do that. Could I help him find it? We loved each other. I still believed that.

If I couldn't help Simon through this bad time in his life, who could? Not his mother, too intimidating. Anyway she was in Saskatoon. Pastor Warkentin or the Lutheran pastor might be able to help but Simon refused to go to them or have them visit. Simon also refused to attend Alcoholics Anonymous meetings in the United Church basement. He was too worried about what people would think of him.

Norine was banging her forehead on the tray of the highchair. She needed her nap. I set the clipping and Valerie's letter aside, took my little girl to the bathroom, and settled her in bed. As I sang to her—*rock-a-bye baby*—I couldn't help wondering what kind of a stepfather Florian would make. Would he love my children? Would he be good to them? Would he read them stories and sing to them?

Simon was a better singer. Actually Simon was the best singer I knew.

Tears trickled down my cheeks as I left the girls' bedroom and retreated to the sewing room to work on a quilt the local marina had commissioned me to make. About two o'clock, my stomach started rumbling. I remembered I hadn't eaten lunch. I was thinking about heating the leftover chicken stew when Simon called from the lean-to. "Shuzee, come and help me." His voice sounded syrupy. He was obviously drunk again.

I drew an exasperated breath, left my quilt, and went out to the lean-to. My husband stood over Emily's bicycle, which lay on the workbench beside an instruction sheet.

Simon looked up, bloodshot. "I'm fikshing Emily'sh bike."

"Good," I said though I doubted his ability to fix anything in his current state.

"Gotta remove thish locknut." He pointed with a shaking hand. "You hold the bike shteady."

I complied though I didn't expect him to succeed. After a few fumbling tries, Simon managed to fit the wrench onto the locknut.

The nut wouldn't turn.

"I think you're turning it the wrong way," I said. "Shouldn't it loosen to the left? *Righty tighty, lefty loosey.*" Emily had learned that expression from Simon. She loved to repeat it in a high sing-song voice.

Simon squinted at the instructions, his eyes unfocusing and refocusing. "No, thish one looshensh clockwishe." A muscle twitched in his jaw. "Maybe it's rushted." He braced himself and gave a mighty heave. The locknut flew off the bracket, bounced against the workbench, hit the floor, and rattled away.

"Shit!" Simon dropped to all fours. "Where'd it go?" He crawled across the floor like a turtle. I glanced around and spotted the locknut beside the bookcase. "Here." I picked it up and handed it to him. "But why don't you leave the bike for now? You should eat something. I'm going to warm the leftover stew."

He lurched to his feet and stood rocking from one foot to the other. "I don't want any shtew."

"Suit yourself." Exasperated, I turned and headed for the kitchen.

"Aw, Shuzeeee." He stumbled after me, smelling like a distillery. "Don't be mean."

I stopped in the kitchen doorway. "I can't put up with this much longer."

"What?"

"Your drinking. What else?"

"The problem ish—" He hung his arm around my shoulders. "You don't undershtand me."

I shook him off and got the stew out of the refrigerator.

"You're right. I don't understand you." I grabbed a wooden spoon to stir the stew. "I don't understand how you can throw your life away." I shook the spoon at him, watching his bleary eyes try to follow it. "And you know what? I almost don't care anymore."

CHAPTER 54

A few days later, I was sitting in my sewing room working on the marina quilt when Emily and Norine came running in. "Mommy, come and see."

"What?" I looked up from embroidering a meadowlark's wing.

"Daddy learned Budge a new trick."

"You mean Daddy taught Budge a new trick."

Emily gave her head an impatient shake. "Right, taught. Come and see. It's a funny trick."

"Come," Norine said.

I wanted to stay in the sewing room; I had work to do.

Norine tugged at my arm.

Poor kid. She and Emily hadn't enjoyed many happy times with their father lately. I sighed and followed the girls along the hall, carrying my meadowlark in his embroidery frame. That meadowlark was my type of bird. He was clean, silent, and under my control. Most important, he wasn't moving.

By contrast, the bird I saw from the living-room doorway was perched on Simon's finger fluttering her wings like a tiny helicopter. His finger stayed steady because he was sober, not yet having returned to the bottles after his half-week of teaching.

As I stepped into the room, Budge stopped fluttering. She gawked around a bit and then pooped on Simon's finger. Maybe she was excited about showing 'Mommy' her new trick. Maybe not. I suspected she couldn't tell one person from another, which was just as well since I hated her. I didn't like the rest of Budge's family either. Thankfully Simon had left Budge's husband and four gawky children in their cage.

Emily tore a bit of toilet paper off the roll that sat on the coffee table and wiped Budge's deposit off Simon's finger. She handed the soiled paper to Norine, who trotted off to the kitchen garbage can and dropped it in. Sisterly teamwork.

Simon stroked Budge's stubby head. "Can you scoot through your tunnel for Mommy?" He laid the toilet-paper roll on its side. Emily and Norine placed a few grains of millet at the far end. Simon nudged the bird toward the near end. "Tunnel," he said.

She gave him a look that might be interpreted as reluctant.

"Tunnel." He nudged her again.

Budge hesitated a second, then fluttered over to the roll, skedaddled through it, and gobbled up the millet.

"She did it," Norine yelled.

I applauded from the doorway.

Emily plucked at her dad's sleeve. "Can you make her do it again?"

"Maybe later. We don't want to tire her out." Simon reunited the feathered performer with her family in the cage, then raised an eyebrow at me. "We'll need a bigger cage soon. The chicks are growing fast."

"So are our girls," I blurted. "Emily's shoes are too small for her. They hurt her feet but we can't afford new ones."

Emily lowered her chin, giving her father an embarrassed smirk, as if outgrowing her shoes was a sign of disloyalty.

I didn't like having the kids hear me badgering Simon about our finances. It would only increase their anxiety but I was upset enough to persist. "And what about Norine's tooth? We should take her to a dentist but we don't have the money."

"I'm a failure, obviously." Sarcasm edged the chagrin in his voice. "I don't even make enough money to take care of my own kids."

"I didn't say you were a failure."

"No, but that's what you meant." He grabbed the door of the cage and slammed it, frightening the budgies into scrambling to the far end. Emily and Norine glanced at each other, then scurried to their room and shut the door behind them.

I felt bad about angering their dad. But he was a grown man. He needed to face reality sooner or later. "My sewing machine quit this morning," I announced. "I phoned a couple of repair shops. They said I might need a new one."

"Right. How do you suggest we buy a sewing machine if we can't afford shoes or a dentist?"

"We'd have money if you didn't keep drinking it up and pissing it away."

My husband gave me a half guilty, half defiant look.

"Simon, we're in rough shape. We're overdrawn at the bank. We haven't paid the rent this month. I can't even finish the quilt for the marina and collect my fee because my sewing machine's busted."

He rubbed the back of his neck. "Wally or Manfred might give us a loan. Or my mother."

"Borrowing from your relatives would just be a band-aid solution." I hesitated, then plunged in. "Valerie offered me a job teaching at Tod College."

Simon barked out a laugh. "That would be a long commute."

"I wasn't thinking of commuting."

He jerked his head up. "I'm not moving to Sage City if that's what you're thinking. You can forget that right now."

"If you won't move, I might take the kids and go by myself." My voice shook. The prospect both frightened and excited me.

"What did you say?" His eyes widened.

"I said I might go by myself, with the girls."

"You'd leave me?" Simon blurted. "What would I do?"

"You'd drink yourself into an early grave, I suppose." I paused. "Of course I wouldn't want that." I went to him, took his hand. "I love you. The girls love you. But I can't stay here and watch you destroy yourself."

He yanked his hand out of mine, stumbled into the lean-to, returned with a bottle, and disappeared into the bedroom.

CHAPTER 55

April brought rapid changes to the Saskatchewan prairie. Emily and Norine waded through puddles on the south side of the house while snowbanks lay like dead sheep on the north side. Mallard ducks swam on reedy sloughs. Farmers fixed up their tractors. A meadowlark perched on a barbed-wire fence, pouring out its lilting song.

An earthy lightness filled the air. For the first time in months, I opened the windows of my sewing room.

I was embroidering a seagull for my marina quilt when Simon burst into the room, his cheeks glowing. I was relieved to see it was a healthy glow, not the bloated flush of drunkenness.

"I got a summer job," he announced, plopping himself down on the floor-bed where I slept when he was drunk, and sometimes when he wasn't.

"What kind of a job?" I hoped the pay was decent. We were barely scraping by. I'd persuaded the marina to give me an extra advance on the quilt, but the money hardly covered the repairs to my sewing-machine. Wally had loaned us a thousand dollars. However, we'd promised to pay it back within two years.

Simon's eyes shone. "It's a singing job. A tour."

"Really?" He sometimes sang solos in the Mennonite church, also in the Lutheran, but he'd never gone anywhere on tour. "Where would you go?"

"Nova Scotia." He paused. "And maybe other places in the Maritimes."

"Really? Don't tell me; let me guess. I'll bet this tour involves Ross Forbes." Who else did Simon know on the east coast?

He shifted on the floor-bed. "Ross is one of the organizers, yes, but he won't go on tour himself. He'll be too busy teaching."

"I hope so," I said, jabbing my needle into my seagull's eye.

Simon gave a nervous laugh. "Are you still worried about Ross and me? There's no need, believe me."

"I wish I could believe you."

"Suspicion doesn't look good on you, Sweetheart." Simon lunged to his feet and began pacing the floor, pink spots of excitement burning in his cheeks. "This tour is going to be great. We'll travel with a full band. We'll have costumes. Our names will be on posters."

"Your name too?"

"Yes but in small print. The posters will feature our star performer, Ziggy Belinski."

"You've been invited to go on tour with Ziggy Belinski?" I was reluctantly impressed.

"Yes. Ross showed Belinski a film of me performing with Callum the amazing opera-singing parrot. I guess he liked it."

"I find it hard to believe that Ross would let Callum go on tour without him. He loves that bird."

"Callum will be fine without him," Simon assured me. "He'll travel with the other animals. They're going to have their own trailer, and a veterinarian to look after them."

I yanked my thread through the seagull's eye. "Are you sure this tour is for real? It sounds kind of far-fetched."

Simon stopped pacing. "Ross would know if it's real or not. He's going to fax me the contract. If I decide to go ahead, I sign it and fax it to the organizers' office by next Thursday."

"What do you expect me to do while you're gallivanting around the east coast?" I was the one who'd been thinking about leaving. Now the tables had turned. I couldn't help resenting the switch.

Simon ran his fingers through his hair, managing to partly cover the thinning area on top. "The tour only lasts six weeks. You'll find lots to do. Maybe you could take the girls on a trip."

"Maybe, if we can afford it. How much does this tour pay?"

Simon grinned and gave me a V sign for Victory. "Expenses plus four hundred a week."

"Four hundred what? Clams?"

He rocked back on his heels. "Come on, Susie. It's good money."

It was. I couldn't deny that. "Do you think you can stay sober enough?"

"I pray to God I can." He gave me an earnest look. "I'm not going to drink anymore. I've decided."

"Really?" I was so surprised, my embroidery frame slipped out of my hand.

"Really." Simon picked up the frame and handed it to me. "Muriel Beasley and I are working on it. She's helping me a lot."

My mouth sagged open. Simon had refused to ask a pastor for help or go to Alcoholics Anonymous. Now he was consulting a psychiatrist? Of his own free will? Maybe Ross had put him up to it.

"That's great," I said, daring to hope that my husband could really quit drinking. "It's wonderful." I paused, considering the practicalities. "How much does Muriel charge?" Psychiatrists didn't come cheap, even retired ones.

"She's not charging. She's volunteering her time. Alcoholics Anonymous helped her through some rough times. Now she's giving back."

"Good for you and Muriel." I rose from my chair and gave Simon a congratulatory kiss though I couldn't help feeling slighted. Why hadn't my love and encouragement motivated him to quit drinking? He could have decided for my sake, and the sake of our kids. Did Ross, Callum, and the tour mean more to him than we did?

Simon headed toward the door, then turned. "I looked at those correspondence lessons. They don't seem too hard. I thought I might try them."

"Really?" He'd ignored the lessons for months. Could he handle them now, suddenly? Maybe so, with the prospect of the tour to inspire him.

But what would inspire me? What were my prospects? I wouldn't be obliged to stay in Dayspring if Simon wasn't here. Maybe I could head off on an adventure of my own. I could go to Sage City. I might get a summer job there. Valerie might help me look into the possibilities.

CHAPTER 56

A couple of weeks later, I was sitting at my kitchen table drinking coffee after breakfast when my mother-in-law phoned. "How's by your spring cleaning, Susie?" She sounded as lively as a grasshopper. Her time in Saskatoon had evidently energized her, not exhausted her, as it would many sixty-nine-year-old women who weren't Adeline.

"Spring cleaning?" I sipped my coffee. "I've heard of that. I'm not sure what it is."

Silence. Adeline seldom appreciated my attempts at humour.

"I gather you think my house needs cleaning."

"You've got dirty marks on your walls," Adeline informed me. "There are smudges on your blinds. Your couch is *shmutzik* and your rugs need vacuuming and shampooing."

"Big surprise. I've got kids and they've got birds."

Adeline clicked her tongue. "I had more kids than you and I naver let my house get so *drakjijch*."

Emily had left part of a boiled egg on her plate. I helped myself. "I've been busy," I said, chewing.

"Busy or *nicht*, you should always find time to clean. Think on Simon and the girls. They'll be happier in a clean house."

"I don't think happiness has much to do with cleaning." Our family had been unhappy in a dirty house. Now we were happier in a dirty house. The difference was that Simon had quit drinking, inspired by the prospect of his Maritime adventure. What would Adeline say when she heard about that?

"It's going to rain next week," she announced. "We can't clean if it's *plaudring* down rain. We can't open the windows. Can't see as good." She grabbed a breath. "We should start today."

"Today? I was going to work on the quilt for the marina." I'd been counting on several hours without interruptions. Simon was at school and the girls were at the petting zoo with the kindergarten teachers.

"You can quilt next week when it's raining."

I sucked a breath through my teeth. "I planned to quilt today and I'm going to."

"That quilt can wait yet," Adeline said. "The marina's not in a hurry."

"Maybe not but I am." I needed to finish it so I could collect the rest of my fee.

Adeline snorted. "You should be lucky you have a mother-law that's willing to help you."

"I appreciate your offer but—".

"So we'll spring-clean, *nicht?* I'll bring detergent, soap, cleanser, rags, vinegar, window cleaner, rubber gloves—"

"We're not cleaning today. And that's final."

Long silence. "What about the sagebrushes and rabbitbrushes in your lawn?"

"What about them?" I asked.

"I can dig them out for you."

"No, thanks," I said.

"They look messy."

"We don't think so."

"So you don't want me to do nothing for you?"

"Not today but thanks anyway."

I got more quilting done that day than I'd expected to. Resisting my mother-in-law's bullying had boosted my energy and sharpened my focus.

By the following Saturday afternoon, the marina quilt was almost done. It just needed a border. I was sitting on the porch piecing together a border of blue and green velvet when Adeline's ancient Chevy came rocking up the driveway.

What did she want? Maybe she'd thought of more jobs that could be done around our place. No doubt there were plenty.

She ground her car to a halt near the sandbox, which Simon and the girls were filling with sand.

The kids dropped their shovels and ran to her. "Oma, come and see," Norine shouted, bouncing on her toes.

"Daddy took us to the lake," Emily said. "We got sand to put in the sandbox."

"So we can play," Norine added.

"You'll get dirty," Adeline said, heaving herself out of the car. "But I guess kids need their fun."

The girls grabbed her arms, one on either side. Simon came to meet her, shovel in hand.

I left my sewing and went to join them. "Hello, Mother Epp."

She beamed at us. "Did the Lutheran pester phone to you already?"

"Not that I know of," Simon said. He glanced at me. "Pastor Norlander didn't call, did he?"

"No."

"He will." Adeline hauled in a breath. "He's got good news. The music director that works usually at the Lutheran Bible Camp can't come this year. Simon, the church board wants you to apply for the job once."

"That's an honour," I said, pleased that the board would consider my husband for such an important role. On the other hand, I'd been looking forward to Simon's absence so I could spend a few weeks in Sage City. My friend Valerie had managed to find me a job there.

"It *is* an honour," Simon said, leaning on his shovel. "Unfortunately I won't be around this summer."

"What?" Adeline stared at him "Where are you going?"

When Simon told her, Adeline clutched at her chest and pretended to faint. "Why would you want to chase around the Marimtides singing with a bird when you could be doing God's work?"

"Bible Camp only lasts two weeks," Simon said as the girls drifted off toward the sandbox. "The tour runs for six weeks and pays better."

Adeline narrowed her eyes. "What would you be singing with that bird? I bet not Christian songs."

"Opera," Simon said. "It's Callum's specialty."

"Opera!" Adeline snorted. "Regular people don't understand opera."

The same thought had crossed my mind.

"I'll be singing other music when I perform alone," Simon said.

"What kind?" Adeline asked. "Songs about Jesus?"

Simon's face coloured. "Not many, I wouldn't think."

"I wouldn't think so," Adeline said. "And the people you'd be travelling with! They wouldn't be Mannonites, I bet, or even Lutherans. Probably drunkards, smokers, drug-takers, card-players, *schlinjels* who take God's name in vain."

"They won't all be like that," Simon said. "There'll be decent folks in the bunch."

His mother shook her head. "I think you'd better stay home."

"I'm going, Mother. I've got my plane ticket."

Adeline shot me a look. "Make him stay, *Meyaalchye*. Tell him you need him."

"Simon's a grown man, Mother Epp. If he says he's going, he's going."

CHAPTER 57

Two weeks later, I was in the kitchen making Mennonite plum soup when Simon phoned from Chester, Nova Scotia.

"How're you doing?" I asked.

"Fine."

I glanced out the window at the girls playing in the sandbox. "How's the star parrot?"

"Callum? He's good," Simon said. "Probably asleep in the animal trailer by now." It was nine-thirty PM Nova Scotia time but only five-thirty in Saskatchewan.

"Do the audiences like him better now?"

"They enjoy his *schtick* about shapes and colours," Simon said. "We've fine-tuned that but I've gotta teach him some new songs. Opera doesn't go over like the organizers hoped it would."

"I'm not surprised," I said, adding cornstarch to the water in the saucepan. Simon wasn't crazy about opera himself. He'd only learned it to please Ross Forbes.

"How's Ross?" I asked, the name tasting bitter in my mouth.

"He's okay as far as I know. I haven't seen him since I got here."

"Thank goodness for that." As I mixed the starch with the water, I heard shouts on the other end of the phone line. "What's going on in that motel of yours?"

"A baseball team is staying on this floor. They're partying in the hallway."

"Hopefully they'll settle down soon," I said, measuring pitted plums into my soup.

"I hope so. The walls are thin."

As I set the saucepan on the stove, I heard thumping noises, then someone pounding on a drum or a garbage can. "Your motel doesn't sound very upscale. Can't the organizers afford something better?"

"They say we need to keep our belts tight until we develop a stronger cash flow."

"Have they paid you yet?" We were managing financially thanks to the loan from Wally but the money was disappearing fast.

"We're supposed to get our first cheques at the end of this week."

"Let's hope they come through." Simon would be four hundred dollars richer once they did. The marina had paid me three hundred when I delivered the quilt, but I'd need some of that for my trip to British Columbia, which I hadn't mentioned to Simon yet.

I filled my lungs with prairie air and blurted out my news: "I'm going to drive out to BC."

Silence except for the thumping and shouting in the hallway. "Why?" Simon asked. "You're not leaving me, are you?"

Did I detect an undertone of worry in his voice?

"How could I leave you, Sweetheart?" I stirred my soup. "You're not here for me to leave."

Out in the sandbox, the wind was whipping the girls' hair into their eyes and out again. The kids were playing with it, turning their faces toward it, then away and back again.

"What do you plan on doing in BC?" Simon asked.

"I'll visit my parents and sister first and then teach summer school at the college in Sage City. Embroidery, knitting, and crocheting. Valerie got me the job."

"You could stay home and teach needlework at the Lutheran Camp. I'm sure the Lutherans would love to have you."

"I'd be a volunteer with the Lutherans," I said. "The college pays seven dollars an hour plus room and board."

"Money isn't everything."

"No, but it's something, especially given our debt load. Anyway I'm looking forward to getting back to Sage City. It feels more like home to me than Dayspring."

"Dayspring is our home. We're married, remember?"

Did being married mean my husband should always decide where I lived and where I travelled? What about what I wanted? "You're not the man you were in Sage City."

My husband blew out a long breath. "Okay, I changed for the worse. I admit that. But I'm trying to do better. I haven't had a drink in three months. I finished two correspondence courses. And I'm working hard here, trying to boost our income. What more do you want?"

I wound the phone cord around my fingers, considering Simon's question. "I want a break from Dayspring."

"How long?" Simon asked over a background of drunken voices singing *Wasted Days and Wasted Nights*.

"A few weeks, maybe five."

Long silence from Simon though not from the hallway singers. "What about Emily and Norine?"

"Your mother wants to keep them at her house while I'm gone."

"What do you think?" Simon asked.

"They'd be better off with her than schlepping around the country with me."

"Your relatives will be disappointed about not seeing them."

"I'll take them another time." I appreciated Simon's concern but I couldn't take the girls to Vancouver on this trip. I just couldn't. My sister didn't have room for us, and staying in the house with my parents sapped my energy. Mom with her anxiety and pill-popping. Dad with his loud TV and long-winded stories.

"What do the girls want to do?" Simon asked. A door slammed in the background, then another.

"They're crazy about the idea of staying with your mother." Adeline was a good grandmother despite her lack of tact and humour. She was a capable person, confident, energetic, and entertaining—the opposite of my mother. The girls would be fine with her though I'd miss them.

"What about the budgies?"

"Your mother's willing to take them." Adeline didn't have bird-sitting experience but the girls would be happy to help and advise. Emily was already a proficient advisor at age four and a half. At the moment, she was overseeing the digging of a trench in the sandbox, with Norine doing the grunt work.

Simon yawned. "I should phone the office and ask them to quiet those guys down. I need to get up early tomorrow. Our bus leaves at seven-thirty." He stifled another yawn. "But about your trip. I'm worried about you driving all that way alone."

"You don't want me to see my family?"

"Of course I want you to see them but why not wait until I come home? We could load up the kids and go together."

"You'll be too tired then. And you'll need to get ready for teaching."

"I'd go with you anyway."

"That's good of you, Simon." I said, sweetening my plum soup with brown sugar. "Thanks but I really need some time on my own."

CHAPTER 58

Teaching at summer school in Sage City brought memories of Florian Bouchard rushing back. Our brief time together had opened windows in my soul. Ten months later, fresh breezes still blew in.

Florian and I had never visited the college campus together, but I pictured him strolling its sunlit paths, long-legged and loose-jointed. When I ate in the cafeteria, I wondered which tables Florian had sat at and what he had eaten. When I taught knitting, embroidery, and crocheting under the ponderosa pines and cottonwoods, I imagined him sitting under those same trees.

At the same time, I scolded myself for playing dangerous mind games—heart games.

My husband wrote to me and phoned. He sent chocolates and pink roses to my room in the college dormitory. Pink roses! Simon was courting me from the other end of the country. "Why so romantic all of a sudden?" I asked the next time he phoned. "Maybe you're seeing Ross and feeling guilty about it."

"Of course not. I miss you, Susie. I love you." His answer came too quickly to be convincing. Or was that my imagination? Without seeing his face, it was hard to tell.

Our daughters were doing well according to Adeline and according to Emily and Norine themselves. I phoned the girls every evening and enjoyed their accounts of playing with the kitties in the barn, helping Uncle Manfred milk the cows, gathering eggs in the hen-house, and picking raspberries with Oma. Adeline even took them to the Lutheran Camp, where they heard Bible stories and sang gospel choruses.

I didn't need to worry about my girls, though I missed them—their sweet weight in my lap, their kid-smell, their energy and innocence, the reflections of Simon and myself in their faces. Did the girls miss me? They said so though I suspected Adeline owned a significant portion of their loyalty. She was a natural with them. So was Simon when he wasn't drinking. I tried to be a good mother but I often felt like an actor following stage directions written for someone else. I hadn't received enough good mothering when I was growing up. Neither had Florian. He and I were alike in that way.

The pottery shop where he worked was only sixteen blocks from the college. I could easily drive there or take the bus.

Obviously that was a bad idea. I should push thoughts of the beautiful man to the back of my mind and focus on my teaching.

Maybe Florian would come and find me. Was he still interested? The only clue I had was the newspaper article about the quintessential woman with the slightly crossed eyes. But that had been written months ago.

He must realize I was in Sage City. The city wasn't that big, and the summer school had been widely advertised. My name appeared on posters in the library, coffee shops, and grocery stores. My picture was in the newspaper, along with those of the other teachers. Even if Florian regarded me as merely a friend and former co-worker, it would be polite of him to phone and say hello. I waited a week for his call.

Nothing.

Three days later, still nothing. Maybe he was out of town or married. Probably not married. Valerie would have heard about it and told me.

On the third Friday of summer school, the teachers and students planned to take a day-long hike into the mountains. They didn't really need me so I begged off.

After the hikers left, I French-braided my hair to make myself look more artsy, then put on my blue flowered dress. Its gathered bodice made the most of my meager bosom. I applied mascara to the lashes of my slightly crossed eyes and put on pearl-pink lipstick.

At nine in the morning, I took the bus downtown and spent fifteen minutes in a thrift store buying T-shirts and picture books for the girls. Florian's shop didn't open until ten so I wandered around for a while. It felt good to stroll those familiar streets again. Not much had changed since I'd left ten months earlier. Most of the shops were the same, selling clothing, jewellery, health food, specialty foods, and hand-crafted items.

Complementing this mix were restaurants and coffee shops, City Hall, the library, and several art galleries. The galleries didn't open until ten or eleven, but one of them displayed an out-of-date notice about an exhibition that included works by Sage City sculptor Florian Bouchard.

At ten o'clock I tidied my braids, powdered my nose, and freshened my lipstick. Then I headed up First Avenue toward the pottery shop. It was a yellow brick building with a green door and an ornamental parapet along the roofline. The window displayed a colourful variety of pottery—bowls, mugs, plates, and teapots. I peered inside but didn't see anyone.

I left the shop and walked around the block, marshalling my courage and gasping for breath because the streets were steep. Back in Dayspring, streets were flat. Walking there didn't automatically include cardiovascular workouts.

At ten-fifteen I returned to the yellow brick building, collected my wits, and eased the door open. As I stepped inside, a buzzer sounded. A moment later, Florian hurried into the shop through a back door. He jumped as if he'd stepped on a nail. "Susie, what a surprise!"

I gave him my little-girl look, chin down, eyes wide. "I happened to be passing by and thought I'd stop and say hello." He probably knew this was a lie.

Florian fingered the ceramic cross he wore over his smock. "I noticed your picture in the paper. How do you like teaching at the college?"

"It's good."

"Is your husband here? What about Emily and Norine?" Florian looked thinner than before. His jaw jutted out more.

"The girls are in Saskatchewan with their grandmother. Simon's in Nova Scotia touring with a band."

"So you're alone in Sage City."

I smiled. "Yes. I've been alone here almost three weeks unless you count Valerie and everyone else at summer school." I drew a careful breath. "I'm surprised you and I didn't bump into each other somewhere."

Florian tightened the leather thong that held his ponytail in place. "I tried to ensure that wouldn't happen." His voice sounded stiff and formal.

"Why?" I asked. "Didn't you want to see me? Too busy?" If he still cared for me, he would have found time.

"That's not it," he said with a bleak smile.

"Are you engaged?"

"No, not engaged, not married." He glanced toward the back door. "Sorry, Susie. You'll have to excuse me. I need to unload the kiln."

"I can wait."

He gave me a long look, his fingers tracing the outline of the cross on his chest. "No need for you to wait."

"So what do you expect me to do? Just leave?"

"Yes, I think leaving would be your best option."

I could hardly believe it. He was blowing me off like dandelion fuzz, after what we'd meant to each other.

Florian turned and headed toward the back door.

I hesitated a moment, then followed him.

The door was heavy. I struggled to open it, slipped through, and found myself in a large screened-in verandah. A ceramic kiln dominated the room. Several metal racks stood nearby. A laundry sink crouched in one corner. Pots of marigolds lined the windowsills.

Without a glance in my direction, Florian put on gloves, cracked the door of the kiln open, waited a few moments, and then opened the door wider. A wave of heat rolled out. I stepped into it, wanting to share it with him.

He nudged me away. "Careful. You don't want to get burned."

"I won't," I snapped. I narrowed my eyes against the heat, peering in at rows of pottery on shelves. Bowls, teapots, candle-holders, crucifixes, vases shaped like mermaids with wavy hair tumbling over their tails.

"Did you make any of those?" I asked.

"Nope." Florian nudged me away again, then reached into the kiln and removed a teapot made in the shape of a clock. "I don't do pottery." He rolled one of the racks closer and set the teapot on it.

"So who made them?"

"My boss and his daughters." A muscle in Florian's jaw jumped. "Susie, could you get out of my way, please?"

I retreated to the corner by the sink. "Are you still doing sculptures? I read about your *hypnotic eye* series." The series that might have been inspired by me, or might not have been.

Florian removed a blue pitcher from the kiln. Did his hand tremble or was that my imagination? "I've moved on from my *hypnotic eye* phase."

"Oh?"

"I've decided to do a modern-day depiction of Blessed Sibyllina Biscossi."

"Who?"

"She was a blind Italian saint who lived in the 1300s."

"That's a switch," I said.

"It is."

"You're kidding, right? You were kidding last time you talked about making religious sculptures."

"Nope, not kidding." Florian removed a mermaid vase from the kiln, flicked a bit of extra glaze off her tail, and set her on the rack. "I've changed since you saw me last."

"It would seem so." Ten months ago Florian was my charming bad boy, tempting me to break my marriage vows. Now he was…what?

Florian straightened the cross that hung around his neck. "I've returned to our Lord Jesus Christ."

I blinked. "Pardon me?"

"I've returned to our Lord, the Holy Catholic church, and the sacraments."

"Really?" Ten months ago I had refused Florian's advances because of my faith. Now suddenly he was the religious one.

"It would be a sin for me to come between you and your husband—" The buzzer sounded. "Excuse me." Florian turned and hurried into the shop. "May I help you?"

"Is Albert around?" A man's voice, Eastern European.

Florian closed the door on me.

I slumped against the sink. I should run away from temptation. Just slip into the back alley and disappear from Florian's life.

But it would be rude to run away without saying goodbye, wouldn't it? As I dithered, Florian burst back into the verandah. "Just what I need, more work." His voice rasped. "Tibor's Restaurant needs forty candle-holders by three-thirty. I've got to find them, pack them, pack all this other stuff, deliver the candle-holders, and then drive all the way to Salmon Arm."

"What's in Salmon Arm?"

"Artisan market tomorrow."

"Can I help you pack?"

"Nope." Florian removed a brown teapot from the kiln and set it on the rack with the other pottery.

I gathered up my purse and thrift-store bag. "I guess I should run along."

"Yes." Florian removed several mugs from the kiln. "You should."

"Okay," I said, trying to sound like my heart wasn't splitting in two. "I'll be on my way then."

Florian turned his back on me, fumbling with one of the mugs. Were his shoulders shaking?

"Are you all right?" I asked.

"I'm fine," he said in a strangled voice.

"Are you sure?"

"I don't want you to go."

His voice was so quiet, I didn't think I'd heard right. "Pardon me?" I held my breath, waiting for his answer.

"I said I don't want you to go."

I felt like a condemned prisoner pardoned at the last moment. "Why not?"

"Because I'm crazy about you."

Fireworks exploded in my heart.

"Albert's back," Florian said as a car rumbled into the alley. His next words tumbled out. "I'm booked into a hotel in Salmon Arm, the small one by the lake. Meet me there, would you? Six-thirty."

"What for?"

"Dinner, just dinner. We've got to talk."

"Right. Okay." I touched his arm, then turned and hurried through the door into the shop and out to the street.

CHAPTER 59

Florian Bouchard still loved me! Every nerve in my body tingled with delight. Adrenaline pushing me along, I set off on foot, heading for the college. I didn't have the patience to wait for the bus. My breath came in fast gasps, more from the joy of knowing Florian loved me than from walking uphill. I caught my reflection in the window of a record store. I was an ordinary-looking woman, so ordinary, and one of my braids had come loose. How could Florian love me? It was a miracle.

No, probably not. Miracles are extraordinary events caused by the power of God. God wouldn't inspire Florian to love a married woman.

I could still meet him for dinner though. That wouldn't be so terrible. The hotel restaurant was always busy. There would be lots of people there, maybe including people who knew Florian and me. They would expect us to act like friends and former co-workers, nothing more.

Of course I wouldn't climb those red-carpeted stairs to Florian's room, even if he begged me to. I was strong enough to resist. I had principles though the thought of his elegant hands on—

No, I needed to get hold of myself.

I rounded the corner near the gym, puffing with exertion. The route to the college was mostly uphill. But the street became flatter as it approached the Roman Catholic Cathedral. It was a solid structure—red-brick walls, stained glass windows, round bell tower—an anchor for souls. Florian lived just a few blocks away. This was probably where he dipped his fingers in holy water, crossed himself, knelt in prayer, and confessed his sins. It would be sinful to tempt him to betray his conscience.

If only I'd met Florian before I met Simon! But in 1970, Florian was still in high school. He would probably have considered me too old for him. By October of that year, it was too late. I was married to Simon, rushed to the altar by his mother's meddling and my fear of becoming a perennial wallflower.

No, that wasn't fair. I'd been in love with Simon when we got married. I still loved him in a quiet, non-explosive way. But I'd been naïve when I walked the aisle, short on parental guidance. I hardly knew my own mind. Maybe I didn't give my consent freely enough. If that was the case, it might be possible to prove that my marriage was invalid. Perhaps it could be annulled. From what I'd heard, annulment and remarriage were acceptable in the Catholic church under certain circumstances.

The Catholic bookstore might have books that dealt with such matters. I crossed the street to the little white building and peered through the window. Bibles, prayer books, rosaries, crucifixes, statue of the Virgin Mary holding Baby Jesus, statue of Saint Francis with birds. Statues of other folks I assumed were saints.

I lingered outside, afraid to go in. Was I supposed to cross myself as I passed the statues? I wouldn't want to call attention to myself by breaking any rules. What if someone spoke to me, asking my opinion of Pope Paul VI's latest pronouncement on something? Should I pretend to be a Catholic? No, I couldn't carry that off. Maybe I could say I was interested in becoming a Catholic.

Actually I might convert if Florian wanted me to.

No, I couldn't do that. Converting would mean giving up the Mennonite faith that had been my family's refuge and support for generations. The prospect of leaving it felt like an icicle jabbing at my heart. I shuddered, left the window, and hurried away from the bookstore.

On the other hand, maybe converting was part of the price I needed to pay for spending the rest of my life with Florian. Could I do that? I wondered, trudging along the sidewalk past flower gardens and neatly painted houses. What would happen to my children if I left their father for Florian? I'd want the girls to live with me but that would be tricky. Simon and Adeline wouldn't willingly let them go. What did other people do in situations like mine? What did Catholics do? My footsteps slowing, I returned to the bookstore.

As I hesitated in front of the door, footsteps clomped up behind me. "Excuse me." A heavyset man led a pot-bellied dog around me. The man clomped inside, not crossing himself. I dithered for a few moments, then followed him.

The store smelled of candle wax. A canned voice sang, "Where charity and love are, God is there." The woman behind the counter (brown skin, torrent of black curls) leaned on her elbows, talking to the heavyset man.

His dog lurched toward me. The man yanked its leash and the animal backed off, giving me a malevolent glare.

The bookshelves were arranged in rows at right angles to the counter. Scanning them, I found a section called MARRIAGE AND FAMILY. A beige book was turned face-out. It bore the catchy title *Your Marriage Is a Sign of Christ's Love for the Church*.

Right. What did that mean in practical terms? If a wife believed in Christ's love for His church, leaving her marriage would be like leaving Christ? No, that was probably too extreme an interpretation. What if her husband was unfaithful, or beat her and drank their money away? How could that marriage be a sign of Christ's love for the church? How many men were Christ-like enough to qualify? How many women were church-like enough?

I flipped through the book, reading at random. *Marriage shows the world God's unconditional love because a couple are willing to grapple with any difficulties and remain united.*

How many couples were willing in this day and age? Even Protestant pastors got divorced and remarried. If they found their marriages unfulfilling, they moved on and presumably continued to serve God.

Our Saviour, spouse of the church, gives Christian spouses strength to forgive each other, bear each other's burdens, and be subject to each other out of reverence for Him.

Admirable ideals but this was 1976. People followed their hearts, pursued their dreams, and strove to realize their potentials.

I flipped to the index, looking for something about annulment. Ah, there it was, several pages. I bought the book, put it in my bag with the T-shirts and picture books for my kids, and left the store under the dog's watchful gaze.

Back in my room at the college, I ate a slice of rye bread with peanut butter, brewed a pot of tea, and settled into the armchair. I was reading about annulment when the phone rang.

I reached over to the desk and grabbed it. "Hello?"

"I'm glad I caught you." Simon sounded breathless. I heard a hum of conversation in the background.

"Where are you?" I asked, setting the book on the desk.

"I'm in a motel lobby in Moncton, waiting for the bus to Halifax."

"Halifax? I thought you and the band planned to be in New Brunswick for another week."

"We did," Simon said, "but Ziggy Belinski had to quit early—family emergency. The rest of the venues we'd booked don't want us without our star attraction."

"That's too bad." A siren wailed on Simon's end of the line. "Will you get paid for that week anyway?" Four hundred dollars was a lot of money to lose.

"Unfortunately we won't but the organizers have offered us a travel bonus. They've arranged to fly us anywhere we want, up to a maximum of four thousand miles, and then home again."

"That's good of them. You could take the opportunity to visit your cousins in Winnipeg or your friends in Whitehorse."

"I'm not crazy about going to Winnipeg or Whitehorse. I'd rather see you."

"What's your hurry? We'll be together at home soon enough." Maybe too soon.

He raised his voice as a vehicle clattered past. "I want to spend some time in Sage City anyway."

"What for?"

"Don't you want to see me, Susie?" Simon sounded like a disappointed child.

Something clogged my throat. I swallowed. "This isn't a good time."

"Why not? I can entertain myself while you work. We'll have our evenings together. And nights."

"The bed in my room isn't big enough for both of us." How could I sleep with Simon while making plans to leave him? It would be the height of hypocrisy.

"We can stay with Jake and Nettie Petkau. They invited us. They have a spare room."

"I don't want to impose on the Petkaus," I said. "Anyway I like my room here."

"We wouldn't be imposing. Their daughter gave them a parrot but they're having trouble with it. They want me to help settle it down."

"So that's what this is about, a parrot?"

"Not primarily, no."

Simon sounded hurt but I almost didn't care. I suggested he fly somewhere exotic like Barbados, Iceland, or Portugal.

"I'd rather see you," he said. "Listen, I've gotta go. I'm on a pay phone. Somebody else wants to use it."

"Okay, 'bye."

"Hold on. Do you have a pen? My plane is due in Sage City at five-forty Monday afternoon, flight 568. Can you pick me up?"

"I guess so." Maybe by Monday I'd have some news about Florian and me. I jotted down Simon's arrival time and flight number, said goodbye, and replaced the phone receiver.

CHAPTER 60

By five o'clock that afternoon, I was driving east out of Sage City, my heart singing with anticipation. In an hour and a half, I'd be in Salmon Arm sitting across a restaurant table from Florian Bouchard.

I wore my grey silk dress with the puffed sleeves, sweetheart neckline, and sash tied in a bow at the back. My mother-in-law called it my Sunday School dress. She was making dresses like it for Emily and Norine but not out of silk. She'd found a blue polyester print in a thrift store. Cheaper and more practical.

Adeline realized I could do a better job of making those dresses. She'd said as much but she barged ahead anyway. Nothing held that woman back. I disliked her pushiness but I had to admit she was a positive influence on my girls. She was a strong person, confident, warm, and consistent—a rock to build one's character on. If only I'd had a rock like that when I was growing up! Not exactly like Adeline but someone with her better qualities.

My mother was shifting sand, afraid of everything. My father was braver. But when I was growing up, he was often away working in lumber camps—washing dishes or cooking. A less sensitive child might not have faltered but I grew up anxious and insecure.

I winced, thinking of the emotional insecurity I was probably communicating to my daughters. By contrast Adeline projected non-stop confidence. If I left Simon for Florian, the girls might not see her very often. Hopefully I could compensate by giving them a happier mother and a lively young stepfather.

I powered the car up a hill, leaving the grasslands behind and entering a pine forest. Actually Florian might not consider a long-term relationship with me. It was one thing to be crazy about a person and quite another to work through the logistics of starting a life together. Accomplishing that would take time, something we didn't have much of. Simon was due to arrive in three days.

A deer bolted out of the trees—a caramel-coloured doe with two fawns, darker brown with white spots. I slowed to see if mother and babies would cross the highway. When they didn't I resumed my speed, my mind racing ahead to Simon arriving at the airport. He'd be wearing a necktie, having kept it in his briefcase and tied it on just before landing. His hair would be neatly combed to cover the thinning area on the top of his head.

Poor old Simon. He'd be fretting over what I'd said on the phone, hoping my attitude had changed in the meantime. He'd be looking forward to hearing about my adventures and telling me his. And making love to me.

How could I tell my husband I was in love with someone else? What if the revelation plunged him back into depression and drinking?

What did God want me to do? I was afraid to ask. Deep down, I knew I should take the high road: Rededicate myself to my marriage and try to work through the problems with Simon until we reached a point where *our union reflected the fidelity of Christ to his church,* in the words of the Catholic book.

But that seemed unrealistic given my situation. My heart and body cried out for Florian. Dreams of his arms around me set off rockets in my mind. As Florian's woman, I could leave my boring self behind and soar to new heights. I'd achieve things I'd never thought possible. He and I would achieve them together. Maybe we'd start a new business, or a charity for disadvantaged children.

I'd never entertained such thoughts about Simon, even when our love was new. Simon was a harbour, not a launching pad. He wasn't even a safe harbour, as it turned out.

The road leveled off and passed several farms, one with an old-fashioned windmill like the one on Simon's brother's farm. Before long I was rolling into the pretty little city of Salmon Arm. With fifteen minutes to spare, I followed the street that led to the waterfront hotel where Florian had suggested I meet him. As I parked in the lot, I noticed a van with a gold and brown sign: *ALBERT COOMBS & DAUGHTERS, POTTERS.*

That must be the vehicle Florian was driving though I didn't see him. He was probably in the restaurant, holding a table for us. The parking lot was almost full so the restaurant might be the same. Three couples walked past my car, the women short-stepping in long skirts, the men sauntering along in jeans and cowboy shirts. One wore a bolo tie.

I drummed my fingers on the steering wheel, remembering a song I'd learned in school: *Once to every man and nation, comes the moment to decide.*

Once to every woman too, presumably. This was my moment to decide. Would I stay true to my wedding vows or follow my heart? Florian was the scarier option, assuming he was an option at all. Maybe once we discussed the hurdles we'd need to clear, he'd back away. Or maybe I would.

I checked my watch. Six thirty-five. I was now five minutes late for our date. I sat in the car for a few moments, watching candles flicker in the restaurant windows. Then I slipped out of the driver's seat, locked the car, and hurried across the street to a florist shop I'd noticed when I arrived.

A beanpole of a woman in her sixties stood outside, locking the door. Her greying hair hung in a ponytail down her back.

"Just a minute," I called, trotting toward her. "Do you have a minute?"

A frown creased her forehead. "I've gotta get home. My husband is barbecuing."

"This won't take long. It's important." I hurried to the shop window and peered in. "What flowers do you have?"

"Almost nothing until tomorrow."

"You must have something. What about those chrysanthemums?" They looked too ordinary but they might have to do.

She sighed and opened the door. I followed her inside. "Do you have a card I can write on?"

She slid one along the counter toward me, along with a pen.

I removed the cap from the pen, wondering what to write.

Mrs. Beanpole was wrapping the chrysanthemums, her movements quick and impatient. Would she have been more sympathetic if she'd known that the rest of my life hung in the balance? I tried the pen on my hand, then turned the card over and wrote, *Go with God, Florian.* I thought for a moment, then added, *Soar like an eagle. Love from Susie Rempel Epp.*

I fumbled the card into the envelope, wrote Florian Bouchard on the outside, and handed it to Mrs. Beanpole. "I assume you deliver."

"Not this late. Tomorrow."

"Please. The flowers are for a man named Florian Bouchard. A good-looking young man. He's in the restaurant just across the parking lot. Tall guy with long blond hair."

She frowned at me like I was a dandelion or a stinkweed. "Why don't you deliver the mums yourself? Your leg's not broken."

"No, please. I can't do it." If I saw Florian, I'd drown in his eyes. I took my wallet out of my purse. "How much?"

"Ten dollars delivered. Five dollars not."

"Five dollars is too much just to walk across the parking lot."

She wiggled an eyebrow. "Suit yourself."

I handed her a ten, followed her out of the shop, and escaped to my car. Watching her lollop across to the restaurant, I wondered what Florian would think when he saw my card. Would he be disappointed? Relieved? Embarrassed to be seen receiving flowers? Maybe he'd come looking for me.

I couldn't let him find me. My lofty resolutions would evaporate at the mere sight of him. I started the car and gunned it out of the lot. As I set off along the road to Sage City, I felt light-headed with relief and resignation. In a small town along the way, Sorrento, I stopped and ate a hamburger in a greasy-spoon restaurant. Lots of raw onions.

CHAPTER 61

On Simon's first evening in Sage City, we went for a walk beside the river. Feeling awkward and out of sync with my husband, I left the space between us as wide as I could without leaving the path. Did he notice? I almost didn't care if he did or didn't.

Simon talked. I listened with half an ear, absent-mindedly watching a squirrel scamper up a tree.

"Treble clef," Simon was saying. "Lyrics...vibrato...brass instruments...audience participation."

I nodded occasionally, making listening sounds. *Uh huh. Yeah. Mmm.*

He droned on. "Band members...better organization...Dayspring."

At the word Dayspring, I jerked my head around. "What'd you say?"

"I said maybe you'd like Dayspring better if we had a better house."

Where had that come from? "We can hardly pay the rent on the house we've got."

Simon reached for my hand, bridging the gap between us. "Manfred said he might give us his cabin."

"Really?" Simon's brother had lived in that cabin for as long as I'd known him.

"He's buying a double-wide trailer. He won't need the cabin anymore."

I pulled my hand out of my husband's. "I don't want to live way out there in the boondocks." So close to Simon's mother.

"Of course we wouldn't live there. We'd move the cabin onto our yard and attach it to our house."

"Would we be allowed to do that? It's Ross's house."

"It's okay with him."

"What? You phoned him and asked?"

Simon kicked a stone along the path. "No, we talked about it on our way to the airport."

I stopped short. "I thought you weren't seeing that man anymore. You promised you wouldn't."

Simon stopped beside me, rocking on his feet like a boxer waiting to go into the ring. "What would you want me to do? Waste money taking a taxi when I could catch a ride with Ross? He was going to the airport anyway, taking other people."

I jammed my hands into my pockets. "Did you ride in the front with Ross or in the back?"

"That's a childish question. Look, Susie, I don't want us to fight. I came here excited about spending time with you. And what do you do? Right away, you start dragging me down with your suspicion and small-mindedness."

I drew a frustrated breath. "I don't mean to drag you down. I'm just trying to be honest. I'm telling you how I feel so we can work through our problems." That was what the Catholic book advised. So far, it didn't seem to be working.

Simon hooked his thumbs into his belt loops. "Just because we're married, that shouldn't mean I'm not allowed to have any friends, or any freedom."

"I like freedom too." I could have flown away with my butterfly, Florian Bouchard, maybe. What would Simon think if he knew that?

"You've got freedom," Simon snapped. "You're in your precious Sage City; you've got our car; you have work you enjoy. You've got your own room, where I'm not permitted to sleep."

"Simon, please, not so loud." A tan-skinned couple were approaching us on the path. They walked arm in arm, casting furtive looks our way—she in a yellow sari, he in a dark suit.

After the couple passed, I said, "I didn't mean you couldn't sleep in my room. I just said the bed is too small for both of us."

Simon gave me a sad smile. "I should have gone to Winnipeg or Whitehorse or Barbados. I would have had a better time."

"You don't mean that. You're just tired." I'd burned my bridges with Florian; I should try harder to make my marriage work. I took Simon's arm. "Come on, let's go to my room." I arched an eyebrow. "I want to show you my embroidery."

"Anything else?" he asked, grumpy but interested.

"We'll see when we get there."

The pink roses Simon had sent me still looked nice, having dried themselves in their vase. As I leaned over to sniff them, Simon leaned in beside me until we stood so close that we were breathing each other's breaths. "I missed you," he whispered, turning my head so our lips met.

Following Simon's lead, I removed his clothes as he removed mine. We made love on the floor; the bed really was too small. Afterwards we took a shower together. Then Simon got dressed, kissed me goodbye, and went to sleep at the Petkaus' house.

I crawled into my little bed smelling of soap and wondering how my husband and I could have talked so much, made love, showered together, and solved so little.

CHAPTER 62

The following afternoon when I returned from teaching, Simon was in my room fiddling with the radio, which seldom worked. On the desk beside the pink roses stood a vase of yellow ones, plump and fresh. "They're gorgeous," I said, leaning over to smell them. "But you shouldn't have."

"I didn't," Simon said, setting the radio on the desk.

"What?"

"I didn't buy those roses."

"Really? Then who did?" Maybe Valerie or one of my students.

Simon shrugged. "I have no idea. A florist delivered them half an hour ago."

"Is there a card?"

He handed me a sealed envelope.

I opened it. Pulling out the card, I immediately recognizing Florian's elegant handwriting. *To Susie, my quintessential woman. Have a wonderful life. I pray for you and your family, a rosary a day. FB*

I pushed the card back into the envelope, trying to look nonchalant though my hand shook.

Simon reached for the envelope.

With a playful grin, I batted his hand away.

"Why can't I read it?"

"It's not from anybody you know."

"I think you have a secret admirer," he said in the teasing voice he sometimes used with the kids.

"Not that I know of." I had an admirer but he wasn't a secret, not to me.

"Come on." Simon crooked a beckoning finger. "Let me see."

I hid the envelope behind my back, then reconsidered. What would be so terrible about letting Simon know he wasn't the only star in my sky? I wasn't the only one in his. I gave him the envelope.

He pulled out the card, stared at it for a long moment, and slumped into the armchair, his head sagging. Out in the street, a siren wailed. Children shouted. A motorcycle roared past.

Finally my husband raised his head. "Who is FB?" His voice sounded as flat as the Saskatchewan prairie and as sad as a hailed-out crop.

"A friend." I clasped my hands behind my back. "A friend who's praying for us." Maybe Florian was praying right now. I pictured his elegant fingers gliding over ceramic rosary beads.

Simon bunched his fists, his thick knuckles whitening. "What's his name? Where does he live?"

"I can't tell you."

"Is he a priest? I hope not if you're his quintessential woman." Sarcasm dripped off the sadness in Simon's voice.

"No, not a priest."

Simon clenched and unclenched his fists. "What's involved in being someone's quintessential woman?"

"It means." I cleared my throat. "It means he's in love with me."

"Have you slept with him?"

"No."

"Do you love him?" Simon's eyes were so full of pain, I couldn't look at him. What could I say? That FB was a love-struck swain whose advances I had rebuffed? No, I couldn't bear to cast Florian in that light. "I love him," I whispered, my voice a scratch in my throat. "But I let him go."

"You let him go?" Simon said in his flat-prairie voice.

I nodded.

"Because of me?"

"Yes, because of you and our girls and your mother and your brothers and the promises I made before God and the church."

Simon managed a wistful smile. "So we're a package deal."

I nodded, slumping down on the bed. "Too big a package to give up."

"Heavy?"

"Sometimes."

The skin under Simon's eyes quivered. "Do you love me?"

What could I say? I loved him like an old pair of slippers. I loved him for marrying me when I couldn't get a date with anybody else. I loved him for giving me two beautiful children.

"Do you love me?" my husband asked again. He looked like a ghost of the Simon Epp I knew.

"Yes, I love you."

"More than you love FB?"

My face warmed. "My feelings for him and you are two different things. Anyway I told you. He's out of my life, gone."

"Not far enough if he's sending you roses. What kind of a turkey is he? Does he know you're married?"

"Of course he knows. That's the point. He sent the flowers to show he plans to stay out of my life."

"But not out of your heart."

"He has no control over what goes on in my heart." Neither did Simon.

"Who is this turkey?"

I said nothing. Telling Simon would diminish Florian, make him seem ordinary. He wasn't. He was thrilling, enchanting, magical as a unicorn. And he was praying for us, his prayers building a wall around a forbidden garden, rosary bead by bead.

Simon grabbed Florian's yellow roses and yanked them out of their vase. As he jammed them head-first into the wastebasket, thorns ripped his fingers.

"That was a childish thing to do," I said, watching the blood blob up.

He gave me a look that could strip paint. With a snarl weakening to a whimper, he turned the basket of roses upside down, gave it a kick, and headed for the door, leaving a trail of blood drops on the carpet.

I took a few tissues from the box on the desk. "Here." I caught up with him, pressing the tissues into his hand.

He jerked them away from me and stormed out, slamming the door behind him. The impact shook my little room.

After Simon left, I paced the floor—up, down, and sideways—avoiding the blood in the carpet and agonizing over what to do. Should I phone the Petkaus and ask them to make sure Simon was okay? No, they'd ask awkward questions. Anyway Simon might not go to the Petkaus. More likely he'd head for the nearest bar or liquor store. Should I go out and look for him? No, that would upset him even more. Better to leave him alone for now.

I spent the rest of that evening pacing, praying, crying until I exhausted myself and fell into a troubled sleep.

The following evening as I washed the blood out of the carpet, a card slid under the door. Simon's handwriting was big, blocky, and sober-looking.

Susie, I'm going to try to be a better husband. Going to finish my degree and get a proper job. Not going to drink again. Not going to see Ross anymore. I hope to make you glad you picked me over FB. Love, SE.

CHAPTER 63

The metallic buzzing of grasshoppers whirred in through our kitchen window. Out on the road, a grain truck rumbled by, hauling wheat to the elevators near the railway tracks. As the dust settled, a smaller truck passed—a blue pickup with cream cans in the box, standing side by side like big-eared soldiers.

Simon and I were back in our house near Dayspring, Saskatchewan. We'd spent the past week with the Petkaus in Sage City, working on our marriage and hopefully making progress.

Simon's mother, Adeline, had brought our daughters over, and was making oatmeal cookies. I sat at the kitchen table writing checks to pay the bills that had arrived while Simon and I were away. He was unpacking the portable organ that he'd arranged to have shipped from Halifax.

"Daddy," Emily asked, "is this organ for me and Emily?" It was a snazzy-looking instrument, chrome with red trim.

Norine grinned at her reflection in its shiny surface.

"It's for all of us," Simon said. "One of the band members sold it to me." He glanced at me. "For a surprisingly low price."

Was that price lower or higher than our water and sewer bill? I wondered, having just paid it. Simon wasn't as frugal as I was.

Adeline tossed a handful of raisins into her cookie dough, scrunched her mouth to one side, and tossed in another handful. "That was nice from him," she said, grabbing a wooden spoon.

"Her actually," Simon said.

"Her?" Adeline's spoon stopped in mid-air.

Simon winked at his mother. "The fire-eating lady." This lady was an invented character in the stories he'd been telling the girls.

"Yuck!" Emily crossed her arms over her five-year-old chest. "I'm not touching a fire-eating lady's organ." She frowned at the keys.

Simon shrugged. "So your sister will learn to play and you won't." He took Norine's right hand and set her index finger on the white key in the centre of the keyboard. "This is middle C."

Norine regarded him with solemn Simon-like eyes.

"Like in the ABC song," he said.

Emily crowded in beside her sister. "Norine doesn't know that song as good as I do." She perched her hands on her hips and sang, "ABCDEFGHIJKLMNOP—"

"You have a nice voice, Emily," Simon said. "It's a pity you don't want to learn to play the organ."

She wrinkled her nose. "I do but—"

"Don't worry. The fire-eating lady is a joke. Actually I bought this organ from a performing monkey."

Emily squinted at him. "That's a joke too. Right, Daddy?"

"Right. Here, give me your hand."

I left my bill-paying to watch the lesson. Simon placed Emily's thumb and middle finger on the E and G above middle C. "Okay." He repositioned Norine's finger. "I'm going to say *one, two, three, go.* When I say *go,* both of you hit your keys."

The first try didn't work because Norine's finger slipped off. However, the second attempt produced a passable chord.

"Good," Simon said. "Stay right there." He scooted around to the lower end of the keyboard. "I'm going to play a song down here. Whenever I nod my head like this, you hit your keys."

He played *Yankee Doodle Dandy,* signaling the timing for the girls.

When the song had galloped to a finish, I applauded though Adeline's face was stiff with disapproval.

"Can we play it again?" Emily asked.

"Okay," Simon said, "but this time—"

Adeline banged a cookie sheet down on the counter. "Why can't you teach the girls a Christian song once? What's *Yankee Doodle?* Just foolishness."

"It's fun, Mother," Simon said through clenched teeth. He grabbed the organ's cover and threw it over the instrument.

Emily glanced from her father to her grandma. "Could you leave it open, Daddy? Please?"

"We'll play it later," Simon said, zipping the cover shut. "After Mrs. Killjoy goes home."

Adeline scowled at him. "That's no way to talk about your poor old *mutta*."

"I'm sorry, I guess." Simon stomped over to the refrigerator and scooped his sunglasses off the top of it. "I just wish you weren't such a spoilsport. I wish you could—"

"I'm trying to learn your kids to be good Christians."

Simon jammed his sunglasses onto his face. "Some Christians actually enjoy life. It doesn't need to be all doom and duty." He turned and stomped out through the lean-to.

The girls glanced at each other, then scampered after their father.

From out in the yard came the squeal of the metal shed-door. Moments later, the lawnmower coughed, coughed again, and then vroomed into puttering mode. Adeline and I watched through the window as Simon began mowing the grass around and between the clumps of sagebrush and rabbitbrush. The girls leapt after him, dodging grasshoppers.

Adeline's sigh ended in a whine. "I wish he'd try to be a better influence on those *kjinja*."

"I think he's wonderful with the kids," I said. "They have fun with him and he's a great teacher."

"Na yo." Adeline clumped over to the oven and slid in a couple of panfulls of cookies.

"I'll get the laundry started," I said. "Then maybe we can take some cookies out to Simon and the girls."

She grunted.

As I threw a load of shirts and T-shirts into the washing machine, I prayed for a brighter future for my family. Simon and I had made some progress in sorting out our relationship. I had recommitted myself to the marriage and resolved to stop thinking about Florian. Simon had made important promises and put them in writing: *I'm going to finish my degree and get a proper job. Not going to drink again. Not going to see Ross anymore.*

As for my mother-in-law, she would probably never change but she had her good points. And she meant well, presumably.

CHAPTER 64

S*eventeen years later*

Dayspring Chronicle, August 23, 1993

Best wishes to Emily and Norine Epp, who recently left Dayspring for Whitehorse, Yukon, where Emily will teach in an elementary school and Norine will continue her college education.

The Epp sisters will also help with young people's meetings in a local Baptist church. Emily's organizational abilities will be an asset in this venture. Norine, whose musical abilities are well known, will undoubtedly find many opportunities to put them to use.

Emily, 22, and Norine, 19, are the daughters of Simon and Susie Epp of Dayspring. Simon teaches in Dayspring and spends his summers touring the Atlantic provinces with a band called The Wylde Atlantick. Susie works as a professional quilt-maker and part-time school secretary.

A farewell service for Emily and Norine was held in the Mennonite church near the home of the girls' paternal grandmother, Adeline Epp. She gave the girls each a smoked sausage, a pail of peppermint cookies, and a German New Testament. Adeline said, "I don't want my grand-girls forgetting their roots halfway up to the North Pole there."

I sat at my kitchen table reading and rereading the newspaper article, my heart swelling with pride. Simon and I had such adventuresome, ambitious daughters. They looked wonderful in the newspaper picture. Emily in her tailored suit, narrow-faced and serious. Norine in a flowered dress, placid and pleasantly plump.

I closed my kitchen curtains against the morning heat, returned to the table, and cut the article out of the paper. I opened my scrapbook, flipped to the most recent photo of Simon singing with The Wylde Atlantick, and glued the article about our girls underneath it.

Simon's birds kept me company with their squawking and chirping. About twenty of them—budgies, cockatoos, mynahs, and parrots—lived in the bird-room across the hall from the kitchen. That room was part of the addition we had built after we bought the house from Ross.

The door between the bird-room and the hall was usually closed. That morning, it wasn't. The birds' caretaker, Penny, had left it open during her visit earlier in the day. She had also switched on the fan in the hallway. The birds needed the breeze from that fan. So did I. The kitchen felt like a sauna already and it was only ten-thirty. I got a pitcher out of the cupboard, dumped ice cubes in, and ran cold water over them. I was slicing a lemon to add when the doorbell rang.

I left my lemon, went to the door, and found Torben from the grocery store standing on the porch. A grin lit his rag-doll face. He offered me a twitchy bow, perspiration beading his forehead. "Roses for Mrs. Epp." He handed me a cellophane-wrapped vase of red roses.

"Thank you, Torben." Dayspring didn't have a flower shop but a florist in Moose Jaw filled orders via the grocery truck. When they arrived at Torben's store, he usually delivered them himself. "I bet they're from your hubby," he said with a wink. "I guess he's tired of sleepin' alone."

"I guess so." I took the vase from Torben. "Thanks again." I gave him a tip, said goodbye, and watched his van drive away.

Back in the kitchen, I set the roses on the table, removed the cellophane wrapping, took out the card, and read. *My dear Susie, I can hardly wait to see you. Only two more weeks. Love, Simon.*

I smiled, thinking how sweet it was of my husband to send roses. This wasn't a special occasion as far as I knew, except maybe the hottest day of the year. As I was adding more water to the vase, the phone rang. I grabbed the receiver. "Hello?"

"'Allo, Mrs. Epp?" A woman's voice, French accent. "Susie Epp?"

"Yes."

"Zis is Constable Mina Gaudet. I'm wiz ze RCMP in Moncton, New Brunswick."

My heart thumped against my ribs. Why would the Moncton police call me? Was something wrong with Simon?

"Mrs. Epp, are you zer?"

"I'm here."

"You are sitting down, Mrs. Epp?"

"Yes." I sank onto a kitchen chair.

"I'm sorry," Constable Gaudet said. "I 'ave bad news. Your 'usband, Simon, 'e 'ad a 'eart attack."

"What?" I gasped for breath despite the breeze from the fan. "Is he okay?"

Constable Gaudet said something I couldn't hear over the fan and the squawking of Simon's birds. "Just a minute." I stumbled into the hallway and turned off the fan. After shutting the door on the birds, I returned to the kitchen and picked up the receiver again. "What did you say?"

"I'm sorry—" Her voice wavered. "Your 'usband, 'e didn't make it."

"No. Please, God, no." My heart left my body and struggled up to the ceiling. The constable was still talking. I heard her words but I couldn't latch onto their meaning. "What did you say?" I asked again, watching drops of condensation run down my pitcher of water. The butter was melting in its dish on the counter.

"I said I'm sorry for your loss."

"Yes. Of course. Thank you." My heart was a fluttering sparrow. A blind sparrow with a broken wing.

"Is somebody zer wiz you?"

"No." Only the birds though I could barely hear their chirping and squawking through the closed door.

"Should I phone somebody to come over?"

"No...I just...I don't know...not now...but thanks anyway."

"All right, I can give you contact information for ze funeral 'ome in Moncton. Dey can 'ave Mr. Epp flown to someplace near you."

"Just a minute. You're going too fast for me. Can you tell me where my husband died? He was touring with a band called The Wylde Atlantick."

"'E was rehearsing, according to Mr. Forbes."

"Mr....Forbes?" What did Ross Forbes have to do with this? Simon hadn't seen him in years. He'd promised not to see him.

"Ross Forbes was ze gentleman who phoned us. 'E said he brought your 'usband some sheet music from 'alifax. Dey were singing it when your 'usband collapsed on ze bed."

"What bed?"

"In Mr. Forbes's 'otel room."

My husband had died in Ross's bed? No. How could he do that to me?

Constable Gaudet burbled on. "Mr. Forbes did everything 'e could. 'E phoned a doctor and ze ambulance. 'E did mouth-to-mouth resuscitation."

Mouth-to-mouth. I pictured Ross bending over my sweetheart, bestowing a *kiss of life* that didn't save his life. Poor Simon. Dear God, why did you let him die? He was only forty-nine years old.

The constable cleared her throat. "Would you be interested to speak to 'im?"

"Who? Simon?" Yes, I wanted to speak to him. I had questions.

"Mr. Forbes. 'E's just down the 'all."

"No, please." Ross was the last person I wanted to speak to. I didn't want his sympathy. I didn't even want to hear his voice.

There was a burst of static from the phone, then Constable Gaudet's voice again. "Should I phone somebody else wid information about ze funeral 'ome? Maybe a priest or—"

"No, you can give it to me." She might as well. I couldn't possibly feel any worse.

Constable Gaudet read out a phone number. I wrote it down with a hand that didn't want to work for me.

After I hung up, I sat staring at the number. I picked up the phone and stabbed a finger at the first digit, then the second, then let my hand drop. I couldn't dial that number, couldn't bear to talk to a stranger about Simon. He had been warm and strong last time I'd seen him. Now he lay cold and lifeless in a funeral home two thousand miles away.

I should phone Simon's mother and my daughters in Whitehorse, poor darlings. How would they take the news that their father had gone to be with Jesus?

Was Simon in fact with Jesus? Maybe not if he'd broken his marriage vows. If Simon had died with that sin on his conscience, where was his soul? Was it on a bus to heaven?

Mennonite theology didn't include praying for the dead but I said a prayer for him anyway. With the Amen still on my lips, I sagged lower on my chair. Lower and lower. "Simon, how could you die? In Ross's bed?" I slumped onto the floor like a sack of turnips. "Talk to me. Say something."

Nothing.

I lay on the floor for I didn't know how long. Finally I hauled myself to my feet. Through a haze of dizziness, Simon's roses caught my eye, taunting me with their beauty.

I didn't want that two-timer's roses. Not in my kitchen or anywhere in my house. I grabbed them by their vase and stumbled outside. My legs shaking, I carried the flowers down the driveway like a bride. But no bridegroom waited at the end of the driveway, just a gravel road and the glaring prairie sky.

A pickup truck approached from the south, the driver slowing. He was one of the Larson twins—I could never tell them apart. Maybe he thought I needed help. I did but not from him. I waved him on and tottered down into the ditch with my roses. Dusty grass and weeds tangled themselves around my feet. I tripped, regained my balance, and dumped the bouquet into a clump of chickweed near the culvert. Grasshoppers bounced into the air like drops of oil from a hot frying pan.

Some of the grasshoppers settled on my roses, some off. The heat was a woolly blanket that felt suffocating. I lifted the vase to smash it on the culvert, then reconsidered. Broken glass would be dangerous to local children who roamed the ditches looking for beer bottles and cans to sell. I left the vase beside the roses, clambered up out of the ditch, and dragged myself back to the house.

In my stifling kitchen, I threw more ice into the pitcher, cut the lemon into it, and carried it into the bedroom with a glass. I switched on the window air-conditioner and picked up the portable phone to start making bad-news calls. "I'm sorry to tell you this but Simon, your son/ father/ brother/ cousin/ friend/ soloist/ choir leader/ colleague had a heart attack. No, I'm sorry. He didn't make it."

CHAPTER 65

According to the clock by my bed, it was six-thirty, time for supper. I dragged myself out of the air-conditioned bedroom and into my stuffy kitchen. There, I started rummaging through the refrigerator, holding the telephone receiver to my ear with my free hand.

"Shall I phone Yash Epp?" asked my sister-in-law Myrtlemay, who was on the line at the moment. She had volunteered to help notify the more distant relatives of Simon's passing.

"Whatever you think." It didn't matter to me.

"Yash is a blowhard," Myrtlemay said, "but Simon always enjoyed seeing him at teachers' conventions."

"So phone him if you want."

"Have you decided about the funeral?"

"Adeline made the arrangements," I said, taking a tub of cottage cheese out of the refrigerator. "Friday, two o'clock in the Lutheran Church." The doors of the Mennonite Church weren't wide enough to let a coffin through. The carpenters hadn't thought of widening the doors when they were transforming the old Bartel School into a church building.

"Why wait until Friday?" Myrtlemay asked.

"Emily and Norine can't get home until Thursday."

"Oh." Myrtlemay's voice softened. "Poor kids. They're too young to lose their father."

"Poor me," I murmured after we'd hung up. I was accustomed to Simon's absences. I actually enjoyed my days and weeks without him. When he was away, I cooked meals he didn't like. I quilted, sewed, and took the girls to British Columbia to visit relatives and friends. But now Simon wasn't coming home, ever again. I would never hear his voice again, never sit at the table with him again, never kiss him, never make love to him.

With tears fogging my vision, I sat down at the table with my tub of cottage cheese. I'd just started eating when a wave of heat rose from my stomach, rolled through my body, and burned out through my face.

That was the second or third hot flash I'd experienced since Constable Gaudet's call that morning. Maybe I was going into the menopause. Or maybe not. I was only forty-two. Maybe my body was just reacting to my grief and the heat of the day. I should open some windows. By this time, it must be cooler outside.

Oh, no! Simon's birds! I lurched out of my chair, my fork splattering cottage cheese. The door of the bird-room had been shut tight since the constable's call. Without the breeze from the fan—which was off anyway—the birds would be cooked by now, or almost. I hurried into the hallway, my nerves thrumming at the thought of what I might find. Shivering with dread, I approached the bird-room, hesitated outside the door, and slid it open.

A wall of heat met me. It stank of feathers and bird droppings. Two of the budgies turned and stared at me, more clueless-looking than ever. The black mynah bird's beak hung open, its mouth a dark cave. One of the parrots shrieked and I saw that its water dish was empty. Some of the other birds' water dishes were empty too. Their caretaker, Penny, had filled them that morning but the birds must have drunk every drop, trying to cool themselves off. I should refill their dishes but I hated the idea of getting that close to the birds. I'd better phone Penny and ask her to do it.

On second thought—I almost smiled as another idea struck me. I could take the birds down to the lake—let them drink all the water they wanted—and flutter away to wherever they pleased. Simon would explode with anger at the mere suggestion. But he wasn't here, was he? Simon the birdman would never be here again. He had died in someone else's bed with someone else's lips on his.

I began with the budgies. Two cages at a time, I carried them through the lean-to and out to Simon's beaten-up truck. "See," I said, setting the cages into the truck-box, "it's nicer out here, isn't it?" A coolish breeze ruffled the budgies' feathers.

I went back inside for the black mynah's cage. The bird whistled in a parched little voice as I carried it through the lean-to and out to the truck. As I loaded the mynah, I noticed that the budgies looked livelier. Their eyes were brighter. One hopped around in its cage.

Up next were the parrots and cockatoos. They were bigger than the other birds, and scarier. However, I steeled myself to my task, lugged them out, and deposited them in the truck-box with the others.

When I'd loaded all the birds, I found some bungee cords in the storage shed and secured the cages the best I could. Then I raised the tailgate, which screeched like a wild animal, prompting shrieks of terror from my feathered passengers. Ignoring their protests, I hopped into the driver's seat. I twisted the key in the ignition until it caught, revved the engine, and roared the truck down to the lake. It bounced up, down, and sideways, the birds squawking protests. Clumps of sagebrush, rabbitbrush, and wolf willow zipped past us.

Near the water's edge, I jolted the vehicle to a halt and hopped out. A balloon of excitement grew inside me as I unloaded the cages and set them on the rocky beach. Recklessness and prudence fought for control of my mind. Should I really open the doors of these cages? Simon would be furious. I could feel his anger from the world beyond.

I ignored it. I had more right to be angry than he did. He'd betrayed me, probably for years on end. I opened the doors of the cages and backed off to wait.

The black mynah was the first to realize it was free to go. With a shriek and a whistle, it fluttered out of its cage and down to the water's edge. It looked almost like a crow in that setting. Foxes, coyotes, hawks, and owls might not notice it right away. The cockatoos, parrots, and other birds would have more trouble along that line but I didn't care.

Within minutes, most of the birds found their way to the water—a cacophony of colours—blue, green, red, orange, yellow, white, and black.

A few of Simon's feathered cronies were too timid or stupid to accept my offer of freedom. Hoping to lure the laggards out, I plucked a few weeds, winnowed out their seeds, and sprinkled them onto a flat rock. Some took the bait. Others wouldn't leave their cages until I shook them out. Laura, the blue and orange budgie, lingered after all the others went. She was a granddaughter of Laurence, one of the hatchlings Simon and the girls had hand-fed. I considered keeping Laura for old time's sake. Then I rejected the idea and tipped her out onto the rock. For a few moments she stood gawking around, flexing her pathetic little wings. Then she hopped down to the water's edge and joined her compatriots.

I took the food dishes out of the cages and emptied them onto the flat rock. "Supper's ready," I called, "whenever you are."

The sun was setting, its rays red and gold on the lake. An owl hooted in the distance. A coyote howled. Another answered. I gathered up the empty cages and loaded them into the truck. "Well, team," I said, "I guess this is goodbye. *Adieu, ciao, tschüss.*" With an airy wave, I called *toodeloo,* then climbed into the truck, coaxed it to life, threw it into gear, and drove home feeling freer and sadder than I had in years.

CHAPTER 66

I tossed and turned for hours that night. By one-thirty in the morning, I'd given up on sleep. I hauled myself out of bed and put on a pair of cut-offs and a shirt of Simon's. The shirt smelled like him, apples and honey. The scent brought fresh tears to my eyes.

Wiping my eyes with the tail of my husband's shirt, I wandered into the kitchen, then across the hall to the former bird-room. The room looked nice without its caged occupants. With its high ceiling and peaked windows, it would make a good display area for the quilts I made.

I leaned against the door-frame, mentally redecorating the room. Norine's portable organ could go along the east wall if and when she and Emily moved back home. Shelves for the girls' books would fit along the opposite wall. The wedding-ring quilt I'd made for Simon could hang on the north wall.

No, he'd hate having his quilt in this room, displacing his beloved birds. "Sorry, Simon." My voice echoed in the empty room. I was sort of sorry.

The room smelled of bird droppings—ammonia and rotten onions. I got a broom from the kitchen and swept up the droppings along with drifts of birdseed and feathers. The task calmed my lacerated nerves. I opened a window, gulped cool night air, and opened more windows. I fetched pails of water, detergent, and cloths, then washed the walls, window frames, light fixtures, baseboards, and floor.

My energy lasted until five AM, when a red sun blinked over the horizon. I dragged myself into the kitchen, ate some cheese and grapes, and made a pot of mint tea. I managed to drink one cup before stumbling into the bedroom and falling into bed.

Heat woke me, some from the sun and some from my own body. Perspiration trickled down between my breasts. Where was my body's thermostat? I wished I knew; I'd turn it down.

If I summoned the energy to stagger out of bed, I could turn the air-conditioner on. I couldn't persuade myself to do that. Instead, I flipped my pillow to the cooler side and drifted off again.

I woke with a start. What time was it? The clock showed almost eight-thirty. Penny would be here soon to feed and water Simon's birds. How would I explain their absence? I struggled into a sitting position, grabbed the phone off the night table, and dialled her number. "Hello, Penny. Don't worry about the birds today, okay?"

"Why not? Emily and Norine aren't home already, are they?"

"No but I made other arrangements for the birds." I wouldn't tell her I'd released them. She might call the police. I could be charged with cruelty to animals. Maybe I'd even be fined or put in jail.

Penny drew a shuddery breath. "I hope those birds are all right."

"They're about as good as can be expected."

"What do you mean?" she asked.

"Well, you know, the hot weather and all. It's hard on them."

"It's hard on everybody." Penny swallowed what sounded like a sob. "Do you think the birds know Simon's gone? Maybe they sense it somehow."

"I doubt that." I grabbed my pillow, shoved it behind my back, and leaned against it.

"How about you? How are you holding up?"

"I'm managing." I appreciated Penny's concern. She had a good heart.

"Shall I come and stay with you for a while?"

"Please don't." I regretted the words as soon as they'd escaped my lips. "Sorry, I don't mean to sound ungrateful. I just mean I need to be alone right now. I hope you understand."

"Are you sure you're okay?"

"As okay as might be expected. I spent most of the night cleaning the house. Couldn't sleep."

"I'm not surprised after the shock you've had. Maybe you should see a doctor. You can probably get a prescription to help you through the worst of this."

"I'd rather try to manage without a prescription. Emily and Norine will be here the day after tomorrow. I need to get ready for them. I should do some more cleaning and mow the lawn. I should shop for groceries and cook." The more projects, the better.

"The girls can help," Penny said. "You don't need to wear yourself out." She paused. "Will you need me for the birds tomorrow?"

"No. Like I said, I made other arrangements."

"Are you sure those birds are all right?"

Should I tell Penny I'd released them? I opened my mouth to confess, then closed it. "Penny, if you don't mind, I've gotta go now."

"Sure, okay. Call me if you need anything."

"Thanks. I appreciate that."

I set the phone on the night table, got up, and turned on the air-conditioner. Slumping back onto the bed, I asked myself when the floor had dropped out of my life? Was it only yesterday? It seemed like a week ago. Maybe praying would make me feel better. "Dear God," I whispered but I couldn't think what to say next. Too tired. Also feeling guilty about the birds. I closed my eyes and let a tidal wave of sleep carry me away.

I woke with a jolt. Somebody or something was tapping on my bedroom window. I bolted upright, heart galumphing, eyelids fluttering. Maybe the birds were coming after me, or their ghosts, seeking revenge. What time was it? The clock said one-twenty. Day or night? Must be one-twenty in the afternoon judging by the sun glowering through the curtains.

Tap, tap. "Susie?"

Oh, no! Mother-in-law. Or was Adeline still my mother-in-law now that Simon was gone? She probably was, according to most people's theory of relatives.

Her croaky voice penetrated the curtains. "Susie, are you okay?"

"I'm managing."

"Penny Kramer phoned to me. She said you might be not okay."

"I'm okay!" I bellowed, lunging out of bed.

I stumbled to the window, yanked the curtains open, and motioned for Adeline to go around to the lean-to door.

"I knocked before," she announced when I met her at the door. "I *klopped* three times. No answer."

"I was sleeping." I ran my fingers through my sinewy hair.

"You look terrible."

"You don't look too good yourself." Adeline's eyes sagged in a way I'd never seen before. Her face was yellow-grey. Her chin trembled. Granted, the woman was ninety, but she usually looked years younger.

"*Na yo.*" She swallowed once, twice, her chin bobbing. "I couldn't sleep last night. Too *trüarijch* about my Simon."

"Me too."

Adeline picked up the cardboard box that sat at her feet. "I baked you some tarts." She thrust the box at me. "Half of them raisin, half walnut."

I took the box from her, surprised at its weight. "It feels like you baked quite a few."

"I wanted you to have enough for the visitors that'll come after the funeral to your house."

"That was kind of you." Excessive but kind.

"Does it give any tea in your kitchen?"

That was my cue to invite her in but I couldn't. She'd notice the silence. No birds chittering, squawking, shrieking.

Adeline fanned her face with her hand. "It's maybe cooler inside."

"This isn't a good time. I'm sorry." As soon as Adeline got into the house, she'd know that her son's birds were gone, disappeared, vanished, *verschwunden, verloren.*

Her eyes ploughed over my face. "How come not?"

"I'm doing some cleaning," I mumbled, setting the box of tarts on a shelf in the lean-to. "I'm not finished."

She barged into the lean-to. "I'm good at cleaning. I'll help along."

I tried to block her path. She pushed past me, charged into the hall outside the bird-room, and stopped short, gaping into the empty room. "Where did my Simon's birds stay?"

I stood up straighter, one army general to another. "I let them out."

"What?"

"I said I let them out." I planted my hands on my hips. "Simon's not here so I loaded his birds into the truck, drove them down to the lake, and released them."

"How could you?" Adeline's look could have curdled borscht.

"I never liked those birds." My words punched the air. "I never wanted them in my house, all those years."

"Simon loved his *foageln.*"

I tossed my greasy hair off my cheek. "This is my house now. I can do what I want."

Adeline extended a cautious hand and patted my shoulder. "I think your nerves are broken down. Losing my boy was too hard on you. It stole your right feelings."

I pulled away from her. "Please don't talk like I'm a basket case."

She frowned. "I'm just trying to understand my daughter-law."

"You never understood me," I muttered. "You never will."

"Maybe not." For a moment Adeline stood like a wounded animal, head down, eyes half-shut. "But what about my grand-girls?" She jerked her head up. "They love their dad's birds."

"The girls aren't here, are they?"

"No, but they will be." She turned and barrelled out onto the porch. "Come on already. We need to drive down to the lake and catch those *foageln.*"

"I don't think we can."

"We should try at least."

"And then what?" I asked.

"Me and Manfred will keep care of them if you don't want them. Or we'll give them to Wally. Come on."

"I don't know where the truck keys are." I really didn't.

"Find the keys once," Adeline barked. "You had them last night. You must have."

I drifted into the house and took my time searching while Adeline loped out to the truck. A few minutes later, she hurtled back inside. "I found them." She jangled the keys in my face. "They were standing right in the ignition. You should be lucky nobody stole Simon's truck with all those expensive cages."

"Nobody did, did they?" I must be losing my grip. It wasn't like me to leave keys in a vehicle.

"Come on already." Adeline flapped outside.

I didn't follow. Let the old bat go by herself. Good luck getting the truck started.

A few minutes later, she flapped back inside, her face pink with exertion. "Here, reach me your phone once."

"What for?"

"I need to call Penny to help me let the truck loose."

"I don't want Penny involved." A shudder of fear ran through me. "She might call the police."

Adeline sucked her teeth, her face working. "Maybe I should phone to the police myself."

I gulped. "Please don't."

"Na yo. If you let the truck loose, I won't phone."

I sighed and followed Adeline outside. We loaded ourselves into the truck. I turned the key in the ignition, once, twice, five times, pumping the gas. When the engine finally choked itself alive, I jostled us down to the lake.

On the beach Adeline clambered out of the truck, gesturing toward clumps of feathers in the weeds. "There some of the budgies are. Skunks probably got them. Or foxes."

One blue budgie was twitching, its beak open, eyes blinking. I felt sorry for it. I wanted to help. At the same time, the sight terrified me.

"We can maybe save that one," Adeline said.

"Maybe." Let her do it if she had the guts.

Adeline fetched one of the smaller cages from the truck-box. With a tenderness surprising in such a ham-handed woman, she made a nest of dry grass in the cage and placed the little bird inside.

A couple of parrots screeched from a willow near the water. They hopped from branch to branch, their feathers carnival green, red, blue, and yellow.

"We can maybe get those parrots in cages back again," Adeline said.

I sighed. "We could try."

Adeline fetched one of the bigger cages from the truck and gave it to me. "You could hold this."

I held it, reluctantly.

Adeline baited the parrots with seeds and insects. She called them the way she called her chickens: "Chick chick chick, CHICK, krruk, krruk, krruk."

They ignored her.

When she finally quit trying, I got a spade from the truck. "Let's bury the dead budgies." Hide the evidence.

"No," Adeline said, "we should better keep them. Emily and Norine might want to give them a funeral yet. They loved their dad's birds." She paused. "They loved their dad." Implying that I didn't.

I returned to the truck, found a plastic bag, and handed it to her. "Put the dead ones in here if you want." I couldn't bring myself to touch them.

CHAPTER 67

I managed to avoid Ross Forbes at Simon's funeral and even during the lunch afterwards. Every time he approached me, I moved away or pretended to be engrossed in conversation. The prospect of speaking to him scared me.

Most people I spoke to me raved about what a great guy Simon had been—wonderful teacher, singer, choir-director, and family man. Their praise echoed a bit hollow considering that he had died in Ross's bed. They didn't seem to know that. All they knew was that he'd suffered a heart attack at a music teachers' conference in Moncton. If they'd asked Ross about it, he must have given them an edited version.

Nobody criticized me for releasing Simon's birds, not to my face anyway. However, during the lunch, Norine bustled around recruiting Ross and others to go down to the lake and try to recapture any birds that were still alive. After she and her recruits left, I asked Emily to take me home. Adeline followed in her car.

Back home in my kitchen, the air was thick with afternoon heat and the cloying smell of funeral flowers. Lilies, roses, freesia, daisies, irises.

Adeline and I wilted onto chairs at the kitchen table while Emily put on the kettle for tea.

"Mom, I'm worried about you," Emily said, fingering the pewter raven that hung on a chain around her neck. "I don't like the idea of you living all by yourself."

"Your nerves are broken down," Adeline informed me though I'd told her to quit saying that.

"I'll be okay." I twisted a button on the bodice of my dress, cobalt-blue with black lace. "I just need time to get over...things." I had survived alone while Simon was away, sometimes for weeks. But this time was different. He wasn't coming back. He wouldn't be here in the fall, winter, or spring. He wouldn't be here for Christmas, Easter, Valentine's Day, or our birthdays. The thought felt like barbed-wire twisting itself around my heart.

"I could move back home," Emily said as she made the tea. "I might be able to get a teaching job in Dayspring or not too far away." She was a dutiful girl, almost too dutiful for a twenty-two-year-old.

"No," I said, "I don't want you giving up your Yukon adventure for my sake. I wouldn't want that for Norine either."

Adeline reached over and laid a heavy hand on my arm. "How about living by me on the farm? Or maybe that wouldn't be interesting enough for you." I detected a note of doubt in her voice. That was unusual.

My insides shrank at the thought of sharing a house with my mother-in-law. "If I lived way out there," I said, "I couldn't keep my job." I enjoyed working at the school. I needed to work for the sake of my mental health. The job got me out of the house, kept me in touch with other people, and structured my time.

Emily poured the tea. Adeline spooned sugar into hers, then clumped over to the counter and returned with a plateful of tarts, half of them raisin, half walnut. "The school board might not want you working anymore by the school, with your broken-down nerves."

"My nerves aren't broken down," I snapped. "How many times do I need to tell you? I'm grieving. Give me a break. Just because you're made of cast iron, that doesn't mean—"

Emily laid a hand on my shoulder. "Easy, Mom. You don't need to decide anything right away. You might even want to move back to Sage City or Vancouver."

"I don't know. Maybe I've been away too long...." My voice trailed off at the sound of voices in the yard. Norine burst into the house, her cheeks pink, curls tousled. "We did it! We caught Dad's black mynah bird, his white mynah, and three of the parrots."

"That's nice," I said, feeling a bit less guilty for releasing them.

"They're in the storage shed, in cages." Norine stopped for a breath. "Uncle Wally and Aunt Myrtlemay will take them home when they leave."

"Lucky birds," I murmured, wondering how they felt about returning to captivity after flying free for three days. I was flying free myself now. Or not flying actually. More like limping.

Adeline swallowed the last of a raisin tart and helped herself to another. "Those *foageln* will be happier living by somebody that doesn't hate them."

"I don't hate the birds," I said. "I just didn't enjoy living with them."

She shrugged. "Same thing."

Norine glanced out the window. "There are quite a few people out in the yard. Can I invite them in for a bowl of Oma's borscht?"

A hot flash danced across my stomach and burned out through my chest. "Is Ross Forbes there?"

Norine tossed her curls out of her eyes. "No, he went to Outlook to see somebody. So can I invite them?"

Adeline surged up from the table. "Invite them already. I made lots of borscht." She took a pot out of the refrigerator, set it on the stove, and turned on the heat.

CHAPTER 68

Three days after Simon's funeral, I drove our daughters to Saskatoon for their return flight to Whitehorse. On my way back, I stopped to visit my husband's grave in the cemetery north of Dayspring. The afternoon was sunny and cool, a relief after the heat wave. The breeze smelled of the clover blooming in the ditches along the road. I parked outside the caragana hedge, creaked open the cemetery gate, and made my way through grass, weeds, and wildflowers to the Epp family plot. A bouquet of plastic geraniums in a concrete vase graced the head of Simon's grave, courtesy of his mother.

I stood at the foot of his grave, praying for his soul using words I'd learned from a Catholic funeral bulletin. *O God, through your mercy, may he rest in peace and may perpetual light shine upon him.*

I hoped God heard my prayer, editing it if necessary. I almost smiled, picturing Simon in heaven singing in a pickup band with some of the prophets or disciples. Hopefully they'd let him take the high harmonies, as he had loved to do when he was on earth.

With a last look at Simon's grave, I stepped over to his father's. I'd never met Isaac Epp but I'd seen pictures of him—a big auburn-haired man with a pie-pan jaw. That jaw hadn't moved much, at least not in speech. *Shtelle Isaak,* the Mennonites called him. Quiet Isaac. His wife, Adeline, did the talking.

I said a prayer for Isaac, then headed back toward my car. As I detoured around a badger hole, I heard a sound that turned my legs to jelly.

That couldn't be Simon singing. Surely not. I glanced around, didn't see anybody. Yet that was Simon's tenor, sweet as honey, singing one of his favourite spirituals. *Dere's a better day a-coming. Fare you well, fare you well.*

Maybe it was a recording. Maybe a ghost. I didn't believe in ghosts but at that moment I wanted to. "Simon? Darling?"

De time shall be no longer. Fare you well, fare you well.

Maybe the singing was coming from outside the cemetery. I hurried to the gate, creaked through it, and stopped short. A blue Toyota was parked on the other side of the hedge. Simon's voice floated out through the open window. *In dat great gittin' up morning. Fare you well, fare you well.*

The blight of my life, Ross Forbes, sat in the driver's seat, tapping a hand on the steering wheel in time to the music.

"Susie!" Ross silenced the tape and hauled himself out of the car. "What a coincidence!" He limped toward me. "I've been wanting to talk to you." His eyes were windows of sympathy where I wanted to see guilt and apology. "How are you holding up?"

I backed away from him. "Not good. My husband died in your bed." My throat felt like it was full of broken glass. "How could you do that to me?"

"I didn't 'do that' to you. Anyway it didn't happen like you make it sound."

"Oh?" I fired the word at him. "How *did* it happen?"

"I can explain if you'll just give me a chance." Ross leaned against his Toyota. "I went to Moncton for the music teachers' conference. I knew The Wylde Atlantick was scheduled to perform there so I brought along some sheet music I'd heard Simon was looking for. After I checked into my hotel, I happened to meet one of the band members. She said Simon probably wouldn't be singing because he wasn't feeling well."

"If my husband wasn't well, why didn't somebody phone and tell me?"

"Apparently it didn't seem serious enough. The bus driver took him to a doctor, who prescribed pills for indigestion and told Simon to rest. I went looking for him and found him sleeping in the bus. The driver thought he should be in bed so I took him to my room." Ross paused. "It was the least I could do for an old friend."

"You could have rented a room for Simon."

He jiggled his bad leg. "That didn't occur to me. Anyway I figured somebody should keep an eye on him. He slept in my room for a while and woke up feeling better. I gave him the sheet music I'd brought. We were singing it when he doubled over with a pain in his chest." Ross's voice broke. "And that was pretty well it."

A crow squawked in a tree and flapped away, its wings snapping at the air.

"Simon was my husband," I said in a voice thick with accusation. "You shouldn't have gone to the conference to see him. He promised me he wouldn't see you anymore. You made a betrayer out of him."

Ross blew out an impatient breath. "I didn't go to see Simon. I went for the conference. I had to give a presentation. And there were people I needed to see."

"You should have skipped that conference, knowing Simon was going to be there."

Ross snorted. "You couldn't expect me to arrange my life according to where Simon was or wasn't going to be."

"Actually you did. You left Dayspring to get away from him."

"That was seventeen years ago, woman."

"You should have made a clean break with him then instead of recruiting him for your band. You knew Simon was in love with you. Why did you have to reopen his wounds? You should have left him alone. You could have found somebody else to sing with your wretched parrot."

"Touring with the band kept Simon from drinking, didn't it?"

"He would have stopped without it." I wasn't sure about that.

"I doubt it," Ross said. "Anyway he did stop, thank God. It was weird, how he went from teetotaler to falling-down drunk. I'd never seen anything like it. If he'd grown up with social drinking, he might have—"

"Don't change the subject, Ross. I want an answer. Why didn't you make a clean break with Simon when you left Dayspring seventeen years ago?"

Ross flicked a fly off his arm, opened his car door, and rolled the window up. "It wasn't the way you seem to think." He closed the door. "There was never anything physical between Simon and me. I'm not gay."

That was a relief if I could believe Ross. Actually I did. I'd suspected as much ever since he'd told me about his lost girlfriend, Isobel. But sex is only part of a relationship. "Simon betrayed me anyway. I don't think I had his whole heart from the day he met you."

"I'm sorry if that was the case," Ross said, his voice as level as a prairie wheat-field. "Truly sorry. But you have to admit Simon and I had a lot in common. Our personalities fed off each other."

"Like his and mine didn't." I stepped on a clump of dandelions, grinding them under my shoe, releasing their bitter scent.

"Probably, but your husband was an honourable man. From the time he promised he'd quit seeing me, he did his best to keep that promise. He never phoned me or wrote to me. Never dropped in at my office or arranged to meet me."

"But you and Simon did see each other during those seventeen years."

A grasshopper jumped onto Ross's pant leg. He brushed it off. "Only when I showed up at a venue where The Wylde Atlantick was performing."

"You should have had the decency to stay away from my husband."

Ross rolled his eyes. "Please. I teach music at the Maritime Conservatory of Performing Arts. The Wylde Atlantic is one of the top musical groups in the Maritimes. It would have been ridiculous for me not to attend any of their performances."

I sighed. "I guess you have a point. I didn't think of that."

"Can you let it go, Susie?"

"I don't know."

"I'll be in Dayspring a few more days. Give me a call at the motel if you like."

"I'll think about it."

CHAPTER 69

I drove slowly on the way home, following the backroads and struggling to adjust my worldview based on what Ross had said.

Flat prairie fields stretched toward the horizon on either side of the road—beige and gold in the late-afternoon light. Durum wheat with its whiskery beards, regular wheat, barley, canary seed.

Harvest-time would soon be here. Sadly my husband wouldn't be around to see it or to start the new school year. Never again would he walk into a classroom with its smell of chalk, textbooks, hairspray, and running shoes. Simon had loved teaching; he was born to teach. I was glad he'd had the opportunity for so many years.

Beyond the barbed-wire fence on my left, a pair of horses raced across a pasture, their hooves flying. Simon's earthly race was done. He couldn't do anything more in this world, good or bad.

How was he faring in the world beyond? He wasn't in hell; I was pretty sure of that. He'd been a believer and he'd done a lot of good in his life. Maybe he was in purgatory. Maybe I should become a Catholic and have Masses offered for his speedy progress into heaven. That way I could pray for my husband on earth while he prayed for me in purgatory, or in heaven if he was there already.

Adeline would be scandalized if I left the Mennonite fold to become a *cat licker*. Then again, her opinion didn't matter so much now that Simon wasn't here to tie us together.

I was only forty-two. I had a lot of years left, God willing, though I might already be in the menopause.

I steered around a dried-up mudhole, wondering if grief and anxiety could have something to do with my hot flashes. I had a history of anxiety. I was born to an anxious mother, grew up anxious, and stayed that way. If I hadn't been afraid of becoming a perennial wallflower, I might not have married the first eligible man who showed an interest in me. Given that I did marry Simon, I should have moved to Dayspring with him. I shouldn't have let my fear of Adeline keep me in Sage City. If I had moved here sooner, Simon might not have fallen for Ross Forbes.

Or he might have anyway.

A more confident woman would have handled her husband's indiscretion differently. A Mrs. Adventuresome might have abandoned Simon for the dashing Florian Bouchard. But I hadn't abandoned my husband, and Florian had married Renee, a tidy blonde accountant who organized conferences and pro-life rallies. Thanks to her connections and his abilities, he made good money creating sculptures for churches, hotels, tourist venues, and city governments.

If I moved back to Sage City, I'd be near Florian, Renee, Valerie, and other friends. But did I really want leave Dayspring? I had years of connections with the place. I knew the prairie like an old hymn. Its stark beauty calmed me in a way no other landscape did.

As I passed a farm with well-drilling equipment in the yard, a truck rumbled toward me from the opposite direction. The driver raised two fingers off the steering wheel, signaling hello. I raised two answering fingers though I didn't recognize the driver or the kids beside him. It was what people did around Dayspring.

As I approached the village, lights gleamed in a few of the buildings including Mahs' Café. Should I stop at the café for supper? No, Ross might be there. I couldn't bear to eat with him. Maybe someday. Not yet.

I passed the café and continued along the seven blocks of Main Street. A lot of things happened in those few blocks. Harvest talk, shop talk, gossip, tourist visits, parades, festivals, farmers' market. I'd miss all that if I left.

I almost smiled as I imagined reinventing myself in this little burg. I could buy a motorcycle and ride it to work, roaring up to the school to the surprise and delight of students and staff.

Or I could quit my job and give sewing lessons, or apply for a job in the library, or run for mayor. I needed to make things happen on my own now. My husband couldn't do anything except maybe pray for me. Tears gathered in my eyes, stinging my sinuses. Never again would I see Simon in the kitchen frying sausages for supper while I cooked the vegetables, or showing me an article in the newspaper, or even switching on the light.

This was an easier thought to contemplate while I was farther from home, more difficult as I approached the house. I dreaded walking in, hearing nothing but my own footsteps. My daughters were in Whitehorse until next spring. My husband was in the cemetery under six feet of freshly dug earth. Simon's birds were gone, many of them dead, some hopefully enjoying their new lives with Wally and Myrtlemay.

I eased the car up the driveway and parked near Simon's truck. I should go into the house and find something to eat. I didn't have the gumption.

A breeze flitted in through the driver's-side window, tinkering with my hair. Crickets chirped in the grass. The setting sun glinted on Simon's truck and on the yellow breast of a meadowlark as he landed on the tailgate. The bird shuffled his feet, perhaps seeking a firmer claw-hold, then threw his head back and poured out a loud gurgling song.

Simon had proposed to me with a meadowlark's song—his version of it. *Come, come, won't you please marry me?* That was twenty-three years ago in Sage City, British Columbia.

What had this meadowlark sung? Maybe Simon would say it was *I'll never forgive you for letting my birds go.*

No, my husband wouldn't be that cruel.

The meadowlark repeated his song, adding a couple of trills. *One step at a time, Susie. God and I are watching over you.*

That probably wasn't what the bird sang. But maybe it was what Simon wanted me to hear. In any case, it was what I needed.

With tears streaming down my face, I stumbled out of the car and trudged up to the house. I unlocked the door, hesitated on the threshold, and ventured inside, one step at a time.

About the Author

Elma Schemenauer was born Elma Mary Martens, a child of Mennonite emigrants from Russia to Canada. She grew up near the prairie village of Elbow, Saskatchewan, halfway between Saskatoon and Regina.

Elma worked in publishing in Toronto for many years and now lives in Kamloops, British Columbia. Elma is the author of 77 published books.

SOME OF ELMA SCHEMENAUER'S 77 BOOKS

Consider the Sunflowers

1940s-era Mennonite novel set mainly in rural Saskatchewan. Some characters are the same as in *Song for Susie Epp*. Publisher Borealis Press of Ottawa.

YesterCanada: Historical Tales of Mystery and Adventure

30 historical and traditional stories from across Canada. Publisher Borealis Press of Ottawa.

Jacob Siemens Family Since 1685

Family history book. Publisher Farland Press. Book includes early Mennonites: Sawatzky, Bergman, Enns, Andres, Dyck, Janzen, Martens, Kehler, Quiring, Neufeld, Friesen, Penner, Goertzen, and more.

Brazil, Canada, England, Ethiopia, Guatemala, Haiti, Iran, Israel, Japan, The Philippines, Russia, Somalia, Uganda

Thirteen factual children's books. Publisher The Child's World of Minnesota.

Newton McTootin and the Bang Bang Tree

Picture book. Publisher MAGOOK, a former division of McClelland & Stewart.

Read more at https://elmams.wixsite.com/elma.